"Mom. What's that TV guy doing here?"

Bianca pulled the boy into a sideways hug, attempting to finger-comb his sleep-tousled hair. A loving, motherly gesture, but her furrowed brow made it clear that the kid's sudden appearance had caught her off guard.

So he answered for her. "I'm Logan Murray, and I just dropped by to thank your mom for helping me at the station the other day."

"Logan Murray, Logan Murray. From the commercial about tires. And the bank with the big green M." The boy held up a forefinger. "And Dogs for Kids, where they match kids like me with helper dogs."

Kids like him. So Drew was aware that his brain functioned differently than other kids'.

Drew quoted the commercial almost verbatim, explaining how the agency spent many months training dogs to open doors and pick up dropped items for kids in wheelchairs, act as the eyes and ears of children who couldn't see or hear … "and keep autistic kids from wandering off or engaging in dangerous activities."

Bianca shrugged one shoulder. "He only needs to hear a thing once, and he can recite it word for word."

"Took me four takes to get it right," Logan said. "And I was reading from a teleprompter."

Bianca hugged Drew tighter and sent Logan a silent message with her eyes: *Thank you.*

Dear Reader,

As you may know, autism affects one child in 88 (one in 54 are boys...including my ten-year-old grandson), and it's the fastest-growing serious developmental disability in the U.S., Canada and Europe today. There is no known cause or cure, and studies conclude that more children will be diagnosed with the disorder than cancer, diabetes and AIDs combined, at an average annual cost per family of $60,000...yet autism receives less than five percent of the research funding of many less prevalent childhood diseases.

According to a recent article in *Psychology Today,* more than 50 percent of parents surveyed believed autism was a contributing factor in their divorce. More often than not, it's the mom who continues to care for her autistic child and, in most cases, other children, as well.

With statistics like that affecting literally thousands of children—and their families—around the world, I couldn't help but wonder if it's possible for the single mom of an autistic child to ever find love again.

In *Devoted to Drew,* I attempted to show a realistic—sometimes stressful, and always challenging—picture of the life of such a mom. If you enjoy the story, I hope you'll be moved to find ways to help an Autism Society chapter in your area.

Until then, here's to happy endings!

All my best to you and yours,

Loree

LOREE LOUGH

With more than four million books in circulation, bestselling author Loree Lough's titles have earned hundreds of 4- and 5-star reviews and industry awards. She splits her time between her home in Baltimore and a cabin in the Alleghenies, where she loves to show off her "Identify the Critter Tracks" skills. Loree has 100 books in print, including reader-favorite series such as the First Responders, Lone Star Legends, Accidental, Suddenly and Turning Points. She loves to hear from readers and answers every letter, personally. Visit her at Facebook, Twitter, Pinterest and www.loreelough.com!

Dedication

This book is dedicated to my daughter, the best mom any on-the-spectrum kid could possibly have, and to all the kids and families struggling to find their path to normal.

Acknowledgments

My sincere thanks to B.J. Surhoff, who during his 18-year baseball career, played every position except pitcher, earning just about every award a major leaguer can win. After retiring from the Orioles, he and wife Polly cofounded Pathfinders for Autism. Now a special training assistant for the team, he agreed to a "walk-on" part in this story, so that he could explain what Pathfinders is, and what it does. Thanks, too, to Shelly McLaughlin at Pathfinders, for some great "what it's like to parent a kid on the spectrum" information (www.pathfindersforautism.org/).

To Rosemary and Burton from National Capitol Therapy Dogs (www.nctdinc.org/new/index.php), to Karen with 4Paws for Ability (4pawsforability.org/), and to Kati and Lauren with Autism Service Dogs of America (autismservicedogsofamerica.com/) for invaluable input that allowed me to provide accurate info about service and therapy dogs.

Thanks to the National Autism Society (www.autism-society.org/) and Judy at the Howard County Autism Society (www.howard-autism.org/). To Kelly Case and Kelly Higgins-Lund, for sharing personal experiences with their own on-the-spectrum sons. And last, but certainly not least, a hearty thank-you to Marty Bass, weatherman at Baltimore's WJZ-TV (baltimore.cbslocal.com/personality/marty-bass/), for insights that helped me write the opening scene. (A rabid Ravens fan and stellar newsman, he knows a few team secrets!)

You're all amazing, and I couldn't have written this novel without you! Thank you, thank you, thank you!

HARLEQUIN HEARTWARMING

Loree Lough

Devoted to Drew

❧ A Child to Love ❧

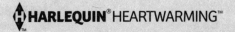

Recycling programs
for this product may
not exist in your area.

ISBN-13: 978-0-373-36653-8

DEVOTED TO DREW

Printed in U.S.A.

HARLEQUIN®
www.Harlequin.com

CHAPTER ONE

LOGAN'S STOMACH HAD been in knots since the day before yesterday, when the general manager's executive assistant had called to schedule this appointment. Now, as he walked through the door, the receptionist's smile—something between pity and dismay—told him contract addendums and codicils had nothing to do with the meeting.

"I know I'm early," he said, "but any way Fletcher will see me now?"

Mandy's I-feel-so-*so*-sorry-for-you expression intensified. "Sorry, Mr. Murray, but he left explicit instructions that they weren't to be disturbed."

"They?"

She shot a glance toward the door. "Just the coaches and the doctors."

Just the coaches and doctors. Plural. His heart beat a little harder as he admitted that he had no one but himself to blame. If he hadn't gone ballistic when that last concussion put him on the injured list, they might not feel it necessary to gang up on him this time.

"It shouldn't be much longer," she added. "Can I get you something to drink while you're waiting?"

In other words, sit tight and keep your mouth shut, like a kid sent to the principal's office for acting up in class.

"Thanks, but I'm fine." In truth, he was anything but. He couldn't remember a headache this bad. Couldn't concentrate. Couldn't sleep. Couldn't hold down anything heavier than soup. Couldn't admit any of it to the guys on the other side of that door.

The phone on Mandy's desk beeped, startling him. Logan added "jumpy" to his list of complaints.

"Yessir, right away," Mandy said. Then, "You can go in now, Mr. Murray."

He was halfway to the door when she added, "Can I at least bring you a bottle of water?"

Logan wondered what sort of Logan Murray gossip had prompted her concerned tone. "Sure. Sounds good," he said. "And please call me Logan."

As he entered Stan Fletcher's office, the five

men who'd gathered to decide his fate stood: the general manager, head coach, doctor, team psychologist and offensive coordinator. Logan hoped, as he shook each extended hand, that they wouldn't notice the tremors pulsing from his hard-beating heart to his fingertips. His agent was in New York, celebrating…wedding anniversary? Wife's birthday? Logan only knew that he'd walked into this meeting alone and unprepared.

The GM pointed at the chair nearest his own. "Take a load off, son."

Logan sat in a buttery leather wingback and did his best to look at ease, despite a strange new empathy for Daniel in the lions' den. Three quick knocks cracked the prickly silence, and Mandy joined them, carrying a cobalt-blue water bottle.

"Here you go, Mr. Mur— Logan."

"Thanks, Mandy," he said, taking it. Once the door closed quietly behind her, Doc Dickerson broke the brittle silence.

"So. Logan. How's the head?"

He nodded. Smiled. Pretended the team doctor's bedside manner didn't need fine-tuning.

"Good," he lied, propping an ankle on a knee. "Fine. Never better."

"I'm surprised to hear that, frankly." He got up and handed Logan a large manila envelope.

He willed his hands not to shake as he removed CT scans and X-rays. "Might as well be reading hieroglyphics," he admitted, holding the films up to the light. He'd seen enough of these things during the course of his career to know how to read and interpret them. But this time, his eyes refused to focus.

"This is your *third* Grade 3 concussion," Gerard continued. And, as if to soften the blow he was about to deliver, the doctor added, "That hit you took when we played the Steelers? One of the worst I've seen in my career."

No one, not the men on the field or fans in the stands that day, would deny it. Neither would anyone who'd seen replays on the news. The ensuing pressure had compelled the Knights' high muckety-mucks to call in a neuropsychologist. Logan wondered why he wasn't now present to reiterate the results of the California Verbal, Rey Auditory, Benton Visual Retention and the Stroop Cognitive tests. Clearly, the sole purpose of this summit was to use the test results to sideline him for a couple of games. Much as he hated the idea, it beat the heck out of the alternative. Logan decided to take it on the chin, without complaint.

Gerard returned to his seat as Fletcher said, "I know it seems coldhearted, dumping the decision on you this way, but I'm afraid that Steelers game was your last."

Logan's heart pounded harder. He sat up straighter. Surely he didn't mean...

"Last game of the season, right?"

The GM slowly shook his head.

His mouth went dry. *What's with the dramatic pause?* Logan wondered, uncapping the water bottle. *Giving me time to let the inevitable sink in?*

"You're welcome to take the films and test results to outside specialists for confirmation," Fletcher said, "but you should know, we've already consulted with the best in the area..."

Logan took a sip of water as Gerard put in, "...and they all concur."

Logan swallowed. Hard. His powers of concentration had been off since the hit. Had he missed a sentence or two? Because surely they weren't trying to tell him that his days as an NFL quarterback were over. He had two more years on his contract. And he'd bounced back from Grade 3 concussions before. Twice before, to be precise.

He faced the head coach, a man he'd come to think of as a friend. "Are they saying what I think they're saying?"

Hildebrand exhaled a shaky sigh. "'Fraid so, pal."

Now the offensive coordinator chimed in with, "Believe me, Logan, this isn't something we *want* to do." A furrow formed on his brow. "You're the best QB in the league, and it's gonna kill us to lose you."

He'd gone toe to toe with Richards nearly every play of every game, all three of his years as the Knights' first-string quarterback. The man was stubborn, but his straightforward honesty had earned Logan's respect. It was the only thing that kept him from lashing out, the way he had last time when they'd put him on the disabled list.

"You're awfully quiet," Logan told the team psychologist. "Waiting till I blow my stack before you put in your two cents?"

O'Riley quirked an eyebrow. "Are you feeling the need to blow your stack?"

Groaning inwardly, Logan ran a hand through his hair. "Save the shrink-speak for one of your other nutcases, and give it to me straight."

"Dr. Gerard already gave it to you straight. you've played your last game."

They took turns spouting excuses and rationalizations, but Gerard's was the only explanation that stuck in his dizzy, throbbing head: "The next Grade 3 could cause significant, irreversible brain damage. Worse, it could kill you."

In the demoralizing hush that followed, Logan heard Gerard's wristwatch counting out the seconds, each tick hammering home the inevitable. But his career didn't have to be over. He was young. Physically fit. He could rebound, as he had before, if they'd give him one more chance.

"I'll sign a waiver," he blurted, leaning forward in the chair, "absolving the Knights from any responsibility if—"

"It's not just the liability," Fletcher injected. "We're talking about your *life* here. The team's reputation. Fan expectation." He exhaled a heavy sigh. "Bottom line, the decision is best for everyone. You, primarily."

Their monotone voices and deadpan expressions underscored O'Riley's hard words: *You've played your last game.*

He stared at the toes of his Crockett & Jones loafers. Without football, what did he have? A big house in exclusive The Preserve development, filled with designer clothes, a three-car garage where his 1955 Corvette and James Bond–like Aston Martin flanked a Harley-Davidson V-Rod. And without football, what would he *do?* During the season, he gave 100 percent on the field; in the off-season, he trained, studied opposing teams and basked in the media spotlight—attention that inspired half a dozen national magazines to name him Bachelor of the Year. These past three and a half years, the game hadn't just provided for him, it had *defined* him.

If he sat for one more second, he'd lose it. For a moment, Logan wished he *was* that trouble-making student, waiting outside the principal's office. A boy could cry when he heard his punishment, but a big tough football player?

He stood, then walked out of the office without a word…because he couldn't talk around the aching sob in his throat. Stunned, he stood swaying just beyond the door's threshold.

"Hey, son," the GM called after him. "You okay?"

And then he heard the shrink say, "Let him go."

"It's a lot for a kid his age to absorb," Richards put in.

He was twenty-five. How old would he have to be before they stopped calling him a kid?

"Give him time," Gerard added. "He'll come around."

Logan wasn't at all sure that was possible. As he passed Mandy's desk, she pressed a hand to her chest and whispered, "I'm so sorry."

Was it really possible that in a matter of minutes he'd gone from being a celebrity athlete to an object of pity? Judging by the receptionist's concerned expression, he had. Nodding, Logan sent her a feeble, shaky smile and hurried to the parking lot, where he sat, silent, and stared through the windshield of his prized sports car.

He thought about calling Willow to let her know what had happened. No...he needed to get his head on straight first. The news would shatter his soon-to-be wife, and he'd need his wits about him to put her back together again. A spiteful thought flitted through his head: if she really loved him, shouldn't it be the other way around?

Movement to his right stunned him back to the here and now. After the SUV's driver backed out of his slot, Logan fired up his engine and peeled out of the lot, swerving in and out of traffic as he raced up Russell Street.

Until flashing lights and a siren stopped him.

And a policewoman stepped up beside the car.

"License and registration, please."

He rummaged through the glove box and his wallet, found what he needed and handed them to her. Before she looked at either, she grinned.

"Logan Murray?" She read the identification while he read her name tag: Mullins.

"*The* Logan Murray?"

And so the pendulum swings back to celebrity athlete, he thought.

"Are you aware that you were doing sixty-five in a forty-mile-per-hour zone?"

"Really?"

"Really."

He tapped the steering wheel. "Sometimes this baby has a mind of its own."

She returned the documents, put one hand on top of his car and said, "You'd better learn to control her, or people might get the impression that all that stuff in the papers is true."

Which stuff? he wondered. The "Murray Moves Fast, Even Off the Field" headline? Or maybe even the "Magic Murray Has a New Lady" nonsense online?

He slid the license into his wallet and put the registration back into the glove box, figuring he had a 50-50 shot of getting a ticket.

Logan turned on what the entertainment reporters called "The Murray Charm."

"You're right, Officer Mullins," he said, flashing his flirtiest smile. "I'll be more careful from now on."

"See that you do." Winking, she tapped the car's roof. "The city expects a Super Bowl win from you this year." And with that, she strolled back to her squad car, hiking her gun belt as she went.

Logan eased into traffic and drove until he ended up in Fells Point, where he parked across from The Horse You Came In On Saloon, Baltimore's oldest bar. Would his agent, or Knights' management, leak the story? he wondered, stepping off the curb to cross the street. How many days before reporters started dogging his heels?

A horn blared, startling him so badly he almost dropped his car keys.

"Hey, idiot! Find someplace else to commit suicide!" the driver bellowed.

"Yeah, whatever," he muttered and continued across Thames Street.

Inside, he took the stool nearest the singing guitarist.

"What'll you have?" the barmaid asked.

"Whiskey, neat."

Either she hadn't recognized him, or she wasn't a Knights fan. A relief either way because it meant he could feel good and sorry for himself while he got good and drunk. As he waited for her to pour a jigger, Logan wondered if self-pity had driven Edgar Allan Poe to this saloon on the last night of his life. Wondered, too, if Poe had decided against calling a woman who wouldn't be there for him.

Self-pity, Logan thought as the barmaid delivered the drink, was a dangerous thing. He lifted the glass, said a silent toast to the sad, sickly author, then tossed back the shot. *Maybe I'll take up writing and drinking, just like you, Eddie,* he thought, signaling the barmaid.

His college roommate, who'd sold a novel loosely based on their campus shenanigans, explained his success this way—"Gotta write what you know, man. Only way to make it in this wacky biz." And since the only thing Logan knew was football, he crossed "author" off his Now What? list.

He put the glass to his lips and laughed to himself. *Drinking...now,* there's *something you know about.*

CHAPTER TWO

Ten years later...

"GREAT INTERVIEW," Marty said. "Hundreds of emails and Facebook posts came in while we were on-air, same as last time. Come on back any time, dude. You're good for ratings!"

Logan shook the newsman's hand. "I'll have my people call your people."

Grinning, Marty checked his watch. "If I didn't have to do the weather in a minute, I'd offer you a cup of coffee."

The assistant producer breezed past them. "There's a fresh pot in the production office...."

Point made and taken: Bianca Wright didn't believe in rolling out the red carpet for the show's guests. At least not once the cameras stopped rolling.

They'd met briefly six months ago, during his first visit to *The Morning Show*. That day she'd been so preoccupied corralling the gaggle of octogenarian belly dancers whose performance followed his segment that she barely had time to escort him to the studio. She was cute. Smart. *Not famous*. Everybody was after him to find a stable woman…someone who didn't jump at every opportunity to draw attention to herself. So, despite the fact that he had a radio interview on the other side of town in an hour, Logan fell into step beside her.

"Marty's right. That was a great interview," she said, scribbling something onto her clipboard. "The kind that will have me answering tons of fan emails for the next couple of days."

Her tone of voice told him she wasn't looking forward to the task. "Next time I'm on the show," he joked, "I'll try not to be so personable."

She made a noise—something between a snort and a grunt. A moment ago she'd been friendly and outgoing. But now? He crossed "sense of humor" off his Good Things About Her list. Women, Logan thought, should come with warning labels. And instruction manuals.

She sat at her desk and adjusted the tilt of a silver-framed photo of a young boy. Must be Bianca's son; he had the same eyes as her. And if the boy's mischievous smirk was any indicator, he was a handful. No photo of a husband, he noticed, but then, there wasn't much room for one on her work-cluttered desk. Maybe a thorny divorce explained her sudden mood shift, or juggling family and career was more than she could handle today. And maybe, he thought, stifling a grunt of his own, she was like every other woman he'd met: impossible.

"Help yourself," Bianca said. "Mugs are in the cabinet above the coffeemaker." She put her back to him and began tapping numbers into her cell phone.

"Hey, sweetie," she said as he filled a station-logoed mug. "It's so good to hear your voice!"

Word for word what his ex used to say... before rehab. Funny how she'd liked him better all boozed up. The reminder was enough to crush all desire to get to know Bianca better. Well, that, and the possibility that she was married.

Logan glanced at his watch. If he left right now, he might just make it to his next interview on time. He waved, hoping to get Bianca's attention so he could mouth a silent thank-you for the coffee before hitting the road.

"I know, I know," she was saying, "but you still have to do what Grandmom tells you to. Rules are rules. We've talked about that, remember?" She covered the mouthpiece and exhaled a frustrated sigh before continuing. "Tell you what. If you do all your chores and don't misbehave today, we'll go out for ice cream after supper. Okay?

"I love you, sweetie. See you in a few hours." Eyes closed, she held the phone to her chest for a split second, then spun the chair to face Logan. "How's the coffee?"

"Better than Starbucks."

Bianca gave him a quick once-over. "If you say so."

"No. Seriously. It's really good."

"Well, I'm two cups over my daily quota, so you're welcome to what's left."

He put the mug on the counter. "So that was your son on the phone?"

"Mmm-hmm." A tiny smile played at the corners of her mouth as she glanced at the picture. "Drew. He's seven."

"I have two sisters. The youngest has a boy about his age. Maybe they go to school together."

"Baltimore is a big city, surrounded by dozens of suburbs."

"You don't buy into the 'it's a small world' philosophy?"

"It isn't that so much as…" And like before, Bianca's smile disappeared as quickly as it appeared. "Drew is autistic."

Logan didn't know why, but his thoughts went immediately to Poe, the service dog he'd adopted when a friend's autistic daughter had died of meningitis complications three years ago. Poe—and dogs like her—were responsible for the pro bono commercials he'd made for the local service dog training facility. Logan pocketed both hands. "I, ah, I don't know what to say." He could have told her that his nephew was autistic, but this didn't seem the time or place.

She searched his face for what seemed like a full minute. It was almost as intimidating as facing a row of scowling linebackers on the football field, which, considering her size, made no sense at all.

"What? I have spinach in my teeth or something?"

One side of her mouth lifted in a faint smile. "You're the first person, ever, to have an honest reaction to the news, that's what."

For the next five minutes, she provided him with a rundown of Drew's situation: at age two, when he wasn't forming sentences, gesturing or responding normally to physical or verbal interactions, Drew's pediatrician put Bianca in touch with a colleague who specialized in childhood developmental disorders. Test results put the boy in the "mild-to-moderate" level on the autism spectrum. After three years of speech, physical and occupational therapy—partnered with sensory and behavioral integration—he was mainstreamed into public school.

Logan then listed similarities between Drew's situation and his friend's daughter, but he didn't share the fact that she had died.

Bianca nodded. "It takes a lot of time, effort and commitment to raise a child with autism and ensure they are happy and comfortable."

At least now Logan understood why she'd chosen a job usually filled by interns and college grads starting out in the industry; the work kept her in the job pool, yet afforded flexibility in case her boy needed her.

"I take it you have good days and bad days?" he asked.

Bianca cast a pensive glance toward Drew's photo. "Mostly good, thanks to some very dedicated, loving people."

"Your husband deserves some credit, then. I know a guy whose kid has cerebral palsy.

Couldn't handle the day-to-day stress, and it cost him his marriage. I'm glad your husband stuck around…that he's doing right by you and your son."

She looked surprised. Hurt. Angry. Which rattled him, until she said, "Jason died three years ago. Pancreatic cancer."

"Oh. Wow. Sorry to hear it," he said, meaning every word.

She lifted one shoulder and one eyebrow. "It is what it is."

Logan had no idea how to respond to that, so he looked at his watch, then blew a silent whistle through his teeth. "Well, I'd better head out. Radio interview in an hour. All the way over on Boston Street."

Bianca looked at her desk clock, then stood and slid his file into a drawer marked ATH-LETES. "Hope you have a helicopter."

Proof that she had a sense of humor after all?

"Just in case," he said, unpocketing his cell phone. "It's not an official guest spot. Just another of those 'we'll put you on air if you're ever in the neighborhood' things. I figured it was a good time to hawk the fund-raiser on the radio, since not everybody watches *The Morning Show*."

"I won't tell Marty you said that."

Logan grinned, wondering why he'd told her all of that. And why he wasn't going outside to make his call. And who the dedicated, loving people in her life might be. Not likely a boyfriend because very few guys had the capacity to commit to a woman with a kid with special needs. His sister's ex was living proof of that.

"Do you have time for a real coffee break?" he asked Bianca as he waited for someone to answer his call.

She looked surprised by the invitation. Not as surprised as Logan was to have extended it. Thankfully, the receptionist spared him the need to say something that would explain *why*.

"I'd like to leave a message in Jack White's voice mail, please."

The woman put him on hold, and while a familiar Eagles tune wafted into his ear, Logan said to Bianca, "You know that great little coffee shop around the corner? It's never busy at this time of day, so—"

"This is Jack," said the recording. "You know what to do."

"Hey, Jack. It's Logan. Can't stop by today after all, so don't count on me to fill air time between Twinkies commercials." Laughing, he added, "See you at the meeting tonight."

He hung up, took a breath, then told Bianca, "My sister's son, Sam, is autistic, and he has a birthday coming up." He swallowed, nervous at sharing this personal information. "I thought maybe you could suggest a toy or a book or something that he'd enjoy."

Logan could almost read her mind, thinking, "Why not ask his mother?"

"And while you're at it," he tacked on, "maybe you can offer a different viewpoint on this idea I have of building a school for kids like Sam. And Drew." He paused long enough to add, "If you're not free, I can wait. Or come back in an hour or two. If you have things to wrap up, that is."

Did his rambling make him sound like an idiot to her, too?

She pointed at her desk. "As a matter of fact, I do have a lot to do before I pick up Drew."

"Oh. Yeah. Sure. Maybe some other time, then."

Silence.

Too truthful to schedule a rain date she wouldn't keep? He might have admired her honesty…if it hadn't made him feel like a babbling buffoon. Much as he hated to admit it, Bianca hadn't given him any reason to think her invitation to grab a cup of coffee from the production office had been anything but. He tried to cover his discomfort by stepping into the hall and looking both ways.

"This place is like a maze. Which way to the lobby again?"

"Are you parked out back or in the garage across the street?"

"Out back."

"Then you don't need to go all the way back to the lobby." She faced the computer. "Turn right and follow the hall to the end," she said, typing, typing, *typing*. "The double doors will lead you to the rear lot."

"Thanks. And thanks for the coffee, too. It really *was* as good as Starbucks."

The keys click-clacked as she said, "Glad you liked it. Drive safely now."

Logan left Bianca to her work, exited the building and got into his car. He'd already acknowledged her intelligence, but based on the smooth, thoughtful way she'd dismissed him, he had to admit that he'd seriously underestimated her people skills.

Movement to the left caught his attention,

and as the driver of an SUV backed out of the space beside his, he was reminded of that day, ten years earlier, when he'd heard the words that changed his life.

His mouth went dry, thinking of the way he'd handled the bad news. How almost four years had gone by before he'd quit treating it with booze. The all too familiar itch started in the back of his throat and his mouth went dry. Logan swallowed. Hard. In the past he would have scratched it with scotch, but AA—and his sponsor—had taught him how to divert the cravings. Logan made a mental note to tell Jack about it at tonight's meeting. Confessing these weak moments had kept him sober for six years, two weeks and five days.

He jammed the key into the ignition and decided to stop by his folks' house on the way home, see how his sister, Sandra, was holding up in taking care of their mom.

The engine emitted a guttural groan that echoed his mood. "Great," he muttered as a series of clicks punctuated the groan, "that's just great." Last thing he needed was a dead battery.

Logan grabbed his phone to call a tow truck. Nothing. No ring tone. No bars. What were

the odds of one guy having two dead batteries in the space of a minute? Slim to none, he
thought, slamming the driver's door.

He could follow the sidewalk around to the
front of the building and ask to use the phone
in the studio's waiting room. Or he could go
into the station the way he'd come out and borrow Bianca's instead.

CHAPTER THREE

RESEARCHING THE GUESTS' business and professional backgrounds was part of her job as assistant producer. Digging into their personal lives was *not*. Mild curiosity had prompted her to find out for herself if the media's assessment of Logan Murray was fact or fiction. She hadn't been surprised at—and quickly dismissed—the juicy tidbits about his romantic escapades. For one thing, her college minor had been PR. For another, common sense told her that if he'd dated as much as the entertainment mags claimed, he'd need forty-eight hours in every day.

Something about his message for the radio DJ echoed in her memory. "See you tonight at the meeting," he'd said. She thumbed through his file, looking for articles that might validate her suspicions. When nothing turned up, she ran a Google search.

Nothing.

Bianca sighed, staring at the list of links. Page after page of photos, bios and academic and athletic awards, but not a word about alcoholism, drug addiction or rehab. If only she could find the article she'd read, months ago, about the time he'd spent in rehab. Well, she thought, they didn't call it Alcoholics Anonymous for nothing.

Or she'd been dead wrong about him.

But why was it so important to find black-and-white evidence that he had skeletons in his closet? Because she needed reasons not to like him. Yeah, he'd said yes to her coffee offer, and yes, he'd invited her to talk autism at the café around the corner. That didn't mean he was interested in her. His file was filled with full-color photographic evidence that he liked his women footloose and flashy, not exhausted and widowed. She tossed the file aside and caught sight of her reflection in the mirrorlike window of the microwave. "You look old enough to be your own mother," she muttered, frowning.

"Talking to yourself again, eh?"

Bianca clapped a hand over her chest. "Good grief, Marty. You scared me half to death!"

"Sorry," he said. "I whistled all the way down the hall so I wouldn't startle you." Then he nodded at Drew's photograph. "How does he like the new school?"

"He's holding his own, I suppose."

"What's that mean...you suppose?"

"Well, he's talking a whole lot more and making eye contact most of the time. Best of all, he lets me hug him, and once in a while, he even hugs me back." Bianca thought of all the years when Drew had turned his face and stiffened when she showed affection in any way. She held her breath to forestall tears. "I just... hoped he'd be further along by now."

He gave her shoulder a friendly squeeze. "I don't need to remind you, of all people, that these things take time, do I?"

She returned his smile. "No, guess not. And I don't need to tell you that I'm not exactly the most patient mom on the planet, do I?"

"No, guess not," Marty echoed.

"So what brings you all the way down the hall to my minuscule cubicle?"

"Would you believe I misplaced Logan Murray's contact info? I forgot to thank him for inviting me to that golf outing last week."

Bianca reopened the file, grabbed a Post-it and wrote Logan's name and phone number on it.

Marty folded it in two and tucked it into the pocket of his crisp white shirt. "Want me to tell him anything for you?"

"Such as…?"

"Such as…you're sorry you turned down his coffee invitation?"

"You were eavesdropping?" Bianca feigned surprise. "I can't believe it!" Then, in a quieter, more serious tone, she added, "That is the *last* thing I want you to tell him."

"So if saying no to his clumsy invite is the last thing, what's the first?"

"I don't want you to tell him anything. Except, maybe, thanks for appearing on the show."

"Uh-huh. Are you forgetting how long we've known one another? I can see straight through you."

Nearly six years. He and Jason had belonged to the same athletic club and often had played doubles tennis. Marty had been at her kitchen table sipping iced tea, waiting for Jason to get home from work, when she took the call from Kennedy Krieger, confirming that Drew indeed had autism. And prior to Jason's cancer diagnosis, they'd been regular guests at Marty's house.

"I'm lucky to call you a friend," she admitted.

"Ditto, kiddo." The note crinkled when he patted his pocket. "Well, I'd better call the guy before I lose this." He rounded the corner, then ducked back in. "You're sure you don't want me to put in a good word for you?"

"Give it a rest, Marty. Even if I had time for a man in my life, you don't seriously think it would be someone like Logan Murray." As if to prove it, she clucked her tongue.

"I happen to know that he has a nephew just like Drew. So he knows all about autism."

"I know. We talked about him. His name's Sam."

Marty paused and said with a frown, "Will you let an old friend give you some advice?"

"Something tells me I couldn't stop you if I tried." Grinning, she crossed both arms over her chest. "Lemme have it, old friend."

"Logan and I have been pals for quite a while now, and—"

"Really. Then why did you need his contact information?"

"Because, Detective Wright, he got tired of the prank calls from crazy broads who want to become Mrs. Murray, so he changed his number. Again." He bobbed his head. "Trust me… I've known him long enough to be able to tell when he's interested in a gal, and when he's *really* interested, if you get my drift."

"Sorry to be so obtuse, but I don't. Get your drift, that is."

"The way he was lookin' at you?" Marty whistled. "He's into you, kid."

"Marty…"

He held up both hands. "Okay, never let it be said I can't take a hint." He gave her a quick hug. "See ya!"

Bianca shook her head. Logan Murray. Interested in her? Ridiculous enough to be comical, she thought as she grabbed her To Do list and read the remaining tasks: call Michael Phelps to remind him what time to arrive for his segment on *The Morning Show* next week; write as much of the teleprompter script as possible for tomorrow's show; order new business cards for herself and her boss; schedule an in-person meeting with Drew's teacher; write Logan Murray a thank-you note for appearing on today's show.

Bianca riffled through her greeting-cards file and found a blank-inside card with a sporty red convertible on the front. *Might as well get the most pressing task out of the way first,* she thought, picking up her favorite ballpoint.

"Dear Mr. Murray, the staff of WPOK thanks you for sharing your time and talents on *The Morning Show.*" That pretty much covered it, but Bianca didn't like the look of all that left-over white space. How would she fill it? she wondered, tapping the pen on her bottom teeth.

Then, remembering that Marty had invited him to come back soon, she added, "We look forward to your next appearance and will con-tact your agent soon to schedule a mutually convenient time." She signed it, "Cordially, Bi-anca P. Wright." If he took the time to read it himself, he'd realize she'd sent two messages for the price of one postage stamp: the station really did appreciate his time and talents, and in the remote possibility Marty was right about him, the signature line would make it clear she didn't share Logan's interest.

She picked up the phone to call Michael Phelps and waited while it rang, thinking.

Taking care of Drew barely left time for sleep, let alone a relationship. Not that she was complaining. Right from the start she and her little boy had connected on a level that no one else had seemed able to reach. Not even his own father. Bianca worked hard to repress memories of Jason's detached attitude toward

Drew, but at times like this, it was difficult to forget the cold, sometimes cruel things he said about his little boy.

A beep sounded in her ear, and it took a second to collect her thoughts. After leaving a voice mail message for Phelps, she sent the swimmer a follow-up text. Experience taught her that, from time to time, even the most organized celebrities let things fall through the cracks. "But not on *my* watch," she muttered, also sending him an email, just to be safe.

After putting in the order for updated business cards, Bianca dialed Mrs. Peterson's personal extension at the school. The note Mrs. Peterson had tucked into Drew's book bag had kept her up half the night, trying to figure out why the boy who seemed content and confident at home had reverted to old behaviors at school. Talking out of turn, getting up without permission, stemming…

"I'd like to discuss Drew's recent, ah, *setback,*" she said after the beep, "so please call me at your earliest convenience." If the recorder picked up the exasperation in her voice, so be it. Neither the staff nor the administration had gone out of their way to hide bias toward kids like Drew. Their misunderstanding of the disorder frustrated her, which inspired her decision to chaperone every field trip and volunteer weekly in the classroom. The hope was two-fold: explain the causes of disruptive behavior, and show them how to diffuse volatile situations by watching how she interacted with Drew and kids like him. Sadly, neither mission had met with much success.

But Bianca had never been a quitter. Not when her college friends told her that double-majoring was a waste of time and money. Not when Jason got sick. And certainly not when Drew was diagnosed with autism. Her son was counting on her now more than ever, and she wouldn't allow anything—or anyone—to keep her from doing what was in his best interests.

She picked up his picture and traced a fingertip over the sweet, crooked smile. "Don't worry, *il mio tesoro,* I'll make things right if it takes—"

A quiet knock interrupted her promise. She was surprised to see Logan, looking rumpled and lost, in her doorway.

"Uh-oh. Couldn't find your way to the exit?"

"Oh, I found it, all right," he said, rubbing grimy hands on a crisp white handkerchief, "but my car won't start. From the sound of things, I'm guessing it's the battery." He held up his cell phone. "Believe it or not, it's dead, too."

He seemed younger, and he looked vulnerable with that lock of near-black hair falling over one eye.

"I have jumper cables in my trunk," she offered. "If that doesn't do the job, I can drive you to my favorite mechanic's shop."

"No, no…don't want to put you out. Just came in to borrow your phone."

She grabbed her purse. "It's no bother. I'm pretty well finished for the day anyway."

For the second time that day, he fell into step beside her. Why did he seem taller than the six-foot-three claimed by his bio? Well-toned thighs flexed with every step. So much for the accuracy of the *Post* article claiming he'd let himself go since retiring from the game.

He held open the door, and as she stepped outside, Logan pointed. "That's my car over there."

She pointed, too. "And that's mine. Be right with you."

In one article about him, she recalled, a reporter had called Logan flamboyant, conceited, a braggart. Yet he was wearing an ordinary navy suit and driving a sedate black sedan. Had he changed a lot since his football days, or were the reports flawed?

Bianca got into her car, started the engine, then parked nose to nose with Logan's Camry, leaving just enough space to stand between the vehicles. How strange, she thought, climbing out of her Jeep, that even her mom drove a flashier vehicle than his. Bianca fastened her keys to the clip inside her purse and popped open the hood.

"So," Logan said, aiming a thumb over his shoulder, "was that Italian I heard when I walked into your office just now?"

"Italian?" It took a moment to figure out what he meant. "Oh, you mean *il mio tesoro*...."

Nodding, Logan pried open his hood, too.

"It's just a little term of endearment. Something I've called Drew since before he was born."

"'My treasure,'" he translated. "I think that's…sweet."

Why the hesitation? She'd met far too many people who considered kids like Drew nothing more than badly behaved nuisances. Some made half-baked attempts at tolerance. Others didn't even try. Which was Logan?

"My mom is Italian," they said at the same time.

Laughing quietly, Logan looked at the sky. "Takes me back…. My mom used to call me *poco terrore*." He met her eyes to add, "Totally different mothering style, evidently."

"Little terror?" Bianca couldn't resist a smile. According to her research, Logan was the youngest of three and the only boy. "So you were a handful even as a kid, huh?"

His expression said, *"Even then"?* But Logan held out a hand. "If you'll give me your keys, I'll get the jumper cables out of the back of your car."

"Thanks, but it'll be faster if I get them."

Bianca knew where the cables were. She had to know *exactly* where everything was—in the house, in her purse, here in the car—because she never knew when a noise, a crowd, a scent might set Drew off and she'd need to put her hands on something else that would quiet him quickly.

She moved both backpacks aside—one holding an assortment of toys, the other stuffed with healthy nonperishable snacks—and unearthed the duffel she'd filled with two outfits for Drew and a change of clothes for herself. Behind it sat the "Just in Case" bin, where she'd stacked blankets, a portable DVD and movies, earplugs and an odd assortment of miscellaneous para- phernalia. Finally, under that, she grabbed the red-zippered pouch labeled Car Kit.

"What's all that?" he asked. "Your bug-out gear?"

She'd seen a cable TV show featuring people who claimed to be prepared for any emergency, including grab-and-go bags.

"I guess you could call it that."

"Drew is one lucky kid."

"Oh?" Bianca grabbed the cables, then slammed the hatch.

"Looks like you're ready for just about any eventuality, which probably gives him a lot of security if things get crazy."

A lucky guess? Or had Logan learned a thing or two from his nephew? Might be nice, she thought, interacting with someone who under- stood what her life was like. How odd that all those articles and news clips showed an entirely different side of him. The negative reports told her Logan had bowed and scraped to garner media attention. What would those correspon- dents say if they could see him now, tie loos- ened and shirtsleeves cuffed, ready for—how had he put it?—any eventuality. Still, there was no escaping the fact that he hadn't just been a top-notch quarterback. He'd costarred in a few box-office hits and earned the moniker "TV's Commercial King" by making every product he advertised on TV seem too good to be true. Maybe what she was witnessing boiled down to two words: good actor.

A gust of March wind took her breath away. If she'd trusted Marty's forecast, Bianca would have worn a coat over her blazer.

"Cold?"

"I'll be fine." Shoulders up to fend off the chill, she said, "I'll get started while—"

He reached into his front seat and grabbed his suit coat. "First put this on."

Tempting as it was to accept it, Bianca said, "No, thanks." If she got dirt or grease on it, she couldn't afford to have it cleaned.

But he draped it over her shoulders anyway. Using his chin as a pointer, Logan added, "You sure you know how to use those things?"

"These," she said, "and every other tool in the shed. Except for the chainsaw." Bianca cringed. "That thing gives me the heebie-jeebies."

"Okay, then...." He got into his car and left the driver's door ajar.

"Everything turned off?"

"Yes, ma'am."

"Emergency brake on?"

"Yes, ma'am."

Bianca connected one red clamp to her battery's positive terminal, attached the other to the positive terminal on Logan's battery, then clipped the black clamp to the negative terminal of her battery and connected the second black clamp to an unpainted bolt on his engine block.

"Okay," she said, "I'm going to start the Jeep."

She stuck the key into the ignition and hesitated. He probably knew to let her car's engine idle a minute or two before starting his. Bianca didn't want to insult him, but she couldn't afford the time or money to replace their batteries if he didn't.

"You know not to start your car right way, right?"

"Yes, ma'am."

She couldn't see him, thanks to the raised hoods, but if his agreeable tone of voice matched his expression, he hadn't taken the question the wrong way.

Bianca fired up the Jeep, then hurried to the driver's side of his car.

Sunshine lit his face, making him squint as he looked up at her. Bianca stepped aside so that her shadow would block it…but not before noticing the pale dots peppering his nose and cheeks. Freckles? At *thirty-five?*

"Think it's safe to rev 'er up now?"

She nodded. "Just don't give it too much gas, okay?"

"Yes, ma'am."

When his car started right up, she fist-pumped the air the way she did every time Drew reached a goal…and Logan's jacket slipped from her shoulders and onto the dirty parking lot.

Retrieving it, she dusted it off. "See? I had a feeling something like that would happen."

Out of the car now, he took it from her and gave it a once-over. "Clean as a whistle."

But she could see the grit and grime that had stained the front pocket. Bianca felt duty-bound to do something about it.

"Just so happens there's a stack of dry cleaning on my closet floor," she said, reaching for it. "I'll drop it off with the rest of my—"

He held tight. "I told you that it's fine. But

even if it wasn't, I have an account with the best dry cleaner in town." He shrugged. "Besides, you already have enough on your shoulders."

Before she could ask what he meant, Logan said, "Can I get you to do me another favor?"

She caught herself staring. "A favor?"

"I don't trust this old beast to fire up again when I need it to, so I was wondering if maybe you'll let me buy you that cup of coffee now to thank you for the jump-start. And to keep you around awhile. For backup. In case this old clunker decides to play dead again when I get ready to hit the road."

The mention of his dead battery reminded her that she hadn't detached the cables. "Oh, for goodness' sake," she muttered. Silently, she ran down the step-by-step process: *remove black clamp from his engine bolt, then black clamp from my battery. Now red clamp from my car and red clamp from his.*

Once finished, she said, "It's been so long since I did this that I wasn't sure I'd remember the right order to do things."

"Now she tells me," he said to the cloudy sky.

In her rush to put everything back where it belonged in the Jeep, Bianca nearly dropped the cables.

Logan caught them. Caught her hands, too.

"You're freezing," he said. "Now you *have* to let me buy you a nice hot cup of coffee. The least I can do is warm you up after making you stand out here in the cold wind all this time. If you have time, that is, before picking Drew up at school."

Bianca checked her watch. By her calculations she had hours and hours!

Logan's lips slanted in a charming, boyish grin. "So you have time, then?"

She was freezing. It would feel good to discuss Drew's condition with someone who really understood it. And she was curious to hear more about this school he wanted to build, for no other reason than to get him on the show to tell the viewers all about it.

"Sure. Why not?"

"Try not to overexcite yourself," he teased, tossing the jacket onto the passenger seat, then climbing into his car. While parallel parking across from the café, Bianca remembered the last time she'd jumped a car battery; it had been three and a half years ago, driving home from Jason's funeral. Drew had gone completely ballistic, drawing the attention of every driver who had passed them on Frederick Road. And the last man she'd shared coffee with? The funeral director, who'd served it in a tiny disposable cup.

Memory of his solemn, monotonous voice prompted a grin because something told her this impromptu coffee date with Logan would be anything but boring.

CHAPTER FOUR

"So LET me get this straight," Griff said, "you spent an hour—"

"Hour and twenty minutes."

"Pardon me. I stand corrected." Griff leaned back in his oversized desk chair and propped both pointy-toed cowboy boots on the glass and stainless-steel desk. "You spent slightly less than an hour and a half with this gal, and already you're feeling...protective."

"She reminds me of Sandra." He shrugged. "So sue me."

Not surprisingly, Griff didn't violate the attorney–client rule, divulging details of his sister's case, even though he and Logan had been as tight as brothers since high school. Logan had seen Griff through a brutal divorce, and Griff had helped Logan survive the first grueling year after the team dropped him.

"But she's a widow?"

"Yeah...."

"Then I don't get it. Your sister divorced her thug of a husband. Do you suspect this Bianca woman was abused, too?"

"No." She hadn't said or done anything to leave that impression. "I can't explain it," Logan admitted. "It's just…" He didn't dare say *It's just something I* feel. Because of the autism connection, and because he was in no mood to fend off his friend's razzing.

Griff put his feet on the floor and leaned both forearms on his desk. "Can I tell you how I feel?"

He sat up straighter. "Suppose I say no."

Griff shrugged. "Then I ignore you, as usual." He aimed a crooked forefinger—the one he'd broken twenty years earlier while playing HORSE in Logan's driveway—and said, "Read my lips: Mind. Your. Own. Business."

Logan winced at the stinging truth of it because he *wanted* her to be his business.

"Chances are, the only thing she has in common with Sandra is an autistic kid. But if there are more parallels?" Griff shook his head. "Then you need to back off. Right now. Or you'll open yourself for a world of hurt. Again."

The not-so-subtle reference to Logan's last

disastrous relationship didn't go unnoticed. Everyone had told him to steer clear of Willow. His parents' main objection had been the eight-year age gap. *She's a lifetime ahead of you!* they'd said. But Griff had been present to witness a few of her outbursts. Despite his friend's objections—and because he'd been young, stubborn and determined to become her protector—Logan had convinced himself that once they got to know her, they'd love her, too. Griff, included.

"Took you a year to recover from what that batty broad did to you."

"You'd think a guy with a hundred degrees on his wall would know *broad* isn't PC."

"And you'd think a guy with a hundred Tinseltown starlets listed in his little black book would know better than to get tangled up with another emotional basket case. Besides, the only way Wacky Willow deserves PC is if it stands for Permanent Confinement in the nearest loony bin."

They'd been down this road enough times that Logan knew it was futile to argue the "Willow was certifiable" point. "So maybe Bianca has some issues. Who doesn't? Doesn't mean she's crazy."

"Or that she was abused."

Logan waited for Griff to repeat the warning he'd issued during those early months with Willow: *Better steer clear of* that *one*....

Thankfully, Griff grabbed Logan's file. "So when are you planning to see this Bianca person again?"

It had been almost a week since she'd sat across from him, sipping cappuccino and talking about her son, but it might as well have been an hour ago. He remembered thinking how the shaft of early-March sunlight, spilling in from the window behind her, gave a halo-like quality to her short blond curls. But then he'd said, "I know a gal who works at Kennedy Krieger, so I know it isn't easy to get an appointment. If you need help getting in, say the word." Instead of saying "Drew is fine where he is," or "We'll see," she'd got to her feet, ice-blue eyes scanning his face as she'd thanked him for the coffee and left.

"Yo. Dude." Griff snapped his fingers. "Earth to Logan, Earth to Logan...."

He met Griff's concerned stare.

"We have work to do, so how 'bout you nap on your own time."

"This is my time," Logan kidded, "bought

and paid for to the tune of one seventy-five an hour."

"Consider yourself lucky. If you weren't a pal, you'd pay double," Griff shot back. He tossed a wad of paper into the trash can. "So as I was saying when you veered off into Bianca-land, when will you see her again?"

"Next time I'm on *The Morning Show,* I guess. Hadn't really thought about it."

"If you say so."

The paperback-sized clock on Griff's desk chimed eleven times. Using the cap of his ball-point, he tapped Logan's file. "Back to business. If you're serious about this autism project, you'll need a clear-cut mission statement." Griff leafed through the will. "What did you do, swallow a leprechaun or something? How does one guy get so lucky in life?"

He'd said pretty much the same thing when Logan had brought him the document naming him sole inheritor of David Richards's assets. A devout Knights fan, the mega-millionaire had often sought Logan's help in raising funds for his pet charities, and as had time passed, he'd begun introducing Logan as "the son I never had." When a team of Hopkins specialists di-agnosed Stage 4 esophageal cancer, David—

recently divorced from his third wife—sent for Logan. In what turned out to be his last self-deprecating joke, David made Logan promise to distribute his wealth "with my big philanthropic heart in mind."

And Logan aimed to do just that.

"The mission statement doesn't have to be fancy," Griff continued. "Just a few short paragraphs describing the purpose of the charity. Who'll run it. Who'll benefit. Once I have it, I can write your Articles of Incorporation, file for your tax ID number—all that legal stuff you pay me the big bucks to do on your behalf." He scribbled something on the inside front cover of the folder, then met Logan's eyes. "Have you decided if this is to be a board-only organization?"

"Unless things have changed since our last meeting, that's the best way to keep greedy stockholders out of the equation."

Griff made another note in the file. "Given any thought to who'll help draft the bylaws?"

Logan rested his elbows on the wingback's arms, then steepled his fingers under his chin. He groaned again, wondering if he'd made a mistake. Funneling the remaining dollars into David's existing charities would be way eas-

ier than building one from the ground up. But
his old friend had been very specific, saying,
"Your heart has never been in any of these proj-
ects of mine. Find one of your own, something
that will make you feel like you're making a
difference, the way mine made me feel." Helping his nephew and kids like him… If Logan
could accomplish something like that, maybe
he wouldn't feel as if he was just taking up
space and wasting the air he breathed.

Griff was still scribbling when Logan added,
"I know a couple people with warehouse space
for sale that could work as a school. But I don't
know if that's the way to go." He paused as
another question popped into his head. "How
many board members do you recommend?"

"I think the two of us can handle it."

"Can't think of anyone else who'll keep their
eyes on the prize and leave their egos—and
self-indulgence—at the door."

"Yeah. They broke the good-guy mold when
they made us, didn't they?"

The friends shared a quiet laugh as Griff
closed the file. "Well, the money is safe in
the bank, so you have plenty of time to think
about it."

Logan got to his feet. "Free for lunch?"

"I wish. I'm due in court at one." He extended his hand, and as Logan grasped it, Griff added, "Be careful, pal."

"Hey. I'll sleep easy knowing you're handling the official stuff."

"I'm not talking about this school project," he said, pointing at the file. "I mean this Bianca woman. You barely know her and already you have that gleam in your eye. Last thing you need is to go head over heels for a woman just because she has a kid like Sam."

Bianca's son was largely responsible for the hours he'd spent this week boning up on specific disorders within the autism spectrum. When he'd deepened the research by interviewing a few experts, he was surprised to learn that more than half of the markers could just as easily describe *him* and other athletes who'd suffered head injuries. The similarities between him and Sam made Logan more determined than ever to build a facility that would help normalize their lives. "Just be careful, okay?" Griff said, walking with him to the door. "I don't have time to put you back together again, Humpty." Then, "Do me a favor?"

"No, I will not give you J-Lo's number."

Griff's eyebrows rose. "Whoa. You mean to say you actually have Jennifer Lopez's—"

Logan only laughed.

"Oh, you're a regular comedian, aren't you?" But he wasn't laughing when he added, "Don't let this one lead you down the primrose path, okay?"

Logan had recently earned his six-years-sober chip, but because he'd seen him hit rock bottom—and stay there for years—Griff had a right to wonder what might shove him off the wagon. And time was the only cure for that.

"Break a leg in court," Logan said, walking backward toward the elevators.

"Chesapeake fishing trip next week. Call me if you're interested."

"Will do," he said, stepping into the elevator. As it dropped toward the basement garage, Logan remembered how, after the Willow debacle, Griff had suggested counseling, "to find out why you're attracted to women with more baggage than an airport luggage carousel." Griff hadn't been the only one who felt that way, which sent Logan on a quest to prove his friend and family wrong. Unfortunately, what he'd learned confirmed their beliefs; according to articles and the results of dozens of university studies he'd read, Logan suffered from what experts called Prince Charming Syndrome. To this day, it remained one of his most embarrassing secrets. Because he'd self-diagnosed the problem, it made sense to prescribe a cure: abstinence.

CHAPTER FIVE

"Mommy?"

Bianca turned down the volume on the tiny kitchen TV. It had been Drew's idea to leave it on while he did homework. "I have to learn to work with distractions around me," he'd said on the first day of school. Amazingly, he'd been right.

She tucked her pen into the checkbook register and traded it for the math assignment he held.

"Finished my homework page," he said.

Not an easy feat, she thought, tears in her eyes. "You answered every question correctly, and it's so nice and neat. I'm so proud of you!"

A slight furrow appeared between his brows as he studied her face. "Then…then why are you sad?"

"Oh, honey, I'm not sad. These are *happy* tears. I'm happy because…" *Because you're looking at me. Straight into my eyes and seeing me!* She got up, walked to his side of the table and wrapped her arms around him. "Because I love you so, *so* much!"

Drew groaned good-naturedly. "I know. Love you, too."

Her three favorite words. He'd been reciting them since before he could walk. They had always sounded hollow, robotic, anything but sincere…until about six months ago, when his facial expressions and voice proved he meant them. How far he'd come since September!

"Can I have a snack break before I do my spelling homework?"

"What would you rather have—string cheese or apple slices?"

"Ice cream! Ice cream! *Ice cream!*" he bellowed.

Bianca laughed. "Okay, how about a healthy snack now and ice cream when your homework is finished?"

He thought about it for a minute, then said, "Do I have a choice?"

"Of course you do—string cheese or apple slices."

"Apple slices will get my pencil sticky," he said, hopping toward the fridge.

She went back to balancing the checkbook,

and he went back to his assignment. His willingness to cooperate made it hard to believe he'd been misbehaving in class. Bianca thought about her recent conversation with Mrs. Peterson. "Is something going on at home, Mrs. Wright," the teacher wanted to know, "that will help me understand why he's acting out?"

Months before his first day of school, Bianca had hand-delivered Drew's file and spent hours defining every test, explaining every result, listing every specialist who'd evaluated Drew and their every conclusion. There were photos. Charts. CDs and DVDs of sessions with occupational, speech and behavioral therapists. She'd been deliberately thorough, for the very reason Mrs. Peterson had mentioned during the meeting: so his teacher would better understand Drew. "He isn't acting out at home," she'd wanted to shout, "so maybe the problem is *at school!*"

Instead, she'd said, "You're too busy teaching and monitoring the other children to keep an eye on Drew every single minute." Bianca promised to spend a lot more time in the classroom so that hopefully, she'd notice something—anything—that would explain Drew's behavior. Because when all was said and done, only one thing mattered: Drew.

She took her son's hands in hers. "So how's school these days, sweetie?"

His pupils dilated before he looked quickly away. And when he started bobbing his head and chanting "school, school, school," Bianca had all the proof she needed that home was *not* the source of the problem.

She adopted a deliberately sing-song tone to break the cycle. "Drew. Honey. Tell Mommy what's going on at school."

An article in *Autism Advocate* explained that kids could sidetrack themselves from stemming, that distracting tendency of autistics to flap their hands, bob their heads and any one of a dozen other repetitive actions. When she explained how the process worked, Drew came up with his own distraction tactics. Dancing, not spinning; jumping instead of running; watching a video to stop himself from staring at lights. It had been months since he'd learned that sitting on his hands put a stop to hand flapping. Longer still since he'd bobbed his head once he figured out that touching his chin to his chest controlled the urge. Yet there he sat, doing both, and it seemed he'd forgotten how to stop himself. Her heart ached, knowing she'd caused it with her ill-timed question.

Then an idea sparked, and she went with it. "What is the boy's name?"

When Drew looked up, his expression said, *How did you know it was a boy?*

"It's okay," she said, scooting her chair closer. "What's the boy's name?"

"His name is Joseph. Joseph is his name. Joseph is the new kid."

Proceed with caution, Bianca thought. Putting ideas in his head to get the information she needed wouldn't help Drew in the long run.

"What can you tell me about Joseph the new kid?"

"I don't like Joseph." Drew sat on his hands but continued shaking his head.

"Why not?"

"Because," he said, sitting taller, "he butts in line and pushes people down and takes other kids' stuff." Drew paused, then pursed his lips. "Joseph kicks. And hits. And uses potty words *all* the time." Frowning, he rested his chin on his chest. "Mrs. Peterson never sees Joseph do any of that. She only sees me get mad when he does it."

Her maternal instinct was strong, and she

wanted nothing more than to hold him tight and promise she'd put a stop to Joseph's bullying. But her desire to help Drew was stronger.

"And you know what else?"

"What else, sweetie?"

"Joseph calls me Flappity Weirdster Weirdo," Drew grumbled. Eyes narrowed, his little hands formed tight fists. "And you know what *else?*"

"What…"

"He bites. *Hard.*"

Bianca gently rolled up his shirt sleeves and stifled a gasp as she saw half a dozen crescent-shaped bruises on each slender forearm.

She wanted to slap Joseph silly. Slap the teacher, too, for allowing this to happen to her sweet boy. Heart pounding, she grit her teeth. *Oh, you are going to get* such *a piece of my mind, Mrs. Peterson!*

The poignant music of a Save the Animals commercial wafted from the television, drawing Drew's attention, and it seemed to Bianca that the abused dogs' and cats' forlorn expressions mirrored her son's mood. She tried to comfort him with a hug, but he stiffened and pulled away.

"Wish I had a daddy who loved me," he said.

Did he yearn for a superhero-type dad who'd

storm the school, demanding protection for his little boy? Or simply someone to tell him that he hadn't invited—and certainly didn't deserve—Joseph's malicious treatment?

Drew stared at the TV as a new commercial appeared on the screen, and in this one, Logan Murray's friendly face smiled out at them.

"Autism Service Dogs of America," he said, "was founded to improve the lives of kids who need a little help...."

She'd heard of the organization and had looked in to getting a dog for Drew. When she had learned that it could cost in the neighborhood of twenty thousand dollars, she'd closed the book on that area of autism research. Not that the dogs weren't worth the price—for the right families—but Bianca wasn't the type to organize a fund-raiser, appealing to friends, family, neighbors and coworkers to help defray the cost.

She'd read Logan's bio cover to cover and knew that it contained a long and varied list of charities. When had he become affiliated with ASDA?

Drew pointed. "Why couldn't I have a dad like *that?*"

She hoped he wouldn't repeat his rendition

of *Daddy Didn't Love Me*. If she hadn't figured out why some parents—fathers, mostly—couldn't cope with autism, how could she explain it to her little boy?

Now Logan squatted and draped an arm around a happy-faced labradoodle. "Isn't that right, Poe?"

When the dog answered with a breathy *woof,* Drew's entire demeanor changed.

"Look, Mom! That dog is *smiling!*"

The only smile Bianca noticed was Drew's.

"Can I have a dog, Mom? That man said it would be good for a kid like me."

A kid like him. She grinned at his ability to make the connection. "We've talked about this before, remember? We can't have a dog because Grandmom is allergic to them."

His shoulders slumped. "I forgot." But he perked up when the curly-haired mutt walked off-screen. "But—but—but—but Mrs. Peterson has a dog like that. I saw the picture on her desk." He paused. "And *she's* allergic."

His grandmother's sensitivity to fur and dander had almost been a blessing in disguise, giving Bianca a good excuse to avoid housebreaking and training a dog and cleaning up after it. Still, if she could find one like the curly-haired mutt grinning into the camera now, she might think about it.

She didn't dare admit such a thing, of course, because in Drew's mind, anything but a flat-out no was a bona fide commitment, one he'd obsess about until something else came along to take the place of his desire for a dog. Bianca decided to divert his attention before mild curiosity turned into fixation.

"Did Mrs. Peterson give you any other homework?"

"She said 'Study for a spelling quiz tomorrow, boys and girls!'" He started reading his list of words as Logan recited the charity's contact information. The camera zoomed in on his face. "The kids need you. Tell 'em, Poe." And right on cue, the tail-wagging dog barked.

"Mom, can we at least *think* about getting a dog?"

She picked up the spelling list. "How about you finish your homework, and maybe then we can *talk* about thinking about it."

"Great. More 'Grandmom is allergic' talk." Drew sighed heavily. "Sometimes," he said, "that mother of yours is *so* exasperating."

"Exasperating," she echoed, mussing his hair. "Do you know what it means?"

"Frustrating, annoying, maddening…"

No wonder every specialist called him The Little Professor, she thought as he assigned a new synonym to each of his fingertips.

Grinning, Bianca started Drew's favorite supper. She grabbed mac and cheese and tomato soup from the pantry and thought about how, in nursery school and pre-K, the county had assigned him to class settings designed specifically for children on the autism spectrum. Almost immediately Drew had sensed that his learning deficiencies weren't as severe as most of his classmates. In typical Drew fashion, he began gathering data, and one day, halfway through his kindergarten year, he put his self-assessment into words: "I can do lots of things those other kids can't do, and I know stuff they don't know." He'd stopped flapping and crossed both arms over his chest to add, "And I control myself way, way better, too." Chin up, he met her eyes. "I think it's time for me to go to *regular* school."

So Bianca met with his pediatrician, his teacher and the school principal and guidance counselor. Thanks to a school board member whose granddaughter was on the spectrum, the team decided to give Drew a chance. His academic performance and personal conduct would be closely monitored. If it was determined that his behavior distracted fellow students, or that he couldn't keep up with curriculum, back to special sessions he'd go. She gave him a lot of credit because he'd held his own...until Joseph was introduced to the mix.

Bianca watched him, eyes squinted in concentration as he whispered *"Mother. M-O-T-H-E-R."* He repeated the process with all twelve words on his list.

"Hey, Mom. Can you do two things at once?"

"Depends what the two things are," she said, stirring elbow noodles into the boiling water.

"Can you mix noodles and test me?"

She turned down the heat under the pot and sat beside him. One by one, she read the words aloud, and one by one, he spelled them. "Great job, honey!" she said when he finished. "You got every single one right!"

"Does that mean I can turn the TV up now?"

Bianca winked. "Okay, but only until I get supper on the table." She gave the macaroni a quick stir, then grabbed three plates and a handful of silverware as the exact same commercial came on, again.

Logan, looking all handsome and savvy in

neatly creased black trousers and a pale blue shirt that brought out the green in his eyes.

"Ninny," she grumbled. "Why would you notice something like that?"

Bianca blamed it on the tiny café table that had put them nearly nose to nose at the coffee shop. Or the sunshine streaming in through the windows that made his eyes glitter like sea glass. Or the long, dark lashes that—

"Look, Mom," Drew said, tugging at her sleeve, "it's *him* again." He narrowed one eye. "Say…isn't he the guy who played a cop in that DVD we watched with Grandmom the other night?"

Bianca's mother walked into the room and grabbed a bottle of water from the fridge. "Why, Drew," Maddy said, looking over his shoulder at the television, "you're absolutely right. That's Logan Murray, and he *did* play the part of the cop who helped Mr. Action save Grand City." She kissed the top of his head. "Your mom is friends with him. Maybe she can get you his autograph."

Drew's eyebrows disappeared beneath thick blond bangs. "Whoa. Mom." He shot her an admiring glance. "You know him? For *real?*"

"Easy, you two," she said, laughing. "I

booked him for *The Morning Show* a couple of times, that's all." She remembered the feel of his big warm hands as he draped his jacket over her shoulders.

"Well," Maddy said, "maybe *friend* was too strong a word."

"But you really, really *know* him?"

"Yes, Drew." Her brain conjured the image of Logan nodding attentively as she rambled on and on about her only child. "But only in a professional capacity."

"Professional capacity," he echoed. "Does that mean you could ask him how *we* could get one of those dogs?" He grinned up at Maddy. "Don't worry, Grandmom," he said, "we'll find one that won't make your eyes swell shut."

As Drew's attention returned to the commercial, Bianca caught her mom's gaze and mouthed, *Let's talk later, okay?*

Maddy squatted beside Drew's chair. "I have a bunch of shopping bags in my trunk," she said, mussing his hair. "After supper, will you help me bring them in?"

His eyes never left the screen. "Mmm-hmm."

Rising, Maddy faced her daughter. "So tell me…is he as charming and handsome in real life as he is on the big screen?" She glanced at the television. "And the small screen?"

As a matter of fact, she thought Logan was more attractive in person than on film, but admitting it would only invite a volley of requests for autographs for her friends...and a repeat performance of "Honey, Jason died *three years* ago!"

Bianca did her best to sound indifferent. "I wouldn't say that." She dished mac and cheese onto three plates. "Supper's almost ready, Drew. Time to wash your hands."

He rose slowly and walked toward the powder room. "A dog for Drew," he said. "A *dog* for Drew. A dog for *Drew!*"

Maddy waited until he was out of earshot. "Good heavens, Bianca, how are you going to talk him out of this *dog* idea?"

"I may not have to," she began. "I've heard good things about these canine companion/autism kid partnerships. Sometimes, if people volunteer to foster these dogs, the agencies bypass the fees. I'll need to do more research before talking with Drew, of course, but if I can work it out..." She met her mother's eyes. "But what about you?"

"What about me? If there's really a breed out

there that won't make my eyes swell shut," she said, quoting Drew, "I see no harm in it. Every boy needs a dog."

"But everything will be different with a furry four-legged kid in the house."

Maddy ladled tomato soup into bowls. "We'll need to make some adjustments, of course. But you know, I think a pet will be good for all of us. It'll give Drew something to focus on besides those ridiculous electronic gizmos of his."

He did spend an inordinate amount of time with handheld games and such, Bianca admitted to herself as she filled Drew's glass with milk.

"I'm not complaining, mind you," Maddy continued, "but it gets lonely around here when you're at work and Drew is in school. Might be nice to have a warm body around that enjoys affection."

Bianca couldn't argue. Drew participated in physical affection—if she was careful not to overdo it—but barely ever hugged his grandmother. All in good time, she thought. Hopefully.

"Bianca…since you need to find out more about these helper dogs anyway, have you considered asking Logan Murray to help?"

"He's the organization's commercial spokesperson, Mom. He might not know anything that might help us."

"How will you know unless you ask?"

Drew hopped into the room, grabbed his napkin and rolled it into a tube. "Grandmom is right," he said through it. "Like you're always telling me…you won't know unless you ask."

Laughing, Bianca rolled her eyes. "Two against one isn't fair!"

"Something else you keep saying and saying and saying… 'Life isn't always fair.'"

She picked up her napkin and waved it like a white flag. "I surrender. Now, can we eat before everything gets cold?"

If she'd known her son and her mom would spend the rest of the meal discussing Logan Murray, Bianca would have a popped a movie into the DVD player and served pizza for supper instead.

CHAPTER SIX

"From the mouths of babes," Deidre said. "And what did you tell him?"

"That he was right, of course, because life isn't always fair."

"Well, if it's any consolation, I've known that Murray boy since he knocked on my door and offered to shovel my sidewalks and driveway…and you know how long and winding *that* is! He couldn't have been more than twelve. Wouldn't take a dime because my husband—do you remember him? Brooke's grandfather?—was in the hospital at the time."

Bianca pictured the regal-looking gentleman who'd helped Deidre raise Brooke and her sister, Beth, after their parents' fatal car crash. The couple attended more events at the girls' high school than most parents, so although she'd never officially met the man, Bianca remembered him well.

"Logan was a sweetheart then," Deidre

went on to say, "and he's a sweetheart now. I'd bet the success of my theater that he'll move heaven and earth to help you get a dog for that terrific kid of yours." She paused but only long enough to take a breath. "So what I'm saying in a roundabout way is, don't be an idiot, girl. Let him help you!"

Thanks to her mother's appetite for the theater, Bianca had had numerous opportunities to interact with Deidre over the years. Almost from the start, the two had forged a strong bond—which perplexed everyone, Maddy in particular—because they had so little in common. But Deidre was everything Bianca wished she could be: energetic and glamorous with a fearless attitude toward life and love… and speaking her mind.

"Okay, lady," she teased, "I can take a hint. Soon as I get home, I'll try calling him."

"'Do or do not,'" Deidre said, quoting Yoda, "'there is no *try*.'"

The back screen door slammed and heavy footfalls moved up the hall.

"Good grief," Deidre said. "You look like something the cat dragged in."

Bianca followed her gaze to the dark-haired man who stood in the parlor doorway.

"Remember when I said we'd make one heck of a couple," he began, "if I were older?"

Deidre blushed. "How could I forget? You made the inane announcement in front of the entire cast of *Guys and Dolls!*"

"That's right. Which is exactly why you owe me one."

"Owe you? For what!"

"For giving the wannabe actors who follow you around a new way to butter you up in the hope of snagging a leading role."

"Don't flatter yourself, handsome. I've heard 'em all. Now, bring your ornery self in here so I can introduce you to my pretty young friend. Bianca Wright, meet Griffin Gerrard."

He stopped several feet from Bianca's chair and cocked his head to the side, as if trying to remember if they'd met before. "Call me Griff. I'd shake your hand, but as you can see," he said, showing his grass-stained palms, "your old friend here is a real slave driver."

"Careful who you're calling old, dollface, or I might show up at your fancy-pants office and tell your fancy-pants clients that their high-priced lawyer didn't read his lease before he signed it."

"Didn't think I needed to, *friend.*" Griff pretended to frown. "If I'd known you had added a Work for Cheap Rent clause…"

"You're so full of stuff and nonsense, I'm amazed it doesn't leak from your ears!" Deidre leaned closer to Bianca to add, "Only reason I tolerate this young rascal is because his father and my dear departed Percy were the best of friends." Eyes on Griff again, she snorted. "You know as well as I do there's no such clause in our lease. And wasn't it just your good fortune when the Patapsco River overflowed its banks and flooded your entire first floor—and an exterminator said he'd need to tarp the house— that you could rent a room from me, instead of checking into a hotel for months?"

"A tarp?" Bianca echoed. The image of a house overrun with bugs sent a shiver down her spine. "Sounds serious."

He sat on the arm of the sofa. "Could have been worse," he began, "if I hadn't caught it early. Kept hearing this tick-tick-ticking in the walls." Griff clicked his thumbnail against the nail of his index finger. "All day. All night. One day it drove me crazy enough to tear down a sheet of paneling, and I found evidence of wood bores feasting on the studs." He counted on his fingers. "So in the past month, I've hired one

contractor to vacuum water out of the basement and seal the foundation, two more to replace the plumbing and wiring and another to
waterproof the cellar walls. And when *they're*
finished, an exterminator will tarp the house
and pump a truckload of insecticide inside. Unless he's a con man, the stuff will kill the wood
bores' eggs, too." He shrugged. "But nobody
forced me to buy a hundred-year-old house."

Deidre leaned closer to Bianca. "Do you believe in coincidence?"

"I suppose. Maybe. Sometimes."

"Well, for your information—oh mistress of
certitude—this handsome lawyer here is like
this," Deidre said, crossing her fingers, "with
your Logan."

What did she mean by *her* Logan?

"Ah, now I know why your name sounded
so familiar," Griff said.

His comment made even less sense than Deidre's. Even after studying Logan's press kit she
knew very little about him, and he knew even
less about her. What could he have shared with
Griff?

She might have put the question to him if
Deidre hadn't chosen that moment to hop up
from her chair.

"Goodness gracious sakes alive!" Bangle bracelets and the hodgepodge of beads and chains wrapped around her neck rattled and clinked as she jogged into the foyer. "I need to be at the theater in half an hour." After pulling a tube of lipstick from her blue silk trousers pocket, she leaned into the big oval mirror and added a layer of bright red to her puckered mouth. "We're doing *Dial* M *for Murder*," she said, repocketing the tube. "If you two want to come on opening night, say the word and I'll save you a couple of tickets."

"Dee. *Dah*ling," Griff said, "you know as well as I do that Hitchcock plays aren't my cup of tea."

"The way you butcher a British accent, it's a good thing you didn't audition for the play!" She fluffed gleaming, chin-length white tresses. "How 'bout *you,* Bianca? Think Drew could sit through two hours of mystery and mayhem?"

Not without earplugs, a blindfold and a prescription for Ritalin, Bianca thought. "Maybe in a few years, when he's a little more mature." Someday, she hoped, the day would come when Drew could enjoy things like movies in a real theater or live performances onstage. "But thanks for the invitation."

Deidre grabbed her cloak from the hall tree. "Tell your mom to call me, Bee-darling," she said, whirling it around her shoulders. "Haven't seen her in weeks. Bet she could use a night off, poor thing."

Poor thing? Not once since her mom moved in had Bianca taken advantage of the situation. She dropped Drew off at school—where he stayed for seven hours every day—and picked him up again. Did the laundry, cooking, shopping and cleaning…most of it in the middle of the night to free up daytime hours for Drew. Poor thing, indeed! Evidently, Logan wasn't the only one talking out of turn.

Deidre slung a huge hand-painted hobo bag over one shoulder and jangled her keys. "Well, I'm off! If I'm not back before you turn in tonight, Griff *dah*ling, make sure the front door is locked, won't you?" She bussed Bianca's cheek. "Don't forget to have your mom call me!"

Then she raced out the door with a dramatic flap of her satiny black cape.

A second, perhaps two, ticked by before Griff said, "She sure knows how to make an exit, doesn't she?"

"The same can be said about her entrances."

"What is she...sixty-five? Seventy?"

"She'll be seventy-six on her next birthday."

"The way she moves?" Griff shook his head. "That's hard to believe, isn't it?"

Bianca nodded, then shouldered her purse. Griff seemed pleasant enough, but she had no desire to discuss the lady of the manor—or anything else, for that matter—with this near stranger.

"Well, I'd better go," she said. "It was nice meeting you." She moved toward the door, but Griff got there first.

"Same here," he said, opening it. "When you see Logan, tell him I said hey...."

He didn't know it, but he'd just provided the perfect opening for her to call Logan and ask for help with the dog. *Met your friend today.... He asked me to say hi.*

"...and that his Articles of Incorporation are ready."

Was it Griff's stance or knowing he was a lawyer that reminded her of the way Jason had loved to bait her with 'are you smart enough to know *this?*' tests?

The memory roused a foul mood, but she shrugged it off.

"Nice meeting you," she repeated and ran down the porch steps. Just how close was he to Logan? Because…birds of a feather and all that.

CHAPTER SEVEN

IT SHOULDN'T MATTER what Call-Me-Griff Gerrard thought of her. Jason had been gone more than three years; the things he'd said and done shouldn't matter, either.

Then why did they?

The ten-minute drive between Deidre's place and her own usually filled her with a sense of calm, especially once she'd turned onto Tongue Row, where centuries-old stone houses hugged the curb and the branches of ancient oaks canopied the road. Not so on this crisp March day.

Shake it off, she scolded. *You don't have time—or the right—to feel sorry for yourself.*

The line of a favorite song filtered from the car's speakers. "…your prison…is walkin' through this world all alone…."

Any other day Bianca would have turned up the volume and belted out the lyrics. This time, the words cut a little too close to the bone. But it wasn't Jason's fault that she'd always been a hopeless romantic.

In the beginning, Jason was Atticus Finch, Sir Galahad and the woodsman who saved Peter from the wolf all rolled into one. She envisioned him as The One who'd turn her little-girl wishes into grown-woman realities: a loving husband, a cozy home, a child to fill its rooms with laughter. During their first few years together, it seemed he shared her dreams. Yes, he was a workaholic, and no, he hadn't been particularly affectionate, but part of the dream was better than none of it. Sadly, Drew's birth forced her to admit the ugly truth: autism hadn't turned Jason *into* a cold, arrogant man; he'd always been that way.

Bianca turned into her driveway and stared at the front of the house—the only home Drew had ever known. The wreath on the door and the mat on the porch said WELCOME. Friends, neighbors and family all praised her for making them feel so much at home that they sometimes lost track of time. When had she last felt that way herself?

Long enough that she couldn't remember.

Once inside her home, she looked around at the rooms she'd redecorated in the hope of filling the gap left by his death. She hadn't been able to control his feelings toward Drew, nor could she control the disease that had taken him from her, but this…this she could control.

The first thing she noticed, walking into the now-sunny kitchen, was Drew's colorful reminder taped to the refrigerator door: A DOG FOR DREW. He'd drawn accurate renditions of not one but *seven* dogs, one for every year he'd lived, "…so we're not stuck lookin' at just one kind."

Smiling, she pressed a palm to a curled corner of the yellow construction paper. Oh, how she loved the boy who was slowly emerging from the lonely shell of autism. If adding a furry, four-legged member to the family would help open the crack of what remained of that shell, she'd beg, borrow or grovel…even to the likes of Logan Murray.

The weather had been glorious these past few days, so she opened the back door and took a deep breath of the sweet spring breeze, then grabbed a notepad and pen from the basket beside the phone and sat at the table. TALKING POINTS, she printed across the top of the pad's first page, and wrote one through ten in the left margin. Her younger sister, Lily, a freelance writer for several local newspapers, had shared the method when Bianca complained about how difficult it was to dig for interview facts that went deeper than the limited information provided by guests' press kits. With a bit of luck, the questions she'd written down for Logan would be answered by the man himself.

She scrolled to his number in her cell phone, took a deep breath and hit the call button. His line rang five times before the now-familiar voice said, "You've reached Logan Murray. Leave a message and I'll get back to you soon."

Bianca hadn't considered the possibility that she'd get voice mail. Without a prepared script, what would she say?

She cleared her throat. "Hi. Logan. It's… This is Bianca. Bianca Wright, from WPOK? When you get a minute, I wonder if you'd give me a call. I, um…there's something…" She pinched the bridge of her nose. "I thought, maybe, since you're affilia—"

The end-of-message beep cut her off midword. Bianca stared at the phone's keypad for a second and considered calling again to pick up where she'd left off. "Right," she grumbled, dropping the phone into her blouse pocket.

"Leave more evidence that you're a stereotypical ditzy blonde."

Bianca turned on the radio sitting on the kitchen counter and dance music filled the air. A glance at her homemade clock told her she had time to start supper before leaving to pick Drew up at school. It also told her that the bowl of a silver spoon she'd tacked into place in the four o'clock spot had slipped out of alignment. Bianca slid a kitchen chair up to the sink and climbed onto the counter.

She reached up to remove the clock from its nail when a DJ-smooth baritone said, "Wouldn't a step stool be safer?"

In one instant she was falling, arms windmilling, too startled to scream.

In the next she found herself nestled in the strong, sure arms of Logan Murray, whose brow furrowed and blue-green eyes were filled with concern. Bianca hadn't been this close to a man in more than a year, when Maddy had arranged a date with her yoga instructor's son; two hours with Davis Blackwell—aka The Octopus—had given her the courage to put a stop to her mother's "A Dad for Drew" campaign.

"You okay?"

Heart pounding, she said, "I will be…when you put me *down*."

Ever so gently, he did as she asked. "Ordinarily, I'd say it isn't a good idea to leave your door unlocked."

She opened her mouth to point out that he'd been the reason she'd lost her balance when he said, "What in God's name were you doing on the counter anyway?"

"The number four came loose." Bianca pointed at the clock.

One long, muscular arm reached up, and with no effort at all, Logan took it down. He was about to hand it to her but hesitated. "Hey." He pointed at her signature. "You made this?"

Smiling, she nodded. It had counted more than three years' worth of minutes, hanging in that same spot for so long that she rarely thought about the night she'd used the last of her art supplies to duplicate the cheese, crusty bread, fruit and wine delivered by neighbors to feed family and friends following Jason's funeral.

"It's gorgeous," he said. His gaze slid to the now-faded splotches of blue-green, burgundy and gold…proof she'd used the oak tabletop as her palette. "And you installed the clockworks yourself, too?"

Bianca nodded.

"You're really talented," he said, handing her the clock.

She put it on the table and moved as close to the door as possible. Just because everybody knew his name and face didn't mean he wasn't a lunatic.

"You're probably wondering why I'm here," he said, leaning on a chair back.

"Actually, I'd rather know how you found out where I live."

"I was just leaving my folks' house when your call came in." A faint, slanted smile lifted one corner of his mouth. "Put my new app to use, cross-checking your phone number with your address." He shrugged. "Mailbox was full, so rather than scroll through and listen to your message, I thought I'd stop by, since I was right around the corner. I knocked, but I guess you didn't hear me because of the radio. What did you need me for?"

What she needed was time. To process all he'd just said. To figure out how to phrase the dog-for-Drew question. To hope he wouldn't mention having witnessed her, shimmying and shaking in time to the music.

"Wonder if I could trouble you for a glass of water," he said, loosening his collar.

Bianca hoped it wasn't a mistake to let him stay. "Where do your folks live?" she asked, grabbing two tumblers from the cabinet.

"Dunloggin Road."

With any luck, the ice cubes drowned out the sound of her gasp, because their neighborhood was walking distance from here.

"Iced tea or lemonade?" she asked, opening the fridge.

"Sweet tea?"

"Is there any other kind?"

"Not in Baltimore," he said, his smile broadening. As she filled their glasses, he picked up the clock. "The detail in this painting is incredible."

She handed him the tea.

"Thanks. Did you study art?"

"No…unless you consider how-to books 'studying.'"

Logan placed the clock back on the table, then leaned his backside against the counter. "Know what else is amazing?"

Bianca had no idea, but he was gearing up to tell her, like it or not.

"I was thinking about getting in touch with you when your call came in."

"Oh?" For a reason she couldn't explain, Deidre's comment, about him being 'her Logan,' popped into her head.

"You remember that school I told you about, the one I hope to build for kids like my nephew and your son?"

How could she forget? His entire demeanor had changed in the coffee shop that day, from quiet and courteous to animated and excited, when he told her about the pipe dream that had gradually become an obsession.

"I need someone to act as point man—sorry, *woman*—and check out some of the leads I'm encountering." He explained the people he'd been lining up interviews with: state and county officials; prominent names in the field of education; experts who'd conducted studies of autism and organizations that linked families with medical, scholastic and counseling services.

"It's not a difficult job," he concluded, "but every phone call is important."

"Like the blue puzzle piece," she said without thinking, "that symbolizes autism."

"Exactly!"

His enthusiasm might have been contagious—if she had time to get involved with his project.

"I'm sure the work will be fascinating, but between my job and the house and errands and Drew's issues…" Did she sound as whiny and self-pitying to him as she did to herself? "I think you're right. About the work being important, that is. But I'd hate to shortchange you," she quickly added. "I don't have time to give it one hundred percent, and I'd hate to let you down."

His expression reminded her of the way Drew looked when she said no to a snack before supper. Bianca didn't like disappointing him, especially when what he hoped to accomplish would benefit so many autistic kids and their families. But there were just so many hours in a day, and she'd already packed each to the max.

Bianca rubbed her chin. "Didn't you tell me when we had coffee last week that your sister was looking for something to do when her kids were in school?"

"She's already at her wits' end, trying to juggle my mom, the folks' house and an autistic son, all without overlooking her daughter's needs." He shook his head. "Sandra isn't like you. She's…she's fragile."

Logan had mentioned that his sister was divorced, and based on his tone of voice, she'd guessed the split hadn't been amicable. Add the stressors of a complicated breakup to caring for a sickly parent, a special needs son *and* another child—all while living under her parents' roof? No wonder Sandra seemed overloaded. But she'd found the strength to leave a bad marriage and had the heart to care for her mother. Anything but fragile by Bianca's definition.

"If time is the only thing keeping you from saying yes, maybe I can help." He stood up straight. "I could hire a housekeeper for you. Someone to run errands. Drive Drew to and from school." He grinned and held a hand up, traffic-cop style. "Don't look at me that way. I'm not a stalker." The smile dimmed and the hand rested on the back of his neck. "If it seems like I'm trying too hard, it's only because I happen to think you're perfect for the job."

Logan could snap his fingers and summon a

bevy of beauties. Could probably do the same to draw in a hoard of assistants. Why did he seem so determined to work with *her?*

"Why *me?* You barely know me."

"I know enough. You're smart. Capable. Efficient." He looked around her kitchen, then nodded approvingly. "And from the looks of things around here, organized, too."

Bianca grunted. "Knowing exactly where things are at any given moment has saved Drew from a meltdown more times than I can count. My so-called organizational skills are the result of desperate necessity, not stellar personality traits."

He lifted one shoulder. "I disagree. And as much as I admire the why and how of your skills, my only interest is *outcome.* And you strike me as a results-oriented kind of woman."

It would feel great to participated in a project that, when complete, would improve the lives of people with autism and their families. Bianca was tempted to say yes. With the extra income, she could hire a housekeeper.

He hadn't said a word about salary. But even if he had, Logan would be her boss…if she said yes.

"Your offer to help me out?" she began.

And Logan brightened.

"Couldn't you make the same offer to your sister? She'd probably enjoy having something to distract her from all the demands on her time."

Frowning, he said, "I told you. Sandra is fragile. One more thing on her To Do list, and she could snap."

"I understand how raising an autistic kid is challenging. And frustrating. Because as moms, we do everything humanly possible to improve life for our kids, despite restrictions put on us by the medical and scientific communities. I think you're seriously underestimating what she's capable of. Have you considered that it might be *good* for her...to help you reach your goal?"

Logan put his glass in the sink. "No disrespect intended, but I think I know my sister better than you do." He walked toward the door, pausing halfway between it and the table. "I'm disappointed you don't want the job, but..." Another shrug, then, "I'm sorry."

For the surprise appearance? For making her feel like a helpless victim by preventing her fall? Scolding her for making him reconsider his assessment of his sister?

"Sorry for what?"

"Barging in here like the proverbial bull in a china shop, for starters. Too late to ask why you called me?"

Logan looked and sounded sincere, but then, he was an actor.

"I, ah, wanted to see if you could..." She told herself, *Do* not *say "help me"!* Instead, she said, "I wondered if you could maybe point me in the right direction. To find out more about service dogs. Like the ones in your commercial."

"Companion dogs," he corrected. "Thinking of getting one for Drew?"

She nodded, and then he filled the uncomfortable silence by telling her everything he knew about them: they provided companionship. Increased levels of independence and confidence. Interrupted self-harming behaviors, such as darting into traffic or sneaking out of the house in the middle of the night.

An involuntary shiver snaked up her spine, remembering the time Drew had done that.

"Your son has done that?" he asked. "Snuck out of the house while you're sleeping, I mean?"

Bianca cupped her elbows. "Only once," she admitted. "The nurse across the street was just getting home from the hospital when she saw him, outside, in bare feet and pj's. If she hadn't been on duty that night..." Bianca's heart beat harder, thinking of the awful possibilities. "The very next day, I installed key-operated locks at the top of every exterior door."

Logan followed her gaze to the one on the kitchen door. "You mean that literally, don't you?"

Bianca didn't like admitting to this self-made millionaire that she couldn't afford to hire a locksmith to do it for her. "Well, sure."

"So you really *do* know how to use every tool in the shed." He smiled. "Except for the chainsaw."

Bianca smiled, too. "Necessity isn't just the mother of invention," she said, waving the compliment away. "Sometimes, it's the mother of peace of mind."

The ticking clock, lying on the table between them, reminded her that school would let out soon.

"I hate to be rude, but I have to pick up Drew at school in a few minutes. He worries if I'm so much as one second late." Bianca thought of the day when an accident had stopped traffic on Route 40 and made her ten minutes late. When she had pulled up to the school and saw the huddle of students, parents, teachers and administrators, she knew exactly who was at the center of it: Drew, kicking and screaming and rolling on the ground. It had been the first—and last—time she wasn't there when the final bell rang. It meant eating lunch at her desk and skipping coffee breaks so that she could leave early, and sitting in the car twice as long as other parents, but it had been worth it.

She grabbed her jacket and purse from the hook behind the door, and Logan held the screen door as she locked up.

"I don't know how you do it," he said, walking beside her to the driveway.

"Do what?"

Touching his thumb to each fingertip, he ticked off her responsibilities. "Full-time job, house and yard to maintain, live-in mom, a kid with special needs… A load like that would crush a lesser woman."

A lesser woman—like Sandra? Maybe, she thought, if his sister had a sibling willing to risk alienating herself by speaking the hard-to-hear truth… Six months after Jason's funeral, her sister, Lily, had grabbed her by the shoulders and said, "If you're determined to suffer, you will. And so will Drew." She'd given Bianca a figurative and literal shake by adding, "So quit wallowing!"

If she knew Logan better, Bianca might ask how he'd formed his opinion of Sandra. But he'd made it clear that he'd made up his mind about her and didn't want anyone poking holes in his theories.

He'd parked beside her and stood in the space between their cars. "Are you in a hurry to get Drew a companion dog?"

She got into her car and buckled the seatbelt. "No, no hurry at all. At this point I just need information, so I can make an informed decision."

"Good. That'll give me time to see what I can dig up."

With one hand on her roof, the other on the open door, he leaned closer.

"Any rules about when I can get back to you?"

"Rules?"

"Sandra doesn't allow calls after seventhirty, which is Sam's bedtime. Thought maybe you had a curfew like that."

"Drew goes to bed at eight, but it usually takes half an hour or so to get him settled in.

No curfew, per se, but between nine and eleven is good because my mother…" Bianca sighed. Why was she telling him all of this?

"Do me a favor?"

Last time he'd said that, she'd ended up spending an hour she couldn't afford sipping coffee and chatting in the quaint little café near the station.

"If I can.…"

"It'll take a few days for me to hunt up the dog info you need, so while you're waiting for me to get back to you, will you think about the job? Think up some ways we can make it doable, and run 'em by me, okay?"

And there it was again—that hopeful expression that made him look more like an overgrown boy than a full-grown man.

"Okay." It was the least she could do, considering he'd agreed to hook her up with companion-dog connections.

He stepped back when she closed the door and said, "Later.…"

Bianca shifted into Reverse and backed down the driveway. Turning to head toward Drew's school, she glanced up at the house and saw Logan, smiling, one hand raised in silent farewell.

A strange sensation engulfed her, like the one she'd always felt when Jason left for work. There was no shame in being lonely, she told herself. No disgrace in admitting that she missed loving and being loved. No dishonor in yearning for someone to share her life.

But Logan Murray had brought the sensations to the surface—after all the hard work she'd done to repress them!

And she resented him a little for that.

CHAPTER EIGHT

"I THINK I made a huge and horrible mistake," Sandra said, jamming her mini-shovel into the dirt, "giving up my job to take care of Mom and the house."

Logan loosened his tie. "At least you and the kids are safe."

She wriggled a lily of the valley plant from the overflowing tray beside her. "Thanks for the reminder, Mr. Silver Lining." Grinning, she dug a little hole and tucked the pod into it.

He had to hand it to her. She'd gone from being Daddy's little girl, to being pushed around by a bullying husband, to being at the beck and call of their ailing mother. All that, and meals to prepare, their folks' house and yard to maintain and two kids to care for. Considering all that, she really didn't complain much.

"So what else is on your To Do list for today?"

"It'll take less time to tell you what *isn't* on it. Suffice to say, I'll be on the move until the kids are in bed and Mom gets her last pill. If Sam doesn't decide to pitch a fit tonight. Again."

He shrugged out of his suit coat, hung it on the porch railing and got onto his knees beside her.

Sandra's brows rose high on her forehead. "Are you out of your mind?"

He relieved her of the garden trowel and dug a hole exactly like hers. "Go pour yourself a glass of wine or something and park your butt in a chair until it's gone. I'll finish up here."

She sat back on her heels and stared at him. "You think because that's a Dolce & Gabbana suit, it'll repel grass stains?"

He kept working.

"Logan. Seriously. That's a two-thousand-dollar suit. You can't just wallow around in the mud that way."

"First of all, it didn't cost two thousand dollars." *It was seven hundred bucks* more *than that.* But no big loss. If he ruined it today, he'd have one less reminder of what Griff jokingly referred to as his I'm a Big Shot years. "Second, I don't see any mud. And you know better than most that the only wallowing I've ever done was after the Willow debacle."

Sandra gave his shoulder a playful shove. "Yeah, you did waste a couple of perfectly good years flexing your self-pity muscles over that lunatic, didn't you? That, and drowning your troubles in Nun's Island whiskey."

The reminder of his battle with the bottle made every muscle tighten. "Sarcasm doesn't become you," he said, slowly releasing a tense breath. "Now get inside and put your feet up, before I change my mind."

She started up the porch steps, stopping at the top. "There's a hose right behind you. Be sure to soak the plants once you get them all in the ground, or you'll have dirtied your hands and stained your fancy duds for nothing."

The screen door creaked closed and he made a mental note to oil it when he finished here. Crawling along the tidy brick-lined bed, he dug and planted and tamped rich black soil around the broad-leafed plants. The work brought him back to his boyhood, when he'd helped his dad plant radishes and spring onions at the edges of the vegetable garden. Wasn't it about this time of year when they began to sprout?

On his feet now, he turned the hose nozzle to

the rain setting, barely noticing as mud splattered on the cuffs of his pants and on the toes of his Ferragamo loafers. The shutters could use a coat of paint, he thought, as he studied the front of the house. The gutters needed a good cleaning and the window screens could use a going-over with a wire brush. He needed to make some time to get over here, take care of some of that. Sandra couldn't do *every*thing.

Logan heard the unmistakable sound of water, plopping into the puddles at his feet. After recoiling the hose, he gathered the tools and carried them around back.

The old wooden shed, like everything else about the quaint '50s rancher where his dad had been born and raised, had seen better days. He added it to his own To Do list, thinking that if the weather was decent, he'd come back on Saturday and tighten the hinge screws and do something about the sticking latch, too.

The scent of gasoline and motor oil, years-old dirt and rusting rakes met him when he opened the wide crossbuck door. He placed the garden shovel on the workbench, but only because there wasn't a place for it on the pegboard above the bench.

To his left sat the dull red lawn mower and

a grimy weed whacker. To his right stood the old yellow tiller that had been the bane of his youth—and his salvation. Smiling, Logan remembered the year he'd turned fourteen, when his dad had gassed up the machine and given him instructions to till the garden. If he'd known how satisfying it would feel, turning rocky, weedy clods into straight, evenly spaced rows, Logan wouldn't have put so much effort into finding excuses to avoid the backyard. Only one other thing in life had ever filled him with such a sense of power and purpose: football.

Slowly, he closed the door on the shed, where shelves of screws and nuts and bolts winked from baby food and Mason jars. He'd closed the door to this—and a whole lot more—when he'd traded home and hearth for the game.

But that was then and this is now, he thought.

It wasn't a long walk back to the house, but Logan took his time. If he knew his sister, she'd repay him for the half hour of R & R by inviting him to supper. And he wouldn't say no to good food and some much overdue family time. He'd barely cleared the bottom porch step when Sandra opened the back screen door.

"Whoa. Stop right there, little brother! If you

think you're gonna waltz in here and muddy up this clean kitchen floor," she said, one hand on her hip, "you've got another think coming!"

Logan looked down at his soggy trouser cuffs and mud-caked shoes. "You're right," he said. "Can you loan me a couple of trash bags?"

"What! Why?"

"So I won't mess up the floor and seats of my car."

"You big goofball. You don't need trash bags. You're staying for supper."

"But…I can't strip down to my skivvies. The kids will be home from school soon." And more likely than not, his niece would bring a few friends.

"Stay put," Sandra said. "I'll get some of Dad's things for you to change into." She started back inside, then came out again. "And as soon as you're presentable, little brother, or we get a minute alone—whichever comes first—you're going to tell me why you came over here in the middle of the day, in the middle of the week, 'cause much as I appreciate the downtime, I'm sure it wasn't to plant posies!"

Half an hour later, her kids poked fun of the too-tight borrowed short-sleeved shirt and pants, and much to his surprise, his dad joined them. Logan gladly went along with it all through supper and dessert. The outfit even roused a round of snickers from his mom, whose stage 4 cancer diagnosis had left her exhausted and with very little reason to laugh.

"I've never seen anything more ridiculous," she said, wiping tears of mirth from her eyes. "Are you doing some sort of clown act for a charity?"

Logan only grinned, letting that be his answer. He couldn't tell her how or why his own clothes had become soiled. Any talk of the flower gardens she could see only from her in-home hospital bed would just depress her more. Her blue-ribbon roses and chrysanthemums had been her pride and joy, but this year, she hadn't had the strength to maintain them and had grudgingly entrusted them to Sandra.

He pulled a chair closer to her bed and sandwiched her hands between his. "So how's it goin', Mom?"

Her lips quavered slightly as the happy smile diminished. "Oh, I'm pluggin' along, taking things minute by minute, you know?"

"Are the drugs helping any with the pain?"

"Oh, honey," she said, squeezing his hand, "stop worrying about me. You're young and handsome. You should be worrying about finding a nice woman, one who'll make you a good home and give you children."

Bianca could give him both....

The thought rocked him because he was in no position to start a relationship with anyone, let alone a widow who was the sole caretaker for a special needs kid and a widowed mother. It was just a random thought, he told himself. A wild notion that was the offshoot of time spent with her and the hours he'd put in collecting data she'd need to get her son a dog. He had to deliver that information soon. That's why she'd popped into his head just now. And that was the *only* reason.

"You know how I hate to nag..." his mother began.

He forced himself to pay attention. She wasn't long for this world, and he needed to spend as much time with her as possible.

"...but you need to put this Willow thing in the past. You threw away a whole year trying to change her. Wasted two more trying to blot what she did to you from your mind by—"

"Mom. Please. Trust me. I'm over it. Okay?" And he was, except for that sliver of humiliation he held on to, a reminder of what happens to guys suffering from Prince Charming Syndrome.

"All right, honey. If you say so." She slipped one hand from his grasp and used it to cup his chin. "Much as I hate to see you go, I'm really sleepy. Could you ask Sandra to come up, bring my medicine?"

"Will do." Logan stood, and after tidying her covers, pressed a gentle kiss to her forehead. "Will do. Get a good night's sleep."

"You'll come back soon, won't you?"

"Just try and keep me away." Tears stung his eyes, and because he didn't want her to see them, Logan walked quickly from her room. In the hallway, leaning on her closed door, he hung his head. She'd looked so small and frail lying there against the pink-flowered pillowcases, a mere shadow of her scared-of-nothing, sturdy self. The woman who'd helped him memorize *The Raven,* whose tutelage had gotten him through calculus and physics, who had taught him to find earthworms on the riverbank, then bait a hook and catch a trout, was slipping away from him. And, oh, how he'd miss her when she was gone.

You're strong and stubborn, like me, she'd

told him in rehab. *You'll beat this thing. I guarantee it!*

That unconditional love and unfailing support explained why every AA sobriety chip he'd earned was in her jewelry box. Logan was due to claim the next one in July, and according to her doctors, she wouldn't last that long.

The question was…would *he?*

CHAPTER NINE

HE MET SANDRA on his way down the stairs. "Always two steps ahead of everyone, aren't you?" he kidded, nodding at the glass of water and assortment of pills on the tray she carried.

When they were side by side, she stopped. "I don't think I've ever been ahead of anyone in my whole life." A blink or two later, she made a "Seriously?" face.

"I get it. She sent you to remind me, didn't she?"

Much as he hated to admit it, his mom hadn't exactly gone easy on Sandra. They'd gone toe to toe on a dozen issues since the divorce: the kids ate too much junk food and didn't get to bed early enough; the laundry should be done on Tuesdays, not every single day; a good housekeeper always vacuumed before she dusted the furniture, not after. Their mom won every round, but only because Sandra was the type who'd walk miles to sidestep confrontation.

Except with Logan.

She narrowed her eyes. "Her doctor was very clear about when and how much medication I should give her."

He held up a hand, and though he hadn't delivered his mother's request, Logan said, "Hey, don't shoot the messenger. You know I'm on your side. And that I believe if anyone else had been taking care of Mom, she'd be gone by now."

Using her chin as a pointer, she looked up the staircase. "Try telling that to *her*."

Logan believed their mom knew that Sandra was trying. But she was in pain. And bored. And annoyed that she had no control over anything—not her house or her gardens and, least of all, her health. Who better to take it out on than her youngest daughter?

Right now, that was the last thing Sandra wanted—or needed—to hear.

"Tell you what," he said, winking. "Next time I stop by, I'll have a talk with her."

"An exercise in futility, but whatever," she said, climbing the stairs. On the landing, she paused. "You're not going home yet, I hope...."

"'Course not. Just going to talk to Dad."

She smiled. "I'll be down as soon as I can." She smirked. "Then you're going to tell me who put that 'I met somebody swell' look on your face."

He would have denied it if she hadn't disappeared into their mother's room. But no big deal. Later, he'd set her straight. Meanwhile, he took comfort in the knowledge that once he delivered the dog-related info he'd dug up, Bianca would slip into the dark recesses of his memory, where she belonged. It was a good thing, he decided, jogging the rest of the way down the stairs, that she'd turned down his job offer.

He was surprised that his dad wasn't in the family room, watching The History Channel over the pages of the evening paper.

"I'm out here, son. On the patio."

He stepped up beside his dad and pocketed his hands. "Nice night."

Carl's gaze remained on the starry sky. "Yes. Yes, it is." Nodding, he turned slightly to ask, "How's your mother?"

"As well as can be expected, I guess." Logan leaned forward slightly to get a better look at his dad's face. "She isn't asleep yet. You can ask her yourself."

"I'll… I…" He drove a hand through his hair. "I'll go up after supper."

Was it his imagination, or was there an un-spoken 'maybe' at the end of that sentence?

Carl leaned on the wrought-iron railing that surrounded the patio. "It's getting harder and harder to know what to say to her."

Logan got it. Finding non-cancer-related top-ics had become a real challenge for him, too.

"I can only imagine how tough it is for you," Logan said. Because she was the love of his fa-ther's life, and soon, he'd lose her. "But you've never dodged a tough situation in your life, and I know you won't dodge this one. Bring the newspaper up there and read it to her. Bet-ter still, get one of her romance novels. She'd get a kick out of hearing you read it out loud."

That inspired a quiet chuckle. Then his dad turned and took a few steps away from Logan. "I'm a lot of things, son, but I'm not a hypo-crite."

He didn't understand, and he said so.

"There are things I can't get into right now, because…because your mother asked me not to tell you kids, and I gave her my word."

How bad could it be? he wondered.

Pretty bad, if the somber silence was any

indicator. The mood surrounding the patio reminded Logan of the night he'd told his parents he'd made the high school football team. *We can't stop you from playing that barbaric sport,* they had said, *but we won't help you hurt yourself...or anyone else.* He was on his own, they'd added, for sports physicals and any other expenses connected with the Centennial Eagles. Balancing school, homework, practice and a part-time job hadn't been easy, but Logan loved the sport enough to sacrifice time with his buddies to earn every dollar and maintain a 3.8 GPA. Four years later, his folks' reaction had been eerily similar when the University of Maryland had offered him a football scholarship, and again when the Knights had picked him in round one of the NFL draft weeks after graduation. Oddly, they were nothing but supportive when the concussion ended his career, and his parents had remained his staunchest allies all through rehab...and every day since.

"Mom doesn't expect anything from us," he said, gripping his dad's shoulder, "except to be there."

"You, Sandra and Sarah, maybe, but not me."

He sounded defeated. But there was something more in his sad, strained voice. Shame?

"Dad. C'mon. She's in pain. And scared. And we both know how vain she is. She probably just doesn't want her best guy to see her looking—"

He met Logan's eyes. "Let it go, son. There are things you can't possibly understand. And I can't explain them because I promised not to. I owe it to her to keep my word about that, at least."

Times like these, Logan wished he could read minds. There was a hidden message, a warning of some sort in his father's peculiar words. He shouldn't have been surprised because his parents had always kept secrets from their kids. About money. About job changes. About illness. The best example of all was waiting until the surgeon had removed fourteen inches of his mom's colon before sharing the bad news: she'd die before the year was out.

"Well," he said, giving his dad's shoulder a slight squeeze, "when you're ready to talk, *if* you're ever ready, I'm here."

Carl nodded. "I know." He placed his hand atop Logan's. "Thanks, son."

His dad turned suddenly and faced the patio doors. "I'm going to bed," he said, his voice laced with regret and profound sadness. "Don't be such a stranger, okay? Your mother needs you now."

Logan nodded, knowing his father needed him, too. Long after his dad had gone inside, Logan sat on a creaking lawn chair, elbows on knees and head down, trying to puzzle out what had just happened between him and his dad.

Movement behind him caught his attention, and he looked up as Sandra stepped onto the patio.

"I feel the same way after five minutes with either of them," she said, handing him a steaming mug of coffee. Taking the seat beside him, she tugged her sweater around her. "Aren't you cold? It can't be more than forty degrees out here."

"No," he admitted, wrapping both hands around the mug. "What do you know about this latest secret they're keeping?"

"Unfortunately, they don't share much. Unless, of course, I've done something they disapprove of, like using too much starch in Dad's shirt collars or letting the kids take long showers."

He reached across the space between them and grabbed her free hand. "You always seem to get the short end of the stick, and I'm sorry about that."

She laughed, a coarse and bitter sound that made his heart ache.

"What's this, your rendition of the pot calling the kettle black?"

"Huh?"

"They made you work like a dog all through high school, never said how proud they were when you earned a scholarship…with no help from them. Never congratulated you when the Knights signed you. Never thanked you for bailing them out when they almost lost this falling-down eyesore of a house. Never offered a word of encouragement or a snippet of moral support when you were cut from the team."

She sipped her coffee and pulled her sweater tighter still. "I don't remember them ever saying they loved us, do you?"

A rhetorical question, evidently, because Sandra didn't wait for a reply.

"And they're the same way with their grandkids. Why, even when they were babies…"

Sandra got up so suddenly, Logan had to grab her chair to keep it from clattering to the pavement. She paced for a minute or two before stopping at the foot of the chair.

"Don't pay any attention to me," she said, her voice soft and sweetly sad. "It's not your fault that Mom has been particularly difficult today."

With Sarah the pediatrician all the way out in Colorado, most of their mother's care had fallen on Sandra's shoulders. He'd offered, dozens of times, to hire a nurse, but his sister had flat-out refused. Yeah, his schedule was crazy, but he found time for golf outings and fishing trips, so...

"I need to help out more. I *want* to help more." He patted the footrest of the chaise lounge. When she sat, he added, "But you know what an idiot I am. You're gonna need to spell it out, tell me what to do and when."

She got up again. "I know you do what you can." And perching on the patio's wrought-iron railing, she met his eyes. "We've been down this road, so pardon my repetitiveness as I say that I don't want your help. And don't give me that 'duh' look. It would take me longer to teach you what to do than it would to do things myself. Besides, it does my heart good knowing *one* of us is living a normal life." She snickered. "So don't be selfish, okay?"

"Selfish?"

"I'm living vicariously through you, you big goof. So don't spoil my fun."

Sandra stared into her mug, ran a fingertip around its rim. "So," she said after a while, "what's her name?"

Again, Bianca came instantly to mind. And again, he had no idea why. "What's whose name?"

"The gold-digging little shrew who has your heart all tied up in knots and turned your brain into a sappy muddle."

Logan snorted. "I'm in no position to link up with anyone." *Least of all a widowed mom. With a kid like Sam.* "My life is a mess. Wouldn't be fair to saddle some poor woman with—"

"You, brother dear, are the *least* messed-up person I know, despite what that crazy Willow did to you. You beat alcoholism!"

"I think that fall you took from the shed roof when we were kids knocked a couple of screws loose. Either that, or you need to update the prescription for your rose-colored glasses." She was only two years older, and the top of her head barely reached his shoulder, yet Logan had always looked up to Sandra. She'd married the wrong guy. Young, naive women had been making that mistake for centuries, and so had stupid, immature guys. Sandra had gone to great lengths to correct her mistake and had continued making enormous sacrifices for Sally and Sam. If he was ever lucky enough to have kids of his own, *they'd* be lucky if he loved them half as much as Sandra loved hers.

She was one of the strongest people he knew, and the admission reminded him of what he'd told Bianca: "Sandra isn't like you. She's fragile." Nothing could be further from the truth, and he didn't know why he hadn't acknowledged it before now.

"Get down from there," he said, patting the lounge chair's footrest again. "I have a favor to ask you." The idea sparked, like rock against flint, and he didn't know why he hadn't thought of it before.

Sandra hesitated but only for a moment. He told her about his dream to build a school for kids on the spectrum. He ran down the same list he'd recited for Bianca, adding that with a little help, he might just succeed at opening a facility that would provide kids like Sam… *and Drew*…the best instructors, the best teaching materials and the best environment, tuition-free.

"Admirable," Sandra said, "but I barely have time to sleep. What makes you think I could help you?"

"I need someone trustworthy," he said, "to chase down some facts and interview a few experts so I'll know what's required to make a go of a facility like that."

She only shook her head.

"Stop looking at me as if I suddenly grew a unibrow. You're smart. You're resourceful. I'd pay you. And provide you with a computer. A printer. A fax machine. Everything you'd need to get the job done. It could be a job-share kind of deal if I can talk a friend into it."

"Ah-ha. A friend, huh?"

He ignored her implication. "I know it sounds crass, but *some*body has to say it: Mom isn't long for this world. You'll have plenty of time after she's gone. Knowing you, you'll stay afterward to take care of Dad. But you can't live here forever. The kids need a home of their own. And so do you. This job won't always be part-time. Once I get things up and running, I'll need someone to manage the office."

She nodded slowly. "It's tempting. But what makes you think I can handle that much responsibility?"

"You handle all of this," he said, gesturing toward the yard and the house. "I know how much effort and energy goes into maintaining all of this without neglecting Dad *or* the kids. Will there be a learning curve?" He shrugged. "'Course there will. But you can handle it."

She grinned. "Because I handle all of this," she echoed.

"I'd pay you well."

"I know that." She paused, as if considering her options. "How soon would I need to start?"

"Tomorrow." He hoped he could talk Bianca into sharing the job. It would require introducing her to his sister, but he had a feeling they'd get along great. "Kidding," he said. "It'll take me a couple of days to line things up, buy some office equipment." For here and for Bianca's house—if she'd stop being stubborn and just say yes.

"Better drag my tight-shirt, short-pants self home," he said, standing. He bent down and pressed a kiss to her forehead. "Promise me something?"

"Maybe." She got to her feet.

"Don't think this to death, okay? You'll scare yourself and talk yourself out of it."

"Okay. I promise. No thinking." Then she

poked a fingertip into his chest. "So you never answered my question."

"Which question?" As if he didn't know.

"What's her name? And don't feed me any of your 'I'm not interested, I'm not worthy' baloney, or I'll think of ways to nag it out of you instead."

She'd do it, too, he thought, grinning. "It isn't what you think. Strictly professional. Not even a 'friend' thing. Single mom, like you. And like you, she has an autistic kid. I'm hoping she'll share this job with you because in my opinion, you're both perfect for it."

"If you say so." She crossed both arms over her chest. "What's her *name!*"

"Stubborn, thy name is Sandra."

"I'm pooped but not so pooped that you can sidetrack me with botched Shakespeare quotes."

He waved an imaginary white flag. "Bianca Wright."

"Well, now, that wasn't so hard, was it?"

Actually, it was. He'd probably be up half the night wondering why his heartbeat doubled when he said her name.

"Go home, Logan. I'm going to bed." She

stepped into the family room. "Lock up on your way out, will you?"

"You lock up, lazybones," he said, starting toward the driveway. "I'm parked over there."

She flicked the patio light on and off as he said, "Sweet dreams, sis."

"I'd say 'you, too,' but that would just be redundant, wouldn't it?"

Sandra closed the door before he could rebut the comment.

In one tick of his wristwatch, she locked the door. In the next, the vertical blinds snapped shut. Then the lights went out and he found himself alone in the dark...

...in more ways than one.

CHAPTER TEN

ACCORDING TO MRS. Peterson, it had not been a good day for Drew.

"I'm so sorry to bother you at work," the teacher said, "but I'm wondering…did Drew take his medicine today?"

Bianca hated taking calls like this at work; it was turning into a not-so-good day for her, too. She reminded the woman of their in-person meeting three months ago, when she'd explained that, at the urging of the behavioral therapist at Kennedy Krieger, she had reluctantly agreed to test a low dose of Ritalin in the hope it would help Drew focus on schoolwork. Almost immediately he had begun complaining about headaches, dizziness and an accelerated heartbeat, and the doctor had weaned him from the stimulant. Drew had been drug-free since.

"Did you move his desk," Bianca said, "as his doctor recommended?"

"Oh. I'm sorry. No, I just haven't had time."

The admission was disappointing but not surprising. The summer before Drew entered first grade, Bianca had attended three meetings with the principal and the school counselor to determine if mainstreaming was best for him. Both women assured her that the Hillsborough Elementary curriculum and staff were exactly what Drew needed, but two months into the school year, it became clear they'd exaggerated their knowledge of autism and their abilities to handle kids on the spectrum. And because Drew didn't handle change well at all, Bianca had taken it upon herself to fill in the gaps rather than move him to another school.

"Have you had time to put a stop to Joseph's bullying?" She pictured the bite marks on Drew's arms. "I'd hate to bring the matter to the attention of the school board...."

"I've had a talk with him," the teacher said, "and his parents." She paused. "Has Drew said something? Because I haven't seen any evidence that the bullying hasn't stopped."

The woman's voice was shaking. Not a good sign. Bianca needed the teacher's cooperation, and alienating her with accusations wasn't the way to get it.

"I remember that we discussed how the constant flicker and buzz of fluorescent lighting is a problem for kids like Drew and how there's nothing you can do about it. But sitting near the pencil sharpener and the open classroom door—where he can be sidetracked by the normal movements of students in the hall—is a problem we *can* solve."

She'd said it all before. Would Mrs. Peterson take her seriously this time?

"Oh, yes, I know I promised to move him." She sighed. "There just always seems to be something distracting *me*." The teacher laughed quietly. "I'm really sorry, Mrs. Wright. I'll do it now, before the children return from the cafeteria."

"You don't know what a relief it is to hear you say that. Thank you! Now, I hate to be a pain…" *But if that's what it takes, that's exactly what I'll be.* "…but you'll need to meet him in the hall. Get him alone, and make sure you have his full attention before you tell him that his mother told you to move his desk to a quieter part of the classroom. He's been expecting it to happen because he and I talk about distractions and how to avoid them, all the time. If he manages to slip inside before you see him and his desk isn't where it was when he left for lunch? Well, I think you know what will happen. And an agitated Drew isn't good for anyone."

"Yes, yes, of course." After a short pause, the woman added, "You have my word—I'll take good care of him."

How many times have I heard that *this year?* "'Thank you' really seems like such a paltry thing to say, considering all the extra effort you're putting in, teaching Drew. It's such a relief to know he's in capable, caring hands when he's away from home." *And if I have to slather compliments a foot deep, I'll do that, too, if it means Drew will get what he needs.*

"Most of the time he's an easy boy to love. Why, he's kept us all in stitches this week, talking about the 'nonsneezy' dog he's going to get!"

She'd been very careful *not* to mention anything about a dog. Why get his hopes up if Logan couldn't find the right one?

"Drew must have overheard my mother and I talking. We're considering a companion dog, but nothing is set in stone." She explained how service dogs benefited autistic kids if the breed and the boy were the right match.

"Well, I'd better go," Mrs. Peterson said, "if I

hope to catch Drew before he reaches the classroom. Just one more thing, though...."

That didn't sound good, Bianca thought,
holding her breath.

"He started out green today, and I had to
change him to red. But since I'm moving his
desk just as soon as we hang up, I think I'll
move him back to green."

The Hillsborough method for encouraging
good behavior—and disapproving of the bad—
probably made sense to the staff and maybe
even to other parents. She was pretty sure that
after a few days of looking at the stoplight
poster, it blended into the background, along
with the card rack that hung beside it. Every
day, all students started out with green cards
in their slots. Cooperation and compliance allowed them to hold on to green. Talking out of
turn or getting up without permission might
demote them to yellow. Things like arguing
and shouting resulted in orange cards. Blatant
disobedience or disrespect earned red.

Exhaling, Bianca said, "Thank you. I know
he'll appreciate that."

Mrs. Peterson laughed softly, but clearly
her heart wasn't in it. "Well, let's just hope he
doesn't lose it again before he gets home!"

Bianca stifled a sigh. "He hates red days, so I'm sure he'll do his best to hold on to his green sticker." Not exactly the truth, but Mrs. Peterson didn't need to know that. Drew had shared his assessment of the system over supper several weeks earlier: *All the teachers and aides really need to do,* he'd said, *is listen to what a kid wants and explain if the answer is no.*

Bianca promised to have a talk with Drew about today's behavior, and Mrs. Peterson would try to get his desk moved.

Try, she thought, frowning as she hung up the phone. Jason had used the word with regularity: *I'll try to get home in time to go with you to Drew's doctor. I'll try not to say things that hurt his feelings. I'll try to spend more time with him....* But he never followed through, and it made her question the veracity of everything else he'd said, from why he arrived home late to why he didn't call while out of town on business.

Though Bianca knew it wasn't fair to measure all men by Jason's behavior, the word made her suspicious of Logan, too. He hadn't promised to get back to her with information about companion dogs, but he'd certainly made her believe he'd *try.*

That had been a week ago.

"Didn't try very hard," she groused. Grabbing her pen, she picked up the phone again and prepared to call tomorrow's *The Morning Show* guests to see if they had any last-minute questions. "Could have *walked* to Mt. Airy," she grumped, mashing the phone's buttons, "and met with the woman myself in the time it's taking him to—"

"This talking to yourself is becoming a habit."

Startled, Bianca nearly dropped her pen and the handset. "Marty, one of these days you're going to be the death of me!"

"Oops." He winced. "Sorry, kiddo." Extending one brown-socked foot, he wiggled his toes. "Those new cowboy boots were bitin' my dogs. Takes time to break in a new pair." He loosened his tie and sat on the chair beside her desk.

"Apology accepted. This time." She added, "Thinking of becoming a signalman, are you?"

"A signalman?"

"You're wearing the perfect neckwear for the job."

He waved the tie's tail at her. "What kind of Baltimorean doesn't recognize the Orioles' colors!"

"Of course. The season *is* in full swing, isn't it?" And before Marty beat her to the punch, she said, "Pun intended."

Shaking his head, Marty clapped a hand over his eyes. "If you ever decide to give up producing, I can hook you up with a pal at the Comedy Factory down on Market Street. I can almost picture you doing stand-up."

Laughing, she said, "I don't know about that, but I'd love to take Drew back to the Inner Harbor. Maybe in a few weeks when the tall ships are in port. If I can find those earplugs he likes."

She thought of their last trip downtown, when a friend who worked at the National Aquarium had escorted her and Drew through the exhibits hours before the doors opened. Bianca would have bet the house Drew would have a grand time in the hushed and dim interior. *Good thing you're not a gambler,* she thought, remembering how one look into the ceiling-to-floor shark tank had been enough to send her son into a tailspin.

Marty patted her knee. "Hey. Don't get all down in the dumps. I know he can be a handful sometimes, but he's making steady progress, thanks to you."

"Yeah." She nodded. "You're a good egg, Marty."

Chuckling, he ran a hand over his balding head. "Hey. I resemble that remark." His expression sobered slightly. "So is Logan Murray the 'he' you were snarling about when I walked in?"

Bianca hadn't told Marty about helping Logan with his battery or how he'd treated her to coffee as a thank-you. Never mentioned that he'd stopped by the house, or that she'd asked for his help finding a companion dog. So how could Marty have guessed?

"No, I'm not a mind reader," he teased, "but I *am* pretty good at math. Logan called last week and asked if I could talk to Denise about that gal in Mt. Airy she interviewed a couple months back. Turned out the name I passed him led to a different service-dog outfit." He finger-combed his mustache. "I just put two and two together and guessed." Leaning closer, he wiggled his eyebrows. "So what's your beef with Baltimore's pretty boy?"

"I don't have a beef with him." The more she talked, the deeper the hole grew. "So that's what you came in here to tell me…that Logan didn't get the name and number he needed from you?"

"Actually, he did. But that isn't why I'm here. I came in to give you these." He reached into his shirt pocket and withdrew two tickets to an Orioles game. "I know how much Drew loves baseball."

"Aw, Marty. That's sweet of you. I appreciate it, really I do, but Drew hates crowds even more than he loves the Os. He's better off watching the game on TV."

"These aren't tickets to a game. They're *passes,* sweetheart, to get you and Drew into the locker room. Let me know if you want to go down there before the game or after so I can stand between you and anybody who's out of uniform." He laughed. "Wouldn't want you blushing, in case there are pictures."

It was a lovely gesture, so thoughtful that it left her at a loss for words. She wanted to accept the gift. But how could she, knowing how Drew reacted to noise and crowds and quite likely the chatter of reporters and the flash of photographers' cameras?

"You can't protect the kid from everything," Marty pointed out. "If you don't let him try new things, how will you find out what he can handle and what he can't?"

Her mother said the same thing. Often.

"If he gets agitated and acts up, nobody's gonna mind. Most of the guys are familiar with autism, thanks to B. J. Surhoff."

She'd heard about how the former Hall of Famer and his wife had founded Pathfinders for Autism to help other parents of autistic kids find services. Several times over the years, Bianca had considered matching their resources with Kennedy-Krieger's, but with everything else she was juggling, change terrified her almost as much as it scared Drew.

Marty tossed the passes onto her desk. "Think about it. If you decide not to go, let me know. I can name ten people off the top of my head who would kill for those things." He checked his watch. "Uh-oh. Better hustle back to the studio. Almost time for the radio weather report on WPOK." On the way to the door, he said, "Have a good one, kiddo. Catch you later."

"You, too, and thanks for thinking of us," she returned, then faced her desk and read the notes she'd made before Marty had popped in. And the ones she'd scribbled while talking with Mrs. Peterson. "Drew talking dogs at school," said one. "Call Logan Murray about dogs," said another.

She ought to be doing a dozen other things, Bianca thought, instead of dialing his cell number. But at least she could cross one thing off her list once she got hold of him.

Three rings, four, then he said, "Marty. Hey. 'Bout time you got back to me." He chuckled. "Wait. Don't tell me. You broke your dialing finger?"

It was refreshing to know he talked to everyone the way he talked to her. "Hi, Logan. It's Bianca. Bianca Wright?"

"Oh. Hey," he said. "Sorry. Saw the station's phone number in the caller ID window and automatically thought it was Marty." He cleared his throat. "Wondering what I found out about the dogs, eh?"

"As a matter of fact, yes."

"I figured to call you tomorrow, after I'd talked with the last name on my list. But I can give you what I have, maybe stop by today to drop off the pamphlets and whatnot."

"Today?"

"Well, I was thinking maybe tonight?"

That would teach her to make snap decisions. Why in the world had she called him!

"Things rarely settle down at my house until eight, eight-thirty." Later, she admitted, if Drew decided not to cooperate with his bed-time routine.

"How's nine, then? I know you'll have put in a full day, so I won't stay long."

She reminded herself that he'd gone to a lot of trouble to help her out. Correction: to help Drew.

"Okay. Sure. See you tonight, then."

"I have back-to-back meetings. No time for supper. Okay with you if I grab some fast food on the way over and eat it at your place?"

Supper, not dinner, she noted. From a guy who'd probably attended a hundred thousand-dollar-a-plate black tie affairs. It made her smile a little. "No need for that. I'll save you a plate. We're having spaghetti and meatballs."

"You're kidding, right?"

"I never joke about food."

Laughing, he said, "Great. Better than great. See you around nine."

She hung up slowly and glanced at the clock: six hours to get everything on her To Do list done…and still have time to get home and touch up her hair and makeup.

CHAPTER ELEVEN

"OH, hello! You must be Logan Murray!"

He accepted the outstretched hand. "And you must be Bianca's mom."

"Please, call me Maddy." She led the way into the family room, where a Hot Wheels track looped across the carpet. "Bianca is upstairs tucking Drew in for the night." She cleared coloring books and crayons from the sofa cushions. "Make yourself comfortable." Glancing around the room, she laughed. "If that's possible in this mess!"

"Doesn't look half as messy as my sister's house," he said, placing a manila folder on the coffee table. He took a seat and hopped right up again. "Ouch," he said, grinning as he put a miniature car on the table.

"Oh, that grandson of mine." Maddy shook her head. "Can I get you anything to drink? Soda? Beer? Coffee?"

"Soda sounds good, thanks."

While she was gone, Logan looked around the room, where a caramel-colored leather sofa was flanked by overstuffed plaid chairs. A wooden clock and framed photographs decorated one polished end table, a vase of spring flowers added color to another and a collection of odd-sized clay pots stood on the coffee table. He liked the tall, wood-shuttered windows and the blue-and-green paisley rug beneath his feet. He admired the clusters of treelike plants in every corner, too. He'd paid a high-priced interior designer to furnish his place with similar pieces, so why did his family room look cold and uninviting, while Bianca's felt warm and welcoming?

"Here you go," Maddy said, placing a wooden tray in front of him. "I wasn't sure if you like sipping straight from the can or if you prefer your soft drinks over ice, so I brought both."

He popped the top of the cola can and poured the liquid into a glass. "You aren't going to keep me company until Bianca finishes upstairs?" he asked.

She sat in the easy chair nearest his end of the sofa. "Well, of course."

Maddy glanced at the ceiling, and he presumed Drew's room was on the other side of it. "I can't imagine why she invited a busy man like you over here on a weeknight. Drew can be…" She bit her lower lip. "Sometimes, after a long day at school, he can be a little…difficult."

Logan leaned back. "Boys will be boys," he said, propping an ankle on a knee. "Besides, Bianca didn't invite me. I sort of invited myself."

"Oh. Really?" Maddy's hands fluttered at her throat. "Well. Goodness."

Maddy pointed at the folder on the coffee table. "Is that the reason you're here?"

Nodding, he said "Yes, ma'am." If he had to guess, he'd say Bianca probably discussed the idea of getting a dog with her mom before asking for his help. But just in case she hadn't, he intended to keep his lips zipped.

"That girl runs around most days like the proverbial chicken without a head."

He followed her gaze, from the toys piled high in a wicker toy box to two pairs of small sneakers lined up side by side next to the TV.

"Now you watch…. She'll come down here, and before she looks into that folder you brought, she'll put all these toys away."

"Can't fault her there," he said. "I'm the same way."

"I've said for years that Bianca is a workaholic. If it isn't Drew this or Drew that, it's something to do with the show. And then she's up half the night trying to keep this place in tip-top shape."

"Because kids with autism crave order in their lives."

She looked surprised, so he said, "My nephew is autistic. Sam. He's about Drew's age."

"Is that right?" Maddy sighed. "Strange, isn't it, the way the number of people with autism continues to grow. Some people blame mandatory vaccinations. I say it's plastic. Everything is packaged in plastic these days. Food. Water. Who knows what's leeching into the things we eat and drink?"

"Something to think about, for sure," he said, looking for something, anything, that would give him an excuse to change the subject. Then he noticed a collection of silver-framed photos on the mantel. "So that's Drew's dad, there in the middle?"

Maddy looked up. "Yes," she said on a sigh.

"Bianca's dad and I didn't have a son of our own, but Jason more than made up for that."

Logan nodded.

"I don't suppose Bianca told you—she positively *hates* talking about herself—but we lost Jason several years ago. Cancer." She shook her head. "Very aggressive. Poor dear suffered horribly at the end."

Bianca had skirted the subject that day in the café and again in her kitchen. He hadn't pressed her for details about her husband—or any other area of her life—but it didn't seem as though she hated talking about herself.

"Guess it must be tough to lose a spouse." With a little luck, Maddy would talk about the more recent loss of her own husband.

"Oh, yes. Yes, it is, especially at first. And having a child like Drew…" She rolled her eyes. "Let's just say dealing with him was complicated even before Jason died."

She rambled on for another minute or so, citing her son-in-law's more stellar qualities and listing all the reasons Drew was such a challenge. Now Logan glanced at the ceiling and wondered how much longer it would take Bianca to tuck the boy in. Unfortunately, Maddy caught him at it.

"See? That's what I mean! When my girls were his age, I said go to bed, and that was that. But Drew? It sometimes takes hours to get him to sleep!" Maddy shook her head, then got to her feet. "I'll just run upstairs and see what's taking so long *this* time."

"Please don't. It isn't Bianca's fault—or Drew's—that I got here early."

Maddy returned to her seat. "Her whole life revolves around that boy. I admire her dedication. She's a wonderful, loving mother, but I don't mind admitting…in her shoes, I'd go mad."

"I don't know Bianca very well," he began, "but from what little I've seen, she's a very responsible, caring woman. She didn't get that way through osmosis. Makes me think if one of your girls had been autistic, you would have handled it."

Blinking, Maddy blushed, then used one hand to fan her face. "That's very nice of you to say."

"What's very nice of him to say?"

"Sweetheart," Maddy said. "I thought you'd never finish up there! This nice man has been waiting for—"

"Sorry to barge in on you earlier than planned," he interrupted, pointing at the file.

"Have you eaten?"

"Actually, they ordered sandwiches for my last meeting." It killed him to say it because he'd been craving a plate of spaghetti and meatballs all day.

"Well," Maddy said, standing, "I think I'll head upstairs." She offered Logan her hand. "It was a pleasure to meet you."

"How long have you *really* been here?" Bianca asked, stooping to pick up toys.

"Five minutes, give or take."

"I hope my mother didn't pester you with too many personal questions." She laughed softly. "My dad used to tease her, saying she should have been a reporter."

Logan laughed. "I can see why."

With the toys put away, Bianca seemed at a loss for something to do. Hands clasped at her waist, she looked at his glass of soda. "Reading two stories and bedtime prayers made me thirsty," she said. "I think I'll pour myself a glass, too. Care for a refill?"

"Nah, I'm good. But thanks." He grabbed his glass and the file and followed her into the kitchen. "So if you don't mind my asking, is your mom ill?"

"Ill?" Bianca carried her soda to the table. "No. She's fine. Why do you ask?"

He sat across from her. "Well, she was bragging about how hard you work. About everything you do around here all by yourself. Guess it made me wonder why she can't help out."

"Mom doesn't help because—how do I put this delicately?—because she hates housework. She's also terrible at it!" Bianca laughed. "I managed it alone before she moved in, and it isn't as though she's a big mess-maker or anything. It's a relief, knowing she isn't rattling around in that big old house all by herself. And it's nice to have a grownup to talk to at the end of the day."

Logan held up one hand, oath-style. "You have my word. I won't tell anyone at the station you said that."

Once again, her big eyes widened as she said, "Oh, my goodness, I didn't mean it that way. I love the job and everyone I work with! What I meant was…it's nice to have Mom here to talk with after I help Drew with his homework, and his bath, and—"

Logan blanketed her hand with his. "Hey.

Bianca. I was pullin' your leg. Don't worry, I get it." He wished he could tell her she didn't owe him any explanations, but that would mean admitting he'd noticed her need to provide them. Last thing he wanted was to get off on the wrong foot—he still wanted her to consider the job he'd offered, alternating days and duties with his sister.

He tapped the manila folder. "This will be a good start for your search for a companion dog."

She sent him a tiny, tentative smile, opened the file and finger-walked through the materials in the folder's pockets. Those same fingers had twisted a paper napkin into a rope that day in the café while telling him about Drew's disorder and how Jason hadn't had time to learn how to interact with his only son.

Bianca's hands were shaking, he noticed, just as they had as she'd tried to remember which cable to remove from his battery that day in the parking lot. If he'd known it would turn her into a nervous wreck, Logan would have done the job himself. But she'd seemed so eager to prove that she could do it that he'd stood back and let her. She'd succeeded at the connection, at calming down, too…until his jacket had slipped from her shoulders. Logan didn't think he'd ever forget the instant of dread and regret that had registered on her pretty face.

As she carefully replaced the press releases and pamphlets into the folder, he tried to understand the disappointment in her eyes. He didn't get it because she'd seemed so interested and excited at first.

And then it hit him: now that he'd done this favor for her, she felt beholden to him.

Not ten minutes ago her mom told him that Bianca was hell-bent on doing everything all by herself. He admired that. Respected it, too. Maybe, if he chose his words correctly, he could get her to agree to do the job...to put things in balance.

Bianca closed the file and wrapped her hands around the tumbler. "This is... It'll save me hours of research. I don't know how to thank you."

"I do."

Eyes wide, she said, "Oh?"

"That job offer I made the other night? Give it a week, and if you hate it, well, we'll call it even. If you like it, we'll talk salary."

She was thinking about it. He could tell by

the way she nodded in sync with her forefinger tapping the file.

"Maybe this will influence your decision. I took your advice to heart—see? Proof I'd be a terrific boss!—and talked to my sister. You were right. She's considering the job, too."

Bianca sat up straighter. He definitely had her attention. And she was definitely interested.

"Job share," he said. "I'll let you two work out the schedule and the logistics. I don't care who works what hours as long as the work gets done."

"You know, that makes sense. A lot of sense." She paused. "And Sandra is okay with it?"

Logan hesitated. "I have to be honest. She agreed to consider it, but she hasn't said yes. Yet."

"Makes sense," she repeated.

"But I have to ask you another favor."

He could almost read her mind: "Another one?"

Logan gave her a quick rundown of the conversation he'd had with his sister. "It hit me like a roundhouse punch that you were right. She isn't fragile at all." He scooted to the edge of his seat, folded his hands on the kitchen table and listed Sandra's duties and responsibilities.

"She went from being Daddy's little girl," he continued, "to being the wife of a control freak. That idiot she was married to blamed her for Sam's condition. Every time the poor kid misbehaved, he punished *her*."

Bianca closed her eyes and cringed, and Logan took it to mean she was imagining what it might be like to take it on the chin—or worse—every time Drew acted out.

"Sandra is a great gal. Smart. Capable. Bighearted. But these past ten years, well, let's just say she doesn't have a very high opinion of herself."

Nodding, Bianca said, "Because she thinks if she'd made a better decision about who to marry…"

Relief wrapped around him. "So if Lady Luck decides I'm worthy, and you guys say yes to the job, I need Sandra to think she's in charge."

He tried to read her reaction to that. Hopefully, the fact that she hadn't recoiled told him Bianca was open to the idea.

"She won't be in charge, of course. No reflection on her intelligence or abilities, mind you. It's just, well…" How would he explain that his sister had allowed others to tell her what to do for so long that he feared she was too weak to take charge when a situation demanded it?

"I hate to lean on a tired old cliché," Bianca said, "but practice makes perfect."

Logan didn't get it and said so.

"Having faith in herself won't come easy at first, but when she realizes she *has* been making smart decisions, her self-confidence will grow."

Bianca leaned forward and explained her rationale. "She decided to leave an abusive relationship, and knowing how kids like Sam react to change, she *decided* to move in with your folks. When your mom was diagnosed with cancer, she *decided* to leave her job rather than put her in the care of in-home nurses...."

She inhaled and let the breath out slowly.

"With a little help, Sandra will figure out that she's always been..." She drew quote marks in the air. "...'management material.'"

"So you're saying... I know it's a lot to ask, especially with all you're already juggling. But you'd be okay with letting her think she's in charge of the project?"

A slight smile turned up the corners of her mouth, and the breath caught in Logan's throat.

"I've never even met the girl," she said softly, "and I like her. So if I can help…"

He'd thought she was a knockout the first time he saw her, but she'd never been more beautiful than she was right now.

"You're pretty amazing, you know that?"

Bianca waved the compliment away. "Just wait till I get my superhero cape back from the dry cleaners!" she said, laughing.

It was a beautiful sound, but not half as beautiful as that face. If she kept looking at him that way, he might just have to thank her for agreeing to help Sandra…with a kiss.

He licked his lips and told himself his reaction was purely physical. What guy wouldn't feel the same way, sitting face-to-face with a woman like this?

She licked her lips, too. Was the moment having the same effect on her?

His stomach growled. Loud. And long.

One second, then two, passed as her expression changed from sweet and caring to amused.

On her feet now, she said, "I take it you didn't eat what they served at your meeting?"

Logan got up, too. If he admitted that he hadn't, she'd offer to make him something. And he didn't want to put her to the trouble. "The food was free, so yeah, I ate."

His stomach rumbled again.

"Evidently, not enough." Bianca headed for the kitchen.

The little clock on her end table said 9:37 p.m. And the weary look in her eyes reminded him that she'd put in a long day. He should leave. Let her get to bed. Promise to check in with her tomorrow, see if, after sleeping on it, she'd made a decision about the job.

Instead, he followed her as a weird thought clicked in his brain: maybe *he* was in need of protection…from *her*.

He'd been a titan on the football field, and earned the kudos of directors and fellow actors for doing his own movie stunts, but when it came to matters of the heart, Logan knew he was a weakling. There was more on the line, lots more, than there had been when he'd been a younger man, and he had a feeling that if he opened himself up to Bianca—and it didn't work out—he'd never recover.

She took a covered dish from the fridge and, balancing it on one palm, said, "Would you rather skip it? It's pretty late to eat such a heavy meal."

This is friendship, he told himself, relieving her of the plate. *Strictly platonic.*

"If my head was as hard as the lining of my stomach," he said, sliding it into the microwave, "my pro football career might have lasted longer than three years."

While the appliance hummed and the food spun in a slow circle, Bianca grabbed a stoneware dish from the cabinet and put it on the table.

"Have a seat," she said, grabbing salt and pepper and parmesan cheese from the pantry.

He started to say dirtying another plate was silly, that he was happy to eat from the one in the oven, but she'd started talking about an article she'd read about the parallels between concussion damage and autism and how she hoped scientists would have more than theories by the time his school was built. So he leaned back and smiled as she placed a fork and butter knife on a napkin beside the plate and changed the subject to the similarities between service and companion dogs and how either one had the potential for improving Drew's life.

The microwave's timer dinged, and he started to get up, thinking the least he could do was take the spaghetti out. But her hand on his shoulder stopped him…and doubled his heartbeat.

"Too hot to handle with your bare hands," she told him. And then she lifted his plate and plopped a colorful pot holder under it.

His skin felt cold when she removed her hand. And when she sat across from him, his entire body felt cold. He wanted her closer. A whole lot closer.

"I hate to eat alone."

"When you're finished, I might have a slice of pie with you."

"Whoa. There's pie, too?"

She nodded. "Cherry."

"I want pie, too," a little voice piped up.

Her voice took on a scolding tone as she said, "Andrew Jason Wright, what are you doing up?"

The boy rubbed sleepy eyes. "I heard something."

He stood beside Bianca's chair and focused on Logan, who'd just taken a huge bite of a meatball.

"Mom," he whispered, "what's that TV guy doing here?"

Bianca pulled him into a sideways hug and made an attempt to finger-comb his sleep-tousled hair, an attempt that was barely tolerated by her son.

Logan could see that his reaction hurt her feelings, so he answered in her stead.

"I'm a friend of your mom's," he said as she slid the file out of Drew's reach.

The action made it clear she didn't want the boy to know about the research just yet, so Logan deliberately skirted the truth.

"I dropped by to thank your mom for helping me at the station the other day."

"What's your name?"

"Logan. Logan Murray."

Drew nodded and began flicking his fingers. "Logan Murray. Tire commercials. Bank commercials. Knights commercials." He looked up suddenly and met Logan's eyes. "And commercials about dogs for kids like me."

Kids like him. It was disconcerting to hear him say it straight out that way. Drew knew, on some level at least, that his brain functioned differently than other kids'. Logan didn't know whether to feel sorry for him—and his nephew—or give him a thumbs-up. Because in his opinion, a lot of adult problems would cease to exist if only grownups had the capacity for honest self-appraisal.

Drew quoted the commercial, almost verbatim, closing with a personal review. "Companion dogs keep kids like me from wandering off or engaging in dangerous activities. And that's why I need one."

"Drew only needs to hear a thing once, and he can recite it word for word. But you're probably used to that."

Because of Sam, he thought. Yeah, he'd experienced the phenomenon before, but Logan didn't think he'd ever get used to the talent that could, within seconds, go from being a very good thing to borderline unbearable.

"I'm jealous," Logan said. "Took four takes before I got it right. And I was reading from cue cards!"

Drew recited the commercial again, then stopped talking as if someone had flipped a switch. Hands clasped, his gaze traveled the room. Sooner or later he'd spot the file folder. And when he did, Bianca would be up all night, trying to explain why he might *not* get a dog.

The ceiling fan captured Drew's attention, and Logan used the temporary distraction to ease the folder closer.

"So, Drew," he said, twirling a noodle around his fork, "is spaghetti your favorite supper?"

He climbed into his mom's lap. "I like pizza better. It's easier to eat."

Logan daubed sauce from his chin and said, "When you're right, you're right."

Bianca mouthed *Thanks* as Drew launched into a string of questions about Logan's role in *Mr. Action:* Had he worn a covert or overt vest under his uniform? Was it lined with titanium or steel? How did he run so fast while wearing so many pounds of protective gear? Did it hurt when he fell from that fire escape? Were the bullets in his service revolver real or pretend? And was he really in love with the woman he and Mr. Action rescued, or was that pretend, too?

Logan couldn't help but laugh. "In real life, she's a very nice lady, and we're friends. But she has a very nice husband and some very nice kids. I only pretended to love her for the movie."

Drew nodded. "Oh. I get it. That's what they call acting in Hollywood, isn't it?"

"That's right. Acting."

Drew faced Bianca. "I like this guy, Mom. Do you like him, too?"

"Yes, of course," she said.

And Logan thought it was charming that her answer produced a blush.

Then Drew cupped a small hand beside Bianca's ear and whispered, "If you like him, then I think you should marry him." He glanced at Logan, then went back to whispering. "You know what Dr. Sharon says...I need a good male role model."

Bianca hid behind one hand. "Oh, Drew," she said as her blush intensified.

When she came out of hiding and fixed those big embarrassed blue eyes on his face, he nearly choked on the bite of meatball he'd just swallowed.

"Awkward," she said. "Sorry."

Not as awkward as his reaction to her. "I didn't hear a thing," he fibbed.

Something Sandra used to say when they were kids echoed in his head: "If wishes were fishes..." An excellent parallel, he thought, to the old "You can't un-ring a bell" maxim. But if he knew what was good for him—and for Bianca—he'd better try.

Drew began flapping his hands and bobbing his head, shouting "I want pie-pie-pie-pie-*pie!*"

Bianca wrapped her arms around him and held him close. Pressing her lips to his temple, she rocked slowly, whispering "Shh, sweetie. Remember the rule?"

A moment of silence before he said, "When I'm calm and quiet, *then* can I have pie?"

"If you can stay calm and quiet until Mr. Murray has finished his spaghetti, yes, you can have a small slice of pie, then back to bed for you."

Just as quickly as the outburst began, it ended. Drew hopped down from Bianca's lap and stood near Logan's elbow. "Are you finished, Mr. Murray?"

Bianca started to reprimand the boy, but Logan held up one hand. "You know," he said, putting down his fork, "I *am* a little full."

"Does that mean you're finished?"

He shoved the plate away, taking care to keep the file folder hidden. "Yup, I'm finished."

Drew ran back to Bianca. "He's done, Mom. Now we can all have pie."

How she managed to collect the spaghetti plate, take the pie out of the fridge and slice it—all with Drew right at her elbow—Logan didn't know. But it told him she had the patience and focus to slog through reports and sift pertinent information from the experts he'd lined up.

When she served Drew his pie, he said, "Can I sit next to you, Mr. Murray?"

"I'd like that," he said, meaning it.

Drew picked up his fork and smiled, exposing three missing teeth and the jagged edges of the brand new one peeking from his pink gums.

"I like you, Mr. Murray."

"I like you, too, kiddo." He meant that, too. "And if it's okay with your mom, you can call me Logan."

He looked at his mother. "Is it okay with you, Mom?"

"Well, sure."

The relief in her eyes, on her face, reminded him of what Sandra so often said: "The parents of autistic kids can't live normal lives." Unfortunately, he understood the mindset all too well because he'd been present, in restaurants, at the grocery store, even during church services—where even people who were *supposed* to be understanding—made her feel like a negligent parent for not knowing how to reel in her out-of-control child. Consequently, Sandra stayed close to home and interacted only with people who understood that Sam really *couldn't* control his words and actions. It made him more certain than ever that building the school was the right thing to do. And when the doors opened, he'd make sure it offered outreach programs geared toward parents like Sandra and Bianca.

CHAPTER TWELVE

LOGAN SCRAPED THE last of the pie from his dessert plate. "Do you make *every*thing from scratch?"

Bianca stood at the sink as she rinsed dishes and flatware. "When I can," she said over her shoulder.

He stepped up beside her and loaded them into the dishwasher. "Be sure to let me know next time you 'can,'" he said, grinning, "so I can head right over."

She laughed as Drew stretched and yawned.

"You need to get back to bed, sweetie," she said, drying her hands. "It's a school night, don't forget."

He looked up at Logan. "Will you tuck me in?"

Logan held her gaze for all of two seconds— long enough for her to read confidence and certainty in his dark eyes. Okay, so his sister's son was on the spectrum, but Drew was different from others with autism in a lot of ways. He didn't reach out to just anyone, but when he did, it was for keeps. Bianca didn't believe most of the love-'em-and-leave-'em stories the gossip rags had printed about Logan, but she couldn't take the chance that he'd get busy— or fall in love *again*—and forget about Drew.

"I'm sure Mr. Murray needs to get home," she said, leading her son toward the stairs. "Besides, it's way past your bedtime, and—"

"I really don't mind," Logan said. "But you're the boss...."

"Please, Mom?"

She looked from Drew to Logan and back again. How odd that she'd never noticed before how many traits they shared: big, expressive eyes, long eyelashes, the talent for looking like a sad, lost puppy...

Smiling, she said, "Well, all right. But only if you promise to go right to sleep."

Drew fist-pumped the air. "Yes!" he said, then took Logan's hand and led him to the staircase.

If you need me... she mouthed.

And he nodded.

She watched until they'd disappeared into

Drew's room before ascending the stairs, where she leaned against the wall right beside the door.

"Mom always sits there," she heard Drew say. She pictured him patting the edge of his mattress. *Her* spot, from the time he moved from the crib to his big-boy bed nearly five years ago.

Logan said, "So when I tuck my niece and nephew in, we read a book. Just one. Then we say our prayers. Is that how you and your mom do it?"

"Yeah, except I already said my prayers, so there's time for two books."

She didn't envy Logan because when Drew was in a mood like this, it wasn't easy to deny him anything.

"Remember the rules," he said.

Nice, she thought. *Firm, but gentle.*

"It's way past your bedtime," he added, "so one book. Okay?"

Silence.

Eyes closed, she took a deep breath and prepared to march in there and avert the chaos that his common-sense approach would surely provoke.

Instead, Drew said, "Then…could you read *Alexander?* It's forty-two pages long."

Logan laughed. "Good thing for you, I've read it before."

Meaning he knew it was mostly pictures. Bianca had to smile at that.

"'It was bedtime,'" Logan read.

Bianca sat on the floor and leaned against the wall, eyes closed. How strange it was to listen to the soothing baritone, to enjoy the story herself for a change. It was so foreign to feel completely safe and at peace...while Drew was awake!

Drew had made many advancements in the past year. But this? Inviting a near-stranger into his room, where previously no one but his mom and grandmother were welcome? Bianca didn't know what to make of that.

Several times since Jason's death, Drew had wished for a dad, one who saw him as he was... and loved him anyway. So it wasn't surprising that he was drawn to Logan's natural, easy charm. He'd starred in a couple of Drew's favorite movies and had appeared so often in TV commercials that he probably didn't seem like a stranger to the boy. But she needed to be careful here. Very careful.

A shadow fell across her crisscrossed legs,

and Bianca looked up, into the smiling face of TV's commercial king.

Logan pressed a forefinger to his lips. "Sound asleep," he whispered as she got to her feet.

She could count on one hand the number of times Drew had gone to sleep that easily. On the way down the stairs, she said, "What are you, a magician? It takes me a minimum of fifteen minutes and two picture books to accomplish what you just did in half the time."

"I can't take any credit. Poor kid was plumb tuckered out."

If only that was the easy explanation. Tired or not, healthy or sick, Drew fought sleep every single night.

"He's a great kid," Logan said, following her into the kitchen. "It's hard to believe he's even *on* the spectrum." He smiled at her. "You've done one heck of a job."

Drew might be too young to exercise caution with this charismatic guy, but Bianca was exactly old enough—and jaded enough—to keep up her guard.

"'On the spectrum' is about all the experts can say. I've lost count of all the therapists and counselors who've worked with him, who've worked with *me,* so I could help Drew achieve his own level of normal." She watched as he leaned his backside against the counter, just as he had earlier. And on the day he'd saved her from crashing to the floor. "He's not there yet," she finished, "but it's good to see he's well on his way."

The dishes were done, and the clock said 10:15 p.m. She had towels to fold and ironing to do before turning in.

"That book Drew chose," Logan said, folding his arms over his chest. "My mom used to read it."

"Funny. My mom read it to me, too."

"Something else we have in common, then."

Bianca knew if she'd stay quiet long enough, he'd tell her what those things were.

"We both have careers in television, Italian moms, connections to autism and the same taste in books."

There was a lot to like about this man, from a certain confidence that was anything *but* conceited to that straightforward way he had of looking a person right in the eye.

"Drew says it was a birthday gift from your dad."

"It's one of my most prized possessions

and one of my favorite childhood memories," Bianca admitted. "Dad was a great guy but not very big on the warm fuzzies—his term for hugs and kisses." But he'd hugged her that day, and she'd never forget the crisp, clean scent of him.

And then she yawned.

Smiling, Logan said, "I'll just take that as my cue to hit the road." He tapped the folder on his way out of the kitchen. "If I can do anything to speed things up, just say the word."

In the foyer, he hesitated, one hand on the curved door handle, the other in his pocket.

"Thanks for the spaghetti. And the pie. And for trusting me with Drew." He nodded. "That was…it was a real treat."

"And thank *you* for the file. I don't know how long it would have taken to dig up the same information on my own."

"Don't mention it." He opened the interior door. "So I'll call Sandra tomorrow, get her to make a decision about the job. If she says she's interested, are you up for a short meet-and-greet to get the ball rolling, so to speak?"

"Sure. Tell her to bring the kids. I'll make pizza, and afterward, while they're playing, the three of us can talk. Be sure to tell her the kitchen and family rooms are connected."

"In case she wonders how we'll discuss business and mind the kids at the same time."

He might just make a pretty good boss, she thought.

A slow smile lifted the left side of his mouth. "I have a birthday coming up. Okay if I bring cake?"

"That might be fun."

"And if there's time before I leave," he said, stepping onto the porch, "maybe you can show me the rest of your paintings."

He pulled the door shut behind him, stopping long enough to add, "I'll call you as soon as I know where Sandra stands on the job thing." And then he winked. "Sleep tight," he said, closing the door.

Bianca locked the knob and the dead bolt and began what Maddy referred to as battening down the hatches. Climbing onto the stool kept in the front hall closet, she turned the key in the lock at the top of the front door, then repeated every step at the back door, the one between the kitchen and the garage and the French doors leading to the deck. After inspecting every first floor and basement win-

dow, Bianca leaned the stool against the foyer
wall and headed upstairs to make sure all the
windows were locked. With Drew, she couldn't
be too careful.

Maddy's door, as usual, was closed. And if
she knew her mother, it was locked from the inside. Not that she blamed her; sleeping with one
eye open and one ear cocked toward the hall
wasn't exactly conducive to productive rest.

She gave in to an overwhelming urge to see
for herself that Drew actually *was* asleep and
not playing quietly with his Hot Wheels or
scribbling in one of his coloring books. Side-
stepping the floorboard squeak outside his
bedroom door, Bianca tiptoed into his room.
Kneeling beside the bed, she watched the
steady rise and fall of his chest, listened to the
calm, quiet breaths…

…and silently wept. Not for herself, but for
Jason, who would never know how much joy
this bright, big-hearted boy bestowed on all
who looked past the tics and noise and unend-
ing questions. Logan, in the forty minutes he'd
spent with Drew, had gained a better understanding of the boy than his own dad had! She
wept for her son, too, because through no fault
of his own, he'd never known a father's love.

He sighed softly and rolled onto his side. In the shard of moonlight spilling in from the window, she saw long lashes that curved toward thick blond bangs. It was too dark to see the freckles scattered across his cheeks and nose, but she didn't need light to know there were exactly one hundred and thirteen golden specks. "One for each angel kiss," she'd told him the day a kid in his class had called him Dotty. The backs of his hands still bore the shallow dimples of his pudgy, baby-boy days. A slight upturn to his pale eyebrows fixed an angelic expression on his perfectly shaped little face. Would he look as innocent in five years? In ten? Or would life's ugly realities replace the sweetness with worry lines?

On her feet again, Bianca resisted the temptation to kiss his sweet face for fear of waking him. Knuckling tears from her eyes, she backed out of his room, taking care not to trip on stuffed animals, toy trucks and colored pencils.

The house was locked up tight, but she'd forgotten to turn off ceiling fixtures and table lamps. The warm golden glow drew her to the first floor. As she walked through the rooms, clicking their switches off, Bianca remembered how Jason had always grumbled about the expense of keeping each lit. Reluctantly, she had given in, but now that *she* was in charge of paying the bills, Bianca lit every shadowy corner of the north-facing house.

After the day she'd put in—seven hours at the station without a break, errands, supper and assorted chores squeezed between Drew's homework and the visit from Logan—she ought to feel weary enough to fall into bed and drift immediately into deep, dreamless sleep. But half an hour later, even after a long, relaxing shower and changing into cotton pj's, Bianca still couldn't relax. Too agitated to read, she looked for something on TV, and when nothing captured her attention, she remembered she had ironing to do. She went to the laundry room and bumped into a stack of cleaning rags, sending them to the floor. When she bent to retrieve them, Bianca saw the legs of her easel and, beside it, three blank canvases she'd put out of sight on the night of Jason's funeral.

Had it really been more than three years since she'd painted?

It had, as evidenced by the thin layer of dust covering the wooden chest that held brushes and tubes of paint. She'd put Jason's tackle box

here, too, thinking Drew might want it someday. He hadn't been interested in lures and flies
or hooks, but he had liked the container. So
she'd gathered up the contents and gave them to
Marty, and Drew used the box to store sparkly
rocks found in the driveway and odd-shaped
coins Maddy brought back from trips to Europe
and Canada. Once, she'd asked if he wanted to
stash his treasures elsewhere and restock the
tackle box with fishing gear of his own. Bianca
would never forget the way he'd crossed both
arms over his chest, eyes narrowed in grim
determination as he said, "He didn't like me,
so I don't like his stuff. And I don't want to be
like him, either."

Nothing she'd said could convince him that
his father *had* loved him, and the same had
been true every time the issue came up in the
years since.

What if she painted Jason's portrait? She'd
make sure he looked like the Jason she'd married, young, happy and hopeful...not the Jason
he'd become when he'd learned his son would
never fit into his plans for the future. Maybe,
if Drew could look into *that* face when she told
him his father loved him, the words would be
easier to believe.

She'd missed the scent of paint, the satisfaction that came from blending colors, the soothing sound of the brush bristling across the canvas, giving life to the images in her mind. When she had packed up all the supplies, Bianca told herself it had been for the best; there were barely enough hours in the day for Drew and work.

"There you go," she muttered, "wallowing in self-pity again." An old D. H. Lawrence quote popped into her head: "I never saw a wild thing sorry for itself; a small bird will drop frozen dead from a bough without ever having felt sorry for itself."

The poet had been right. She needed to get over herself. Hopefully, a cup of herbal tea would calm her down. On the way to the kitchen, she spotted an old issue of *Autism Today* lying faceup on the kitchen desk. She grinned at Drew's attempt at subtlety. His disappointment at missing last year's autism walk was all but forgotten when he realized Maddy would move in on race day. Still, he'd saved the paper—and made sure Bianca would find it—so they wouldn't miss it this year.

An idea sparked. Why not feature the race on *The Morning Show?* She grabbed a pad and pen and began scribbling notes. The minute she got to the office tomorrow, she'd see about arranging prerace interviews with organizers, and talk to the noon and evening news producers to see about coordinating reporters and camera crews. Sipping her tea, she looked at the wall calendar and smiled. This year, with Maddy's help, she could work one of the concession stands, and maybe Drew could help out.

Bianca's cell phone buzzed and did a slow crawl across the table, stopping when it bumped into the folder Logan had delivered earlier. Bold white letters glowed from its black screen: 11:03 p.m. Below it, smaller text said Logan Murray. He'd just left; had he forgotten something?

"Aw, gee. I'm sorry you answered."

"Gee. Thanks," she said, smiling.

"Wait. That isn't what I meant. Well, it is, but…I figured you'd be in bed by now, and I could leave a message without calling the house phone and waking everyone."

Bianca held the teakettle under the faucet. "I hardly ever go to bed before midnight." Putting the kettle on the front burner, she added, "So what's up?"

"I feel like an idiot. The list of names and

addresses—most important thing in the file—
fell out of the folder." He explained how, on the
way over, the driver in front of him had come
to a dead stop. "Thought I'd found everything
on the floorboard, but I missed a page."

She didn't want him to come back. There
wasn't time in her life for anyone but Drew.
Logan looked good on the surface, but so had
Jason…at first. She had to protect her son from
ever having to experience that kind of rejection
and disappointment again. If he had friends
who could connect Drew with a companion
dog for a reasonable price, she'd be a fool not
to accept his help. Beyond that…

"Can I call you when I get to the station in
the morning?" she said. "I might have a few
minutes after the show. Although the only predictable thing about that place is that it isn't
predictable! After all you've already done, I
feel awful even suggesting that you drop it off.
On second thought, can you scan the contacts
list and send it in an email?"

"Um, Bianca?"

She almost said, *Thank you for stopping me,
or I might never have shut up!*

"I'm on your back porch."

CHAPTER THIRTEEN

HEART THUMPING, she whirled around. And sure enough, there he stood, waving a single sheet of paper.

"Love those li'l clouds on your pj's," he said into the phone.

She looked down at the big-eyed baby sheep that decorated her pajamas.

"They're not clouds. They're lambs." *Oh. Fine,* she thought. *There's a man on your porch, at eleven o'clock, but* that *matters.*

"Well," he said, "that's a relief. Because in my opinion, there's way too much personification in the world."

Personification? What *was* he talking about?

"I thought it was weird that the designer gave the clouds eyes. With eyelashes. And itty bitty smiles." He jiggled the doorknob. "Left my jacket in the car, and it's kinda cold out here."

Bianca had already locked up for the night, so she had two choices: Tell him to return to his car and drop the file in the mail, or get this over with, here and now. Groaning to herself, she dragged a kitchen chair to the door and, using the key that dangled from the chain around her neck, unlocked the door.

Two panes of glass—one in the entry door, the other in the storm door—separated them. "Aw gee," he said into the phone, wincing as she stepped onto the chair seat, "be careful, okay? If you fall again, I can't catch you from out here."

A rational person would have let his call go to voice mail. A sane woman wouldn't be opening the door at this hour to a man she barely knew. Bianca stepped aside as he walked into the kitchen. Clearly, she was neither.

"Sorry to be such a pain," he said, holding up the page, "but I know this could be important for Drew. I didn't want you to have to wait to look through this." Logan handed her the second folder. "'Cause I'll be out of commission for a couple weeks."

While gawking through the door, his face had been backlit by the golden glow of the porch light. Now, illuminated by the bright beam of the ceiling fixture, she noticed bloodshot eyes and a certain weariness that sagged his broad shoulders.

"Out of commission? As in…recovering from a surgical procedure?"

"No, no," he said. "Nothing like that. It's just…" Frowning, he shook his head. "It's business stuff. Driving back and forth between here and DC. Dozens of meetings. A couple of trips to New York…" His lips slanted in a boyish smile. "But I'm touched that a woman like you would worry about me."

Bianca did her best not to frown. "I wasn't worried."

He didn't believe it, and the proof was written all over his handsome face.

"Just a little curious about what might put you out of commission and what it would take to correct it and how long it might take to recuperate after the procedure. Since you don't need one, well, that's a good thing." She exhaled a sigh of frustration. "But really, it was a natural assumption because you look exhausted."

"Up since four-thirty, so I'm not surprised to hear I look a little done in." The smile grew. "But I'm not the one carrying on a cell phone conversation with a person standing two feet from me."

Why hadn't she noticed that he'd put his phone away? Bianca felt the heat of a blush color her cheeks as she snapped her cell phone shut...

...and caught sight of her silhouette on the refrigerator door.

After her shower, she'd pulled her hair back to pluck her eyebrows—and forgotten to remove the stubby ponytails.

"Oh, good heavens," she said, holding her breath. Because if she looked half as silly to him as she looked to herself...

"If it's any consolation, I think you look cute." And then he pointed at the stove. "The teapot is about to whistle."

How could he possibly know a thing like that?

Almost immediately she saw the telltale puff-sputter that always preceded the whistle. She'd made it her business to notice things like that because the price to pay—for Drew—was simply too high. Bianca turned off the burner and glanced at the clock. A moment ago, he'd teased her for talking on the phone to a person who stood mere feet from her. It had been unsettling then, seemed more so now. It had been years since she'd been alone with a man. Longer still since she'd been this close. And Jason had been the only male to see her in pajamas.

"I should go," he said, "so you can enjoy your tea."

"Actually, I'm more in the mood for hot chocolate." She wasn't, but Bianca couldn't let him think he was right about everything. Courtesy and gratitude had motivated her earlier invitation, but taking his call and opening the door to him just now had been a mistake. Besides, if things went as expected, he'd be her boss in a few days, and this popping in and out of her private life—uninvited and unannounced— could not continue. Bianca knew she had to set some boundaries. But at the moment, she didn't know *how*.

"I'd say you remind me of my mom, standing there, looking all stern, but…"

Do not take the bait, she told herself. *Don't ask him why—just let it slide.*

"Stern is tough to pull off…in lambie pajamas."

Bianca stared at her toes. Well, she had no one but herself to blame. And because she was in this deep, why not go for broke?

She grabbed her favorite mug from the cabinet—the huge, lumpy red blob Drew had made in kindergarten—and said, "So tell me more about your mom."

"Did I tell you she has cancer?"

"Only in passing." She got another mug out of the cabinet. "Coffee or tea?"

"Actually, I'm more in the mood for hot chocolate. Especially if I'm going to tell you about Mom's illness."

Had she imagined the hitch in his voice? Bianca filled both mugs with powdered cocoa mix and carried them to the table.

"You might as well have a seat." She took two spoons from the silverware drawer and handed one to him. "Especially if you're going to tell me about your mom's illness."

"It's stage 4 colon cancer. At least, stage 4 is what it was when they first found it. It's metastasized, so things don't look good. Not good at all."

Two words came to mind as she studied his weary face: *defeated* and *helpless*. Bianca patted his hand. Was it her imagination, or were his eyes shimmering with unshed tears?

Logan glanced away and cleared his throat.

"I know how hard it is," she said, "watching someone suffer."

"Especially someone you love."

Love.

The word hit her like a cold slap. How long had it been since she'd truly loved Jason? Years, she admitted. When he'd first told her how ashamed he was to have a son like Drew, she had blamed the shock of hearing he had cancer and had told herself he'd come around once he adjusted to the news. If anything, he had grown even more cold and distant.

"That's terrible," Logan said. "Sorry you had to go through all that. Sorry *Drew* had to."

Maybe she was in the middle of a wicked nightmare because surely she hadn't just said all of that *out loud!*

If the look on his face was any indicator, she had.

It didn't seem like she could do anything right tonight. But she'd opened the door to the macabre subject, so Bianca decided to listen for as long as Logan needed to talk about his mom's illness.

"Are we friends yet, Bianca?"

They'd spent, at most, the equivalent of one day together, sharing most of that with other people at the station and here at her house. Of course they weren't friends.

"Sorry. Didn't mean to put you on the spot. I

just want you to know…you don't have to pretend with me."

Pretend? She'd just bared her soul to him, every word 100 percent truth.

"No offense, but I know the signs. My sister had a husband like yours."

Oh…now she got it.

"Jason could sometimes be a self-centered jerk," she admitted. "What man isn't?"

He cocked one eyebrow.

"He wasn't the best husband in the world, but he never laid a hand on me…never even tried. He wasn't the best father, either, but he never, *ever* touched Drew."

Logan sat back and, hands up like the victim of a holdup, said, "I'm sorry. I was out of line."

"Yes, yes you *were*."

Logan lowered his hands. "It won't happen again. You've got my word on it."

"So when was your mother diagnosed?"

"A little more than a year ago."

"And Sandra has been taking care of her all this time?"

"Pretty much."

"It can't be easy, tending to the needs of a dying parent."

"Whoa." His dark eyes widened. "You don't

mean to say…you took care of your dad *and* your husband?"

"No. My dad was a test pilot." He already knew far too much about her. She wouldn't add those details of the crash and the long, agonizing battle he fought to come back afterward…a battle he didn't win.

"How much help does your sister get with taking care of your mom?"

"Susan, our oldest sister, lives out of state. I pitch in now and then, and Dad…" He shrugged. "Dad does what he can."

"I know how difficult it can be," she said, "to find ways to do your share when there are so many other demands on your time."

He held her gaze for a moment. "You managed."

"A person doesn't reach your level of success without knowing how to set priorities."

"In other words," he said, "I don't do more because I choose not to."

"I wouldn't have put it quite that way, but…"

"Mind if I give you a little friendly advice?"

As he'd pointed out, dressed in baby-blue lamb pajamas, she was hardly in a position to object.

"You're a great daughter, a super mom." He

patted his stomach. "And feed hungry strangers. So how 'bout taking care of *Bianca* for a change?"

Logan opened the door and pointed at the folder still sitting on the table. "Remember, if you need any help getting an appointment with those folks, call me." He stepped onto the porch, then leaned back in. "Need to get home and let the dog out." He aimed a thumb at the secondary bolt at the top of the door. "Don't forget to lock up, okay?" He shrugged. "Because, well, y'know...."

Yeah, she knew. "If Drew sneaks out because I forget, it's on me, not you."

Logan shook his head. "Like I said, you're too nice. If I had the sense God gave a flea, I wouldn't have come over so late, and you wouldn't have unlocked an already locked door. So if Drew sneaks out, it *is* on me."

She could admit that he'd made a good point or restate the obvious: Drew was her responsibility, 24/7, even if their normal schedule was slightly altered by an unexpected visit.

"Close the door," she said, dragging a kitchen chair behind her, "and I'll lock up right now."

Voice muffled by the closed doors, Logan said, "Sweet dreams, Bianca."

For a moment there, it looked as if he wanted to add something. But she must have been mistaken because he stepped out of the golden glow of the porch light and was swallowed up by the darkness.

"Sweet dreams to you, too," she whispered. And she meant it.

CHAPTER FOURTEEN

LOGAN LIFTED HIS mom from her bed and gently deposited her in the big recliner near the window. "Feet up or down?"

"Up. And close the blinds."

It wasn't even nine in the morning, and already Sandra looked done in. Logan filled both of his mom's requests, then proceeded to help his sister change the bed linens.

"If you really want to help," she whispered, tugging sheets from the mattress, "you could fix her a cup of chicken broth."

Logan was only too happy for the excuse to leave the room. While puttering in the kitchen, he wondered if she'd made the request to spare herself the back-and-forth trip or because she'd seen his reaction to their mother's unappreciative behavior. The latter, if he knew Sandra.

He chose a lightweight cup and dumped a spoonful of chicken bouillon into it, dropped a teabag into a matching mug and added hot water to both. On the way back upstairs, he grabbed a handful of saltines from the pantry and put them on the tray, whistling *The Pink Panther* theme as he climbed the steps.

Sandra met him on the landing. "Shh!" she hissed. "Mom's asleep, and I need the rest more than she does!"

Despite the gleam in her eyes, something told him she wasn't kidding. He held up the tray. "But...I made the broth. And tea. Where should I put it?"

Clutching the rumpled sheets to her chest, she grinned and continued downstairs. "Careful, little brother, or I might just tell you."

Logan followed her to the laundry room. "So have you had a chance to think about the job offer?" Once she'd stuffed sheets into the washer, he followed her to the kitchen. "I talked with my friend, and she's on board."

He slid the tray onto the counter and started a pot of coffee. It had finished perking when she faced him, red-eyed and sniffling.

Sandra blew her nose. "I just wish I could do *some*thing to make her happy in her last days!" Nodding at the tray, she slumped onto a counter stool. "The tea's too hot, or the broth isn't salty enough. Her room is stuffy. Or cold. Too much light coming in, or not enough. One minute she's lonely. The next, she wants privacy." Groaning, she held her head in her hands. "I swear, Logan, I'm out of ideas and nearly out of patience, too."

It showed. Sandra looked as defeated as she sounded. Logan opened his cell phone and pecked in a number.

"Who are you calling?"

He held up a forefinger. "The cavalry."

She sipped her coffee as Griff picked up.

"This better be good, Murray. I was just about to seal a sweet deal with a cute little blonde and—"

"At nine in the morning? Good grief, man. Pace yourself. You're not in college anymore."

"Real funny, but I repeat—this better be good.…"

"Okay, Mr. Cut-to-the-blonde. I need you to reschedule my meetings."

"Which meetings?"

"All of them. New York. DC. Everything we scheduled for next week. See if you can move things to week after next. Get back to me when—"

"Uh, you'd better check your phone's contacts list, pal. I think you called me by mistake when you meant to dial your secretary."

"I don't have a secretary."

"I've nagged you about that for years. Because scheduling meetings, making phone calls and rearranging schedules is what secretaries do, not attorneys."

Logan met Sandra's eyes, reached across the table and squeezed her hand.

"Look. Griff. You're right, and I'm sorry. I just figured because you set up the meetings, you could rearrange them faster than I could. This isn't a good excuse, but it's all I've got— I'm going to spend the week here with Mom. Give Sandra a much-needed break."

His sister slapped a palm onto the tabletop. "Logan! Don't be ridiculous. I'm having a bad day, that's all. I'll pull myself together in a few minutes. I always do."

He gave her the universal "shh" sign as Griff growled something unintelligible into the phone.

"I'm gonna hold you to that hiring-a-secretary thing," the lawyer said, "right after I take care of the rearranging. Soon as I have new dates, I'll get back to you. And I have a good mind to charge you the going rate." Another pause, and then, "Speaking of getting back…"

Logan heard a click, and looked at his phone. "Well, how do you like that?" he said, dropping it into his pocket. "The dude hung up on me!"

Sandra picked up her mug. "I don't blame him one bit. Sometimes you behave as though you're his only client. Not a very best-friend attitude, you know." She shook her head. "Rearrange a week's worth of meetings? Why would you ask him to do such a thing?"

He considered saying *Because Mom is running you ragged, and you're beginning to look more like her sister than her daughter.* But Sandra had programmed herself to please, even if it meant working to the point of exhaustion. Logan had been the first person she'd told about the abuse, and when he had threatened to show her husband what it felt like to be the victim of a bully, she'd made him swear to guard her secret. She promised to leave, but first, she'd needed a safe place to go. He'd invited her and the kids to move in with him, and they would have…if their mother's diagnosis hadn't changed Sandra's mind.

But he would change her mind about not taking time for herself. "So where would you rather go and relax, Deep Creek Lake or Ocean City?" He owned a condo in the mountains and another at the beach.

Sandra rolled her eyes. "Oh, for goodness' sake. I don't need a vacation. I told you, all I need is a little time to cool off and get hold of myself."

"What makes you think this is about what *you* need? I'm doing this," he fibbed, "because I feel guilty letting you do everything. And I have to tell you, I don't much like the feeling."

Her eyes sparkled with unshed tears. "We both know that's a bunch of malarkey."

"Whatever." Grinning, he shrugged. "So which will it be, the mountains or the beach?" Logan hoped Bianca wouldn't back out of the job when she found out about this latest turn of events.

Sandra sighed. "What about Poe?"

"What about her? She's housebroken…."

"The kids have school."

"Yeah. So?"

"So, they live here, too."

"And…?"

"I don't think you realize what you're proposing."

He was determined to counter every objection with logic. "I'm not fool enough to believe what you do is easy. Make a schedule. Write down tips." With his right hand forming the Boy Scout salute, he added, "And don't go easy on me."

She only sighed.

"If you're worried that I'll let the kids skip school or feed them nothing but junk food the whole time you're gone, well, don't."

She started counting on her fingers. "In addition to homework, Sally has dance lessons, and Sam has softball practice and games. Dad is like Hansel, leaving a messy trail everywhere he goes. Then there's the cooking and the laundry. And shopping and cleaning and *trying* to meet Mom's never-ending demands."

She ran out of fingers and started over again. "You'd have to make sure Mom takes her meds and eats and gets enough fluids into her so the pills will do their job. Seriously, Logan, it's a cycle of nonstop craziness that starts the minute you open your eyes and doesn't stop until you drop, bone-tired, into bed."

She paused, then crossed her arms over her chest. "You could hire someone, you know."

"Yeah. I could. But I don't want to."

"Why not?"

"Because it's high time I did my share, and hiring someone would be the easy way out." He shrugged. "Besides, you've been doing all that and then some, all by yourself, for more than a year. I can handle it for a few days. But even if I can't, it won't kill anybody to get off-schedule for a week."

"But—"

"No buts. I need to do this, if for no other reason than to prove to you—and myself—that I can. So pick one. Ski resort or ocean? We're only into the first week of April, so it'll be quiet in both places. You'll get plenty of R & R. And don't worry about how you'll break the news to Mom. I'll do it. I'll tell Dad, and if you want me to, I'll tell the kids, too."

Frowning, she bit her lower lip. "I have to admit, it's a tempting offer, but—"

"You know how much I hate to repeat myself. No buts." Logan sandwiched her hands between his own. "Sandra. Use your head. Mom is…" He couldn't bring himself to say *dying*. "These next few months will be ten times tougher than the past few." He gave her hands a squeeze. "I thought you knew every tenet of good manners."

Her nose crinkled with confusion as, one finger in the air, he recited, "'It is discourteous to look a gift horse in the mouth.'"

It was good to hear her laugh.

"So now you're making up rules of etiquette? You're crazy, you know that?"

It was as close to a yes as he'd hear. "If I had to guess, I'd say you're going to the condo at Deep Creek."

"You know me too well." She squeezed his hand. "You're a great brother and a good friend. And I love you to pieces."

"Ack," he said, standing. "All this mush is making me nauseous." Logan put their mugs into the dishwasher. "I'm going home. Make a few calls. Throw a few things in a duffel for Poe and me. I'll be back first thing in the morning, and then we can sit down. Make some lists, fill in some calendar blocks." With that, he left before she had a chance to change her mind.

When he returned the next day just before lunch, Logan was surprised to see two suitcases beside the front door. He could hear her humming in the kitchen and took that opportunity to throw her bags into the back of his car.

"Want some tea or coffee?" she asked when he joined her.

"All I want," he said, pressing the keys to the

condo and his car into her palm, "is for you to hit the road. Right now. If you make tracks, you'll have time to stop at the grocery store before you settle in."

She stared at the key ring. "I have my own car, you know."

"But it isn't gassed up. Or a four-wheel drive. The road to the condo can get muddy and rutty this time of year, you know." He touched a finger to the tip of her nose. "Besides, your suitcases are already in the trunk."

"But...I thought I'd leave after the kids got home from school, so I could say goodbye again."

"Again? That means you've already told them you're going?"

"Yes, but—"

"There you go, *butting*." He laughed. "If I know you, you were up half the night writing a detailed manifesto. Where is it?"

"On the kitchen table. With the baby monitor. You'll need to carry the receiver everywhere and always."

"Refresh my memory...that thing you say every time you and the kids leave the house?"

"You mean, 'do you need to use the bathroom?'"

"Yeah. That. Well, do you?"

"No."

"Good." Hands on her shoulders, Logan turned her to face the porch and gave a gentle shove. "Call me when you get there."

Sandra was smiling when he closed the door. Knowing her, she'd stand there for a minute or two trying to decide whether or not to go. So he locked the knob. And the deadbolt. "Remember…call when you get there," he hollered through the door.

A moment of silence was followed by her quiet laughter. The car had no sooner started up before his mom's voice crackled through the baby monitor.

"Sandra? Sandra, where are you?"

"And so it begins," he said, heading for the kitchen. According to Sandra's list, his mom wasn't due another dose of morphine until noon.

He took the stairs two at a time, thinking to kill two birds with one stone: find out what she needed, and let her know she'd have to put up with him for the rest of the week.

"Hey, Mom. What can I do for you?"

She said she was surprised to see him. Then

she thumped a fist onto the mattress when he told her that Sandra was on her way out of town.

Poe took the thump as an invitation to hop up. She made herself comfortable on the bed and rested her chin on Nancy's lap.

"I can't believe she'd leave me high and dry this way." She stroked the dog's head. "How selfish and self-centered. I might have known I couldn't count on her when—"

"Mom, that's ridiculous, and you know it as well as I do. Sandra has put her whole life on hold to devote herself to you all these months." Even the doctors agreed that if not for Sandra's unique brand of TLC, it wasn't likely their mom would have lasted this long. "She needs a break, and you know that, too. Besides, I'm perfectly capable of waiting on you." He stepped up to the bed and thrust out his chin. "At your service, madam," he said, bowing. "Coffee? A soda? Some tea and crumpets, perhaps?"

"That's the worst impersonation of an English butler I've ever heard."

"Beg pardon, madam."

"The worst British accent, too." But she was smiling when she said, "It's time for my soap opera."

Logan dropped the accent to say, "The remote is right there on your nightstand."

"But…but Sandra always turns it on for me."

"This seems as good a time as any to set a few things straight." He crossed the room, tuned the TV to her favorite channel, then sat on the edge of her bed. "Look. Mom. I love you. Wouldn't be here if I didn't. But I'm not Sandra."

"What does that mean?"

"That you can't bully or guilt-trip me."

"Bully? Guilt trip! Why, I've never—"

Logan silenced her with a stern you're-not-fooling-me look, then pressed a kiss to her cheek. "I'm going to get you a bowl of the soup Sandra made this morning," he said, handing her the remote. He tapped the baby monitor. "If you need anything, just whistle."

Poe followed close on his heels, and on the landing, Logan patted her head. "Think she'll actually whistle?"

"Do what?" his dad said, hanging his coat in the hall closet.

"You're home early."

"Just here for lunch, same as every day. What are you doing here?"

So in addition to everything else she did around here, Sandra prepared their dad's lunch, too?

Leading the way into the kitchen, Logan explained the reason for his presence in the house. "Don't mind telling you, wasn't easy watching how Mom treats Sandra. She's doing her best, but you'd never know it by the way Mom talks to her." He lifted the lid to the soup pot. "I know Mom's in pain. And scared." He grabbed the ladle. "But she's running Sandra ragged. Things keep up this way, Sandra will be in the hospital when Mom needs her most." Filling the bowl, he added, "So I sent her to Deep Creek, with strict orders to get some rest." He dipped his dad a bowl of soup, too.

"And you think you can take her place?"

Logan knew that tone. He'd heard it all his life. It was a challenge, and he credited it for every success of his youth.

"It's only a week," he said, placing his father's bowl on the table. "Sandra will get some fresh air. A chance to get her head on straight. Catch up on her sleep." He filled another bowl. "And *we'll* be fine, too. Overdose on pizza and Chinese takeout, maybe, but—"

His dad laughed. "Sandra will have a fit. You know how she fusses over those kids."

The way Bianca fusses over Drew and Maddy. Logan shook his head. Where had that crazy thought come from?

"I don't want to be around when she finds out you've pumped them full of junk food for seven days."

Logan shrugged. "So we won't let her find out."

"You know I don't do things that way."

No. Of course he didn't. Carl Murray believed blunt honesty was a good thing, solicited or not, even when it hurt. How Sandra managed to remain civil in the face of dual paternal disapproval, he didn't know. Could he could take a lesson from her and get through the week without blurting out something rude or hurtful?

Only one way to find out, he thought, picking up his mother's tray. He was halfway to the hall when his dad said, "Son, before you take that to your mom…"

Logan hesitated.

"I know she can be…difficult. But cut her some slack, will you?"

He chose his words carefully. "Dad. C'mon. Have you ever known me to be anything less than respectful with you *or* mom?"

Carl pursed his lips, and Logan prepared

for a recitation of insolence, committed at age five or ten, or both. Instead, his dad said, "You might want to add the salt shaker to your tray. The soup is pretty bland." Then he plucked his keys from the hook beside the back door. "Better get back to the office. See you at dinnertime."

Logan looked at his dad's still-full bowl and the spoon that sat beside it.

"Would it have killed him to say thanks?" he said to Poe.

The dog answered with a breathy bark.

"Gonna be a long week."

Another quiet woof.

"Well," his mom said when he walked into her room, "it took you long enough."

Logan hesitated for a moment before sliding the tray onto the adjustable overbed table. He considered telling her, as he raised the head of her bed, that Sandra made the soup before leaving for the mountains. But knowing his mom, she'd find a reason to reject it for no reason other than to make a point: her daughter had left her in a lurch.

Logan rolled the table close, tucked a napkin under her chin...

...and waited for her to react.

"Stop that," she said, smacking the back of his hand. "I'm not a helpless baby."

Baby. He blamed the word for conjuring the image of Bianca with her tiny ponytails and sheep-covered pajamas. *Not sheep,* he corrected, grinning, *lambs.*

"What's so funny?"

"Nothing." He waved a hand in front of his face. "So what can I get you? Something sweet to eat after your soup? I saw some cookies in the pantry."

"There were cupcakes, unless Sam and Sally ate them all." She sipped her tea. "You'd think they were lumberjacks, the way they pack away food."

"You used to say the same thing about Susan and Sandra and me, remember?"

She grew pensive as tears filled her eyes. "Yes. Yes, I remember."

He'd seen her cry before—when she had lost her folks, after her favorite cat died—but this was different. Her days were ticking down to a precious few, and no one was more aware of that than Nancy.

"So when was the last time you saw the grandkids?"

"Oh, couple days ago, I guess." She flapped

her blankets. "I hate being so feeble that I'm susceptible to every bug that comes down the pipe."

Logan frowned, remembering how an ordinary cold, caught on Christmas morning when the family had crowded around the tree, had turned into full-blown pneumonia. It had been a scary few days, and more than once, they'd thought the illness would take her before the disease had a chance to. Always a fighter, Nancy had muscled through and came out of it just in time for her second round of chemo. The powerful drugs lowered her resistance even more, so if anyone had so much as the sniffles, they were barred from her room.

"I miss them," she admitted. "I know it's for my own good, but sometimes I'd rather risk catching something than sitting up here all alone, all day, every day."

"Well, hang in there. Mother's Day is right around the corner. Your treatments will be over by then, so maybe we can pull something together to celebrate."

He'd call Sarah, insist that she fly in for the weekend, invite Deidre, Bianca and her mom, sister and son. He'd buy a gross of paper facemasks and surgical gloves in case sniffling and sneezing had nothing to do with spring allergies.

"That might be nice."

Her soft, sad voice told him she was only too aware that this would be her last Mother's Day.

It wouldn't be easy on any of them, least of all his dad. But they'd muddle through and do it up right and make a happy memory they could talk about for years.

CHAPTER FIFTEEN

BIANCA HAD SPENT the morning cooking up casseroles that could be frozen, then heated up for supper during the week. The afternoon had been devoted to cleaning closets and scrubbing floors. She'd just finished vacuuming the living room when the doorbell rang.

Drew thundered into the foyer, shouting, "Mom, there's somebody at the door!"

"Why don't you find Grandmom," she said, "so she can ask that rude salesman why he ignored our No Soliciting sign?"

"But Grandmom is outside reading a book, 'member?"

Yes, she remembered because when Maddy announced her intention to head into the yard, she had two choices: point out all the things she'd be doing while her mom enjoyed the breezy sunshine, or ask for some help with the housework. Bianca had two choices now, too:

answer the door in her grimy sweat suit, or bellow "Go away!" through the door.

She peeked into the foyer mirror. No smudges on her face, at least. After tucking perspiration-dampened hair behind her ears, she opened the door.

And there stood Logan, looking like a *GQ* cover model in his snug jeans and a University of Maryland T-shirt. If she'd looked out the peephole, there'd be no reason to wish she'd put her second choice into action. What was it about this guy that made her drop her guard time and again?

Drew wriggled between her and the doorjamb. "Hey, you're back. Did you forget something?"

"No, I have something to tell your mom. Something I didn't want to say over the phone." He held up a white paper bag. "I brought you a cupcake. My sister made it." Logan met Bianca's eyes. "If it's okay with your mom, maybe you can eat it in the kitchen while we talk?"

"What kind of cupcake?"

"Chocolate with butter cream frosting."

Drew tugged at her hand. "Is it okay, Mom? I promise to be quiet, and I won't interrupt."

He glanced back at the bag and licked his lips. "You know chocolate is my favorite…."

She was about to agree when Maddy stepped up behind her.

"Logan, what a lovely surprise." She elbowed Bianca. "Don't let him stand out there like a common salesman," she teased. "He'll think I didn't teach you any manners at all!"

Bianca stepped aside, and as Logan entered the foyer, he leaned close to her ear. "Sorry," he whispered. "This is exactly what I was trying to avoid by not calling first. I won't stay long. Promise."

She was far more interested in why he'd stopped by than how long he'd stay.

"He brought me a cupcake," Drew said. "His sister made it for me. Because he wants me to behave myself while he talks to Mom alone." He smiled up at Logan. "Isn't that right?"

"Couldn't have said it better myself."

Bianca relieved him of the bag. "C'mon, sweetie," she said, leading Drew into the kitchen. "I'll get you set up at the table."

"Can I watch TV while I eat my cupcake?"

"If you promise to drink a cup of milk, yes, I'll put a movie into the DVD player for you."

"Shrek!" he said. "I *love* that one!"

Maddy laughed. "He's only seen it a dozen times. Haven't you, cutie?"

"How many is a dozen again?" Drew asked.

Logan said, "Twelve."

The boy looked at his grandmother. "Then I've seen it a dozen plus three times."

"I guess that explains why you can recite every line of dialogue!" She kissed his temple. "I'll be out back, sipping lemonade and reading a book," she told Bianca. And facing Logan, Maddy added, "Good to see you again. Don't be a stranger!"

Bianca stared at the toes of her once-white sneakers and summoned the willpower to exercise those rules of etiquette Maddy had drilled into her head.

Bianca peeled away the cupcake paper and put the treat on a plate. Then she dampened a paper towel and put it on the table. "Remember to wipe your hands on that," she said, "and not your shirt, okay?"

"Okay, Mom," he said around a mouthful of cake.

Bianca headed into the family room with Logan close behind her.

"So the reason I disrupted your Saturday morning," he said, "is my sister."

"Oh?" His tone of voice at the door had made her wonder if maybe his mom's condition had deteriorated.

"Stopped by Thursday for a routine visit with my mom, took one look at Sandra and knew if I didn't do something fast, she'd snap." He drove a hand through his hair. "So I sent her to my condo in Deep Creek for the week. She left yesterday morning." Then, arms akimbo, he said, "You're lookin' at her replacement."

Bianca studied his face. His easy smile told her he could do the job and that he felt satisfied he'd done the right thing. The image of him packing the kids' lunches, shuttling them to the school's carpool lane, then folding towels and washing dishes produced a smile.

"Who's with your mom now?"

"She just got her morning morphine dose, so she'll be out for an hour, maybe two. If she comes around before I get back—which, according to Sandra's instructions isn't likely— Dad's right there."

And because they lived so close, Bianca realized, he was confident he'd be home long before his mom woke up.

"I'm guessing you'll need to postpone this job-share thing."

"No way. Sandra will be back in a week. I ordered some equipment for you. But before I deliver it, I want to make sure you're okay shouldering the work alone until she gets back."

"Equipment?"

"Laptop, printer… Stuff to make the job easier. I wanted to see how you feel about a separate phone line so we can route calls through it. Less disruption for you and Maddy and Drew, y'know?"

"No need to go to all that expense. I could use my cell."

"Maybe. We'll see." He cocked his head. "Does that mean you're on board?"

She had no idea what he'd set into motion, but she trusted that whatever it was, he'd kept her crazy schedule in mind.

"What does Sandra say about me running the show while she's on vacation?"

"I didn't give her a chance to voice an opinion, but I know she'll be fine with it."

Because it was true? Or because she didn't want to disappoint her amiable brother?

"Okay, then…"

"Excellent!" he said, clasping his hands. "I'll just say bye to Drew and Maddy and let you get back to work."

Logan walked into the kitchen and stood at the table beside Drew.

"Well, didn't you make quick work of that cupcake?"

"It was delicious," he said around the last bite. "Tell your sister thank you."

"Will do. See you soon, kiddo."

Drew waved, using one chocolate-covered finger, as Logan crossed to the patio doors.

He slid the screen aside and leaned out. "Good seeing you, Maddy. Enjoy this nice weather while you can. I hear we're in for one heck of a storm later."

Maddy fired off a tiny salute and went right back to reading her book.

"Be nice, Mom," Bianca called, "or Logan might think I didn't teach you any manners."

"Touché," Maddy called back.

On the way to the foyer, Logan said, "You guys have a cool relationship."

Smiling, she nodded. "Yeah, we do. I'm pretty lucky."

"So is she. Not every daughter would open her home to a widowed mom." He smirked. "Especially a strong-minded mom."

"Well, for the most part, we're like-minded, so that's cool, too."

He grabbed the doorknob. "Your laptop and other stuff should be delivered on Monday. I'll give you a heads-up, and maybe soon after that, I'll bring it over and help you hook it up. Meanwhile, how 'bout if I email you the names of the experts you'll interview? If they check out, that is."

At first she'd balked at the idea of letting him provide office equipment. But it made perfect sense from a business standpoint; her computer was old and slow, and the printer was on its last legs. And a separate phone would greatly reduce any chance that incoming calls would interfere with day-to-day activity around here. Besides, it was a temporary arrangement; after delivering the information Logan needed, she'd return it.

"Sounds good," she told him. "That way I can get a head start on the research, save the interviews for later."

He was half in, half out the door when he added, "Oh. One last thing. I'm thinking of doing something special for Mother's Day. Deidre, Griff, my sisters… If you guys don't already have something planned, I hope you'll join us. Nothing fancy. Burgers and dogs on the grill… No pressure. I'm just thinking the more, the merrier, y'know? So give it some thought, okay?"

And with that, he was gone.

Bianca went back to dusting. She'd heard the pain in his voice and had a pretty good idea what put it there: this would be his mom's last Mother's Day. Attending the party meant meeting his dad, Sandra and her kids and the sister who lived in Colorado. She warned herself not to read anything into the invitation. Bosses invited employees to their homes all the time.

"You'll never get anywhere with a man like Logan looking the way you do."

Startled, Bianca spritzed furniture polish far beyond the end table. "Mom. You're as bad as Marty. Do I have to hang a bell around your neck, too?"

"You can't distract me that easily. Just look at yourself. His picture is everywhere with socialites and movie stars, recording artists and Victoria's Secret models. How do you hope to snag him if every time he sees you, you're wearing holey sweat pants and a baggy T-shirt? You could have at least run a comb through your hair!"

She might have said, "He has seen me in a business suit" or "I'm not interested in Logan," but the image of herself in Pippi Longstocking ponytails and blue lambs pajamas silenced her. She could remind her mom that there hadn't been time to make herself presentable, but what would be the point?

She glanced at the paperback in Maddy's hands. "So how's the book?"

Her mother groaned, then wrapped Bianca in a motherly hug. "I give up. If you want to spend the rest of your life alone, there's nothing I can do about it."

"Alone?" She patted her mom's back. "But Mom...I have you and Drew!"

Maddy feigned a long-suffering smile and started up the stairs. "If you need me, I'll be in my room praying for a miracle."

"My mom the comedian," she said, standing beside Drew. "Lucky me."

She looked over his shoulder at his puzzle. "How's it going, sweetie?"

"It's a tie."

He liked playing games against invisible opponents. Sometimes he taught them his own version of the rules; other times he did everything in his power to win.

Drew stopped working and looked up at her. "Why is your hair wet?"

"Because I was working really hard and got a little sweaty."

"Then you should get a bath. You'll be surprised how much better you'll feel afterward."

Laughing, Bianca wondered how many times she'd said the same words to him.

"Are we really going to Logan's house on Mother's Day?"

So he'd overheard the conversation, had he?

"I haven't decided yet. Would you like to?"

"Heck, yeah! I really like Logan." He focused on his puzzle again. "Do you think he likes me?"

"Of course he does. He said he thinks you're a great kid."

Smiling, Drew gave a satisfied nod.

"Do you like Logan?" he asked.

She had to choose her words carefully here. If the endorsement seemed too positive, he'd pester her for more time with the guy. Not enough, and he might repeat her words verbatim.

"Yeah, he's okay. Why do you ask?"

"Do you think he'd make a good dad?"

She didn't have much to go on, but based on the way he connected with Drew, Bianca said, "Yeah, I think so."

He sat, quietly adding pieces to his puzzle. "Is it too soon after the cupcake for chocolate milk?"

"Yeah, I think maybe it is."

Shrugging, he snapped the last piece into place. "That's okay. I'd rather have white milk anyway." He leaned forward, admiring the cartoon rendition of SpongeBob and his pals. "I'm sure glad this is just a picture."

She poured his milk. "Oh? Why's that?"

"Because SpongeBob's voice is annoying. And pictures don't talk." Tucking in one corner of his mouth, he nodded. "Patrick has an annoying voice, too, but I like Sandy's." He grinned. "Sandy is cute." He looked up at Bianca. "Do you like Sandy?"

"Of all the cartoon squirrels I know," she said, putting the glass on the table, "I like Sandy best."

Drew grinned. "Heh. You're funny, Mom."

She helped him disassemble the puzzle, and they took turns dropping the pieces into the box.

"So if you like him so much," he said, examining a piece, "why don't you marry him?"

No way could she have prepared for a question like that. Sometimes she could distract him without answering.

This wasn't one of those times.

Drew repeated himself twice as she slid the lid back onto the puzzle box.

"How about helping me put your toys away?" she said, hoping this attempt at evading the subject might succeed. "The family room is a mess, and we wouldn't want Grandmom to come in here and trip on something."

His expression told her things would go one of two ways: he'd want to know why he had to do the work, or he'd ask the "marry him" question again.

Drew surprised her by going into the family room, where he got busy moving toys from the floor to his toy chest.

"If you tell Logan that I cleaned up my mess, do you think *then* he'll want to get married to us?"

Interesting, she thought, that he'd said "us." If she didn't know better, Bianca would say that Drew realized she yearned for a normal family life, too. What made him think *Logan* would fill that desire, though, she couldn't say. He was pleasant enough to be around and seemed like a decent guy. The fact that he knew how to inter-

act with an autistic kid was another point in his
favor, but she couldn't risk letting him get too
close to Drew. More accurately, couldn't risk
letting Drew get too close to him. Drew still
hadn't recovered from Jason's rejection, and
Bianca refused to expose him to hurt and disappointment like that again. And then there was
the elephant in the room: Logan hadn't given
her any reason to believe he was interested in
anything but a professional—albeit friendly—
association.

"Logan is a busy guy," she began. "His mom
is very sick, and he helps his dad and sister take
care of her. Plus he has a house of his own to
maintain, and filming TV commercials means
he puts in long days and travels a lot."

"Like Dad used to do?"

She was mildly surprised that he remembered the long hours, overnight trips and other
work responsibilities that had put physical and
emotional distance between him and his dad.
At times like these, she wondered if, with time
and understanding, Jason would have learned
to love Drew one day.

"So what would you say to pizza for supper?"
Bianca hoped he'd let the Jason and Logan conversation threads fall by the wayside.

"I'd say yes!"

"And afterward, we can have movie night."

"With popcorn and hot chocolate in the dark?"

"You bet. We'll even put sleeping bags on the floor."

"Grandmom, too?"

"We can ask her."

He rubbed his hands together. "Cool." Then he raced for the stairs.

How many seconds, she wondered, before he knocked on Maddy's door?

She didn't have to wonder long, and it warmed her heart when Maddy's animated voice blended with his.

Surrounded as he was by nurturing, unconditional love, surely he'd succeed in life, even without a dad.

Right?

CHAPTER SIXTEEN

BASED ON THE dimensions of the desk Logan had ordered for her, Bianca made space in the corner of the family room. If she'd known a stately armoire would arrive with the office equipment, she might have moved her windmill palm and ceiling-tall ficus.

"Man, oh, man," Logan grunted, hugging the tall, slender pot that housed her Pachira tree. "This thing must weigh a ton. Quick...tell me where you want it before I burst my spleen!"

She slid an end table out of the way, and he wasted no time putting the tree down. Straightening, he rubbed his back. "What *is* that thing?"

"The botanical name is *Pachira aquatica*."

"The leaves remind me of my grandmother's chestnut tree."

"Some people call it the giant chestnut. Others call it the money tree."

He leaned in for a closer look. "That," he

said, pointing at the feathery red accents of a white blossom, "looks like a flower, not a nut *or* money."

Grinning, Bianca said, "You're lucky you got here when you did. In another half hour or so, it'll close and won't open again until it's dark."

Nodding, he stepped back.

"It was one of the plants someone sent to the funeral home. I've babied it and braided the trunk, but this spring is the first time it bloomed. I'm hoping it means I'll see a few nuts this year, too."

"Does it cost a lot to take care of?"

"No. Just water and a little fertilizer three or four times a year."

"Then why do they call it the money tree?"

"Because some people think the leaves look like groupings of dollar bills. I think it's the feng shui philosophy."

"Fung schway?" he echoed.

"It's an ancient philosophy," she began. "'Feng' means wind and 'shui' is water. According to the Chinese, they're the most basic and natural elements...both required for human survival. The theory is, everything—people, animals, plants and things—exists in a world of energy. If our lives are in balance, we invite good energy. Luck, to put it another way. Which attracts other good things."

"Ah-ha," he said. "Like money."

"Right."

Logan opened the laptop box. "Funny."

"What is?" She tore into the printer carton.

"I never figured you for that type."

Bianca frowned slightly. "What type?"

"You know, one of those—" he drew quote marks in the air "—'find your center' Yoga disciples." He folded his hands, closed his eyes and moaned, "Aum-m-m-m."

And then he laughed. And *laughed*. "Bet you're awfully cute, though, doing the cobra and the thunderbolt."

"I'll have you know I attended one yoga class. *One*." Later, when he was gone, she'd analyze what he might have meant by "cute."

Eyes narrowed, Bianca smirked. "How do *you* know so much about the positions, *boss?*"

Logan wiped tears of mirth from his eyes and went back to unpacking the laptop. "My ex-fiancée was into all that meditative, path-to-wisdom hogwash."

He wasn't smiling when he added, "She was the second woman I knew who went down self-realization road. Promised myself if I ever got interested in another woman, first question I'd ask wouldn't be 'How about dinner sometime?' It'd be 'You're not into yoga, are you?'"

Well, *that* cleared a few things up. Bianca could hardly wait to share his outlook with Maddy, who thought feng shui was a bunch of nonsense.

On his hands and knees, Logan fished the electric cord through the back of the armoire and plugged it in.

"Do me a favor, will you?"

She peered around the cabinet and waited to see which cord or tool he'd ask her to hand him.

"Don't call me boss ever again, okay? We're peers. I'm in it for Sam. You're in it for Drew. And hopefully, what we accomplish for the boys will benefit a whole lot of kids just like them."

Peers? Bianca thought not! She couldn't recall his exact words, but he'd asked her to think about sharing the job with his sister. Hadn't he said that if she decided to work with him, they'd discuss salary?

"Hand me the printer cord, will ya?"

As she fished the plug through the hole in the back of the cabinet, Bianca accepted that Logan had spent a lot of money on the beautiful armoire and everything that it would house. She intended to make a commitment, too—of time and energy and enthusiasm—because she believed in the project as much as he did. Could she afford to make that investment *without* remuneration?

He crawled out from behind the armoire and began connecting the wires to the corresponding electronics.

"Guess you didn't hear what I said." Logan leaned over the printer. "About not calling me boss."

"You were two feet away. Of course I heard you."

He lined up the printer, the laptop and the mouse pad, then stood back to admire his handiwork. Then he rolled the desk chair toward her.

"Let's see how much adjusting it'll take before we find the right height for you."

Bianca plopped onto the seat. He'd said "let's" and "us," reminding her of the way Drew had asked if Logan would get married to "us." Was it a male trait, this tendency to draw people into groups? Or did it mean something more?

The better question, she thought as he pumped the chair's height-control handle, was why it mattered. Despite asking her not to call him boss, Logan had made it clear that he saw her as an employee. And she'd underscored the relationship by wondering how much he'd pay her to do the job.

"There," he said, rolling her up to the desk tucked into the armoire. "How's that?"

She curled her fingers over the laptop's keyboard. "Perfect."

"You'll like this chair, I think. It's ergonomically correct, so you should be able to sit here for hours before discomfort sets in."

She looked over her shoulder and grinned. Logan looked the way Drew did when he finished his homework or picked up his toys without being asked. Proud.

Logan's left brow rose slightly. "What?"

"Don't tell me," she teased. "You made a commercial about this nifty piece of ergonomic furniture."

Now he looked hurt, and she felt bad about that.

Bianca got up. "Sorry. Sometimes my sense of humor leaves a lot to be desired."

"Nothing to apologize for. I *did* record a radio ad for the manufacturer." He smiled. Not an "It's okay" or "Don't worry about it" grin, but the kind that said, "I know something you don't know." She'd misread his expression a second ago and didn't want to repeat the mistake. Maybe she'd heard the commercial while driving Drew to school or on the way home from work.

"Really?"

His grin grew. "Guess we have something else in common."

Something else? Bianca ran a short list of the things he might mean: an involvement with television. A close-knit family. A desire to make life better for the autistic kids in their lives…

"Sometimes," he said, "my sense of humor leaves a lot to be desired."

Bianca wasn't sure how to react…until he reached out and gave her shoulder a playful shove. She laughed. And when he joined in, she laughed harder still.

"Goodness! I could hear you from the backyard!" Maddy said.

Instantly, the laughter stopped. Logan caught Bianca's startled gaze and took a step left, effectively putting his back to her mom. "Sorry," he said under his breath, "didn't see her come in."

"I guess you two finished setting up, and that's why you have time to laugh and joke." She slid an arm around Bianca's waist. "But really, what does it matter? It's just *so* good to hear you enjoying life for a change!" She looked at Logan. "I have you to thank for that."

It seemed he didn't know how to respond, and that surprised Bianca. The man who'd looked so comfortable shepherding Emmy and Oscar winners down the red carpet, at a loss for words?

She returned her mother's sideways hug. "My hands are all grimy, so I wonder if you'd mind getting Logan a bottle of water."

"Mind? It's my pleasure!" As she walked toward the kitchen, Maddy winked at Logan. "Small price to pay for this happy mood my girl is in."

The minute Maddy was out of earshot, Logan shook his head and leaned close to Bianca. "That mother of yours," he said, smiling, "is a piece of work."

"She takes after me, not her father," Maddy called.

Logan and Bianca exchanged another surprised glance.

She delivered the water and, giggling, said, "So aren't you the lucky duck."

Bianca waited until the screen door slid shut behind her mom to say, "It's like she has no censorship filters. If it's in her head, it's out her mouth."

Logan chuckled. "Reminds me of Deidre."

They spent a few minutes sharing some of the inappropriate comments their elderly friend had made.

He started bagging the Styrofoam while she broke down the boxes.

"So what's that?" he asked, pointing.

Bianca glanced at the easel that she had covered with a sheet and the table beside it that held her palette, which stood in the opposite corner of the family room.

"I'm painting something for Drew."

He walked toward it. "Do you mind?"

"No, but keep in mind it isn't finished," she said as he tugged at a corner of the sheet.

Logan looked from the painting to the picture of Jason on the mantel and back again.

"Man," he said, bending for an even closer look. "You sure this isn't a photograph?"

She showed him her acrylic-stained fingernails. "Absolutely positive."

"Well, wow. It's fantastic." He replaced the cover. "You're really talented."

Bianca shrugged and went back to folding the boxes into stackable squares. She wouldn't be satisfied until she'd painted *love* into Jason's eyes. It wouldn't be easy because with every brush stroke, she was reminded of the man she'd thought he was, before their wedding, before Drew's diagnosis....

"So have you heard from your sister?" she asked, hoping to change the subject.

"Talked to her last evening. Mom broke down when they hung up. Said she's glad Sandra's having a good time and admitted that after a year without a day off, she'd earned the break." A half-hearted smile lifted one corner of his mouth. "Guess having me in charge makes it easy to see what good care Sandra took of her."

"I'm sure you're doing fine. It can't be easy, running the whole house, taking care of the kids, all while making sure your mom gets her medicine, and meals, and…"

"…and baths? Don't tell anyone, but I hired a home nurse to come in once a day to give her a sponge bath, make sure I didn't screw anything up."

"If I was a betting woman, I'd wager she hasn't found a thing."

"Yet."

"You'll be fine. Besides, it's only another couple of days."

He nodded. "Had a chance to call any of the companion-dog people yet?"

"As a matter of fact, I haven't. But it's high on my To Do list."

"I had a notion to bring Poe over here," he said. "See how Drew behaves around dogs."

"Poe?" The name sounded familiar.

"She's my dog. The one in the commercial." He smiled. "One of my closest friends, too. She belonged to friends whose child was on the spectrum."

So the dog in the commercial really was his? But, wait… Had he said his friend's child *was* on the spectrum?

"They moved in with me when their house went into foreclosure. Took a year, trying to find a place that allowed dogs like the one you're thinking of getting for Drew. About the time they found one, Holly was diagnosed with bacterial meningitis." He stared at the floor. Examined his hands. Heaved a huge, sad sigh. "She was one great kid."

Now Bianca understood: they hadn't found a solution for her autistic traits.... Holly had died.

"The dog reminded her folks too much of their loss. They were going to send Poe back to her trainers, but because she was used to me—and I missed having her around—I adopted her."

"How old was Holly?"

"Six. Barely."

"Did she... Did it happen recently?"

"Three years ago, come August."

So. Just about the time she'd lost Jason. Bianca searched for words of comfort, but all that came to mind were the strange, insensitive things people had said when Jason died: "How lucky he is not to be suffering anymore" and "Now that he's in a better place, you can get on with your life." They'd meant well, and even at the time she'd realized their discomfort with her loss was what prompted the inappropriate comments. But what was wrong with simply saying, "I'm sorry?"

It's what she said to Logan.

"Thanks. You know, it's weird, but I haven't heard from them since I picked up Poe." He pressed the pads of his fingers together, pushed them together and apart, together and apart, like a spider doing pushups on a mirror. "Guess I'm a reminder of their loss, too."

"Losing Jason was tough," Bianca admitted, "but to lose a child?" She glanced at the photos of her husband and son, side by side on the mantel. Meeting Logan's eyes, she said, "They'll come around in time."

"It's been three years. But a guy can hope."

Maddy walked into the room, grabbed a book from one of the shelves that flanked the fireplace and said, "Yes. I'm available to babysit if you guys want to grab a bite to eat later."

When she was gone, Logan took a gulp from the water bottle and, while replacing the cap, said, "I don't know how you do it."

"Do what?"

"Put up with…" He pointed in the direction Maddy had gone. "If I'm over the line here, say the word. It's just, well, she's pretty outspoken, y'know?"

She couldn't very well accuse him of overstepping his bounds when Maddy had interrupted every time he'd visited. Well, except for the one she'd jokingly dubbed "Mission: Lamb pj's."

"She is what she is," Bianca admitted.

"Lucky for me, the good far outweighs the bad. And to be fair, I'm even weirder than Mom."

He returned her smile. "I haven't seen one example of your weirdness. But seriously. What's your secret, you know, for keeping a respectful tongue in your head?"

"When she says something inappropriate or intrusive, I just tell myself she means well, that she's trying to help and everything she does comes from a place of love and affection."

Smirking, he said, "So you lie to yourself."

Bianca laughed. "Semantics. It's easy as pie."

"I made a pie. Once." He waved his hand like a flag of surrender. "Nothing easy about it. But I get your point. I'll keep that in mind next time my mom gives me what-for when her tea is too hot or the soup is too cold."

The mantel clock pealed two times. "I'd better get back. Time for another dose of morphine. And Dad's probably pulling out his hair by now."

Bianca looked at the armoire. "Thanks for all of this. It'll make the job a lot easier." Good time to talk money? she wondered.

"No, thank *you*. But don't do anything until we have a chance to talk salary. In the meantime, give some thought to what that might be, based on, oh, four or five hours a week. And don't shortchange yourself, hear?"

"Don't worry. If you can't meet my price, I can always rely on my trusty money tree."

"You're something else," he said again, heading for the back door.

"The front door is closer, and nearer your car, you know."

"Yeah, but your mom's room is at the top of the stairs."

Bianca didn't know what that had to do with anything.

"She might decide to check up on you," he said, opening the kitchen door.

"I'm used to it."

"Well, I'm not," he said, "and I don't want to take the chance that she'll misinterpret this."

He wrapped her in a big, warm hug, then stepped back and smiled. Not the practiced grin reserved for print and film cameras, but a sincere, affectionate smile.

"Person can't have too many friends," he said, closing the door behind him.

CHAPTER SEVENTEEN

HOLDING HER CLOSE reminded him of how he'd felt kissing Amy Thornton behind the bleachers in eighth grade. Come to think of it, not even his first kiss had made him feel this way.

He hadn't kissed Bianca. But he'd wanted to. Man, but he'd wanted to!

Logan had been up most of the night trying to make sense of the way she made him feel. His pulse quickened just thinking about her. Other women he'd known had aroused a similar reaction but not because of fear.

It had lasted but a moment, just long enough to feel her heart beating hard against his chest and hear her short, trembling breaths. Would she have stayed as long in his arms if he *had* given in to the urge to kiss her?

His phone rang before he could complete the thought. "Saved by the bell," he told Poe.

"Got a pencil?" Griff asked over the phone.

Logan wrote down every new date and time.

Every new venue, too. "So I'm guessing all these free lunch meetings are my price to pay for canceling?"

"You guess right. Small price to pay, if you ask me." Griff laughed. "How're things with your mom?"

"She's holding her own."

"And you?"

He understood the good intentions of the question because *he'd* asked it in the past. His mother's condition motivated his decision to come up with another way to check on the well-being of friends who faced the ugliness of a family member's terminal diagnosis.

"I'm good," Logan said.

"Free for lunch?"

"Yeah…if you can come here. I can't leave Mom alone."

"That'll work. I've been meaning to pay her a visit anyway."

Griff hadn't seen Nancy since Thanksgiving, after the second round of chemo had ended. Her hair had grown back, but she'd lost another fifteen pounds since then. Better to warn folks, Logan decided, so she wouldn't have to cope with their shock…or pity.

"She's down to seventy-two pounds," Logan said. "Just so you know."

A moment of silence, and then, "What can I bring? I'm guessing she's still not a fan of cut flowers."

He remembered the time Griff had tried to wake him up by tossing pebbles at his bedroom window. When one had cracked the glass, he'd felt so badly that not only had he replaced the pane, but he'd also brought a bouquet of roses to show his mom how sorry he was. Would she have gone easier on Griff if he'd been ten or twelve—instead of a junior in college? Probably not. But Griff didn't need to know that.

"She loves ice cream," he said. "Anything that's nut-free."

"Allergic?"

"Nah. She just doesn't like 'em."

"So…burgers? Pizza? Subs?"

"The fridge is filled with luncheon meat and salad fixin's. My crazy sister must have run to the twenty-four-hour grocery store once everyone was asleep."

"She's a prize, all right. But…I'm not in the mood for healthy food. Besides, if I know Nancy, she'll keep you hoppin' until I get there. I'll pick something up on my way over."

Griff had been right. Since ending the call, Logan had run up and down the stairs so many times he'd lost count. He was changing the batteries in the baby monitor's receiver when his pal showed up balancing a cardboard tray of sodas, burgers and fries on one palm and carrying an insulated ice cream bag in the other.

The old friends climbed the stairs together. "Let me go in first, make sure she's combed her hair and hasn't dribbled something on her nightgown."

When Logan closed the door behind him, Nancy said, "Did I hear Griffin's voice out there?"

"Yep. In the flesh."

"Get in here, you ruffian," she hollered. "Unless you have a pocketful of pebbles…."

Logan couldn't remember when she'd last looked as happy.

He left them alone to visit while he prepared Nancy's lunch: pureed chicken, sweet potatoes and triple-blended applesauce. He saved Griff's ice cream as a surprise, and once she'd had her fill—two generous scoops of cherry vanilla—he administered another dose of morphine.

After she'd dozed off, Logan and Griff returned to the kitchen.

"Can't believe how small and frail she looks," Griff said around a mouthful of burger. "Hard to believe I ever had nightmares about her."

"Nightmares. About Mom? You're kidding."

"I wish. You have no idea how many times I woke up in a sweat after a king-size Nancy chased us with her feather duster."

They shared a good laugh over the memory of the time she'd done just that.

Griff balled up a burger wrapper and tossed it at the trash can. "Hoo-ha," he said when it bounced off the rim and dropped out of sight. He helped himself to another burger. "Heard from Sandra since she left?"

"She calls two, three times a day. Sometimes more."

"She's waiting for you to beg her to come home, you big idiot. You don't expect her to admit you can't cut it, do you?"

"Yeah, well, it isn't easy, but I'm soldiering through it." Logan used a French fry as a pointer. "Though I have to admit, I might have yelled uncle days ago, if not for some solid advice from a good friend."

"I don't recall doling out any advice." Then he stopped midchew and groaned. "Aw, man. No way. The widow? Say it ain't so."

Should have known better than to try to hide something from him. Griff knew Logan better than his parents and sisters—even Sandra, who'd always been more friend than sibling.

"You're out of your ever-lovin' mind. You know that, right?"

"Never felt more sane in my life." Funny thing was, Logan meant it. "But let me put your mind at ease—she's a nice gal. Takes good care of her kid. Treats her nosy mom with respect. And gave me a few pointers so I could avoid confrontation with you-know-who." He aimed a thumb at the ceiling. "But that's it. I wouldn't even go so far as to call her a friend."

Logan remembered that sweet, soul-stirring hug and took a gulp of his soda.

Griff did the same. "Her advice must have been pretty good, then, because things looked pretty peaceful between you and Nancy."

"And it's gonna stay that way until…"

Griff frowned. Nodded. Leaned back in his chair and shook his head. "You know it's impossible, right?"

"She's got a month left, two at best. If I can't keep a civil tongue in my head that long, I'm one sorry excuse for a son."

"I wasn't talking about you putting up with

your mom's infernal nagging." He held up both hands. "Sorry. That came out wrong."

"No apologies necessary. I know what you meant."

Griff nodded again. "Yeah. Guess you do." He got up and tossed the rest of the lunch papers into the trash. "I was talking about—"

"Bianca?"

His friend drilled him with a long hard stare.

"Yeah. Bianca. It's impossible," he repeated, "for a man and a woman to be—" he drew quote marks in the air "—'just friends.' You know that, too, right?"

"I don't know if I agree with that, but I guess we'll find out. If I decide to take things even *that* far."

He waited, hoping his friend wouldn't hear the half-truth in his statement.

"Ah-ha. If you say so." Griff opened the screen door. "Hey, it's really nice out here. Want some help carrying your mom to the chaise lounge so she can get some fresh air?"

"Just dosed her with morphine. She'll sleep for an hour. But it's a good idea. If she doesn't wake up in a foul mood, I'll carry her down here."

"Well, I'm only five minutes away. No court today, so if you need a hand…"

"She's light as a feather, but thanks. Thanks for lunch and for stopping by. You made her day."

Griff started for his car, hesitating halfway there. "Do me a favor, will ya?"

Logan had a feeling he knew what his friend would say.

"I have a couple dozen court cases in the next couple of months, so don't fall stupid in love with this one, okay, Humpty? 'Cause I won't have time to put you back together again."

"Yeah, yeah," he said as Griff slid behind the wheel. "The yolk is on you, pal, because I'm not interested."

His grin faded as Griff drove away. In truth, the joke was on *him*…

…because he had a feeling it was already too late.

CHAPTER EIGHTEEN

"UNLESS I hit construction traffic," Sandra said, "I should be home by dinnertime tomorrow."

He'd done a fair-to-middlin' job of keeping up with things, but she'd find that out soon enough. The kids were in their family room doing homework, his dad had fallen asleep in the den and the last load of towels was about to come out of the dryer.

"We'll all be relieved to see you."

"Even Mom?"

"Especially Mom. Seems I wasn't gifted with your nursing skills."

He heard the smile in her voice when she said, "You're a sweetheart to make up a story like that, but it's okay. I've got my head on straight now, thanks to you. Can't wait to get back. I really miss you guys!"

Laughing, Logan said, "Give me a break. You talked to everybody three, four times a day. That's more than you talk to us when you're *here*. When did you find time to miss anyone?"

Sandra told him she'd already packed the car and that the minute she finished her morning hike, she'd grab a shower and hit the road. He'd no sooner hung up than the back doorbell rang.

"Well, if it isn't my favorite old Broadway actress!" Logan said to the stylish elderly woman.

"Better watch who you're callin' old, kiddo," Deidre said, bussing his cheek. "I've decked younger men than you in my day...."

"I was just about to bring Mom her afternoon snack. Wouldn't it be a cool surprise if you delivered it instead?"

"I know it's been a few weeks since I popped by to see her, but that isn't why I'm here today." She sniffed. "Not sure if this is spring allergies or if I'm coming down with a cold, but I don't want to risk exposing her."

Deidre plopped her enormous red tote on a kitchen chair and removed a multicolored scarf that could double as a tablecloth. "You're the one I'm here to see, handsome. Sit with me a spell, and I'll tell you why."

In typical Deidre fashion, she didn't get right to the point. Instead, the former actress talked about Felix, her fourth husband. Changed the subject to Griff, who'd been renting the garage apartment at her boardinghouse while his place was being remodeled prior to fumigation. Finally, she brought him up to speed on what her newly married granddaughter had been up to.

"Brooke and Hunter just found out they're going to have a baby!"

He pictured the couple. "No kiddin'. That's great news. I'll have to send Hunter some cigars. And flowers for Brooke." A twinge of envy snaked up his spine, and he wondered why he'd never felt that way when other pals announced engagements, weddings or pregnancies.

"How's that other li'l monkey of theirs?"

Deidre clasped both hands under her chin. "Connor? Oh, he's an absolute angel, I tell you. He can't wait to have a little brother or sister. Why, the way he acts…"

She grabbed the suitcase she called a purse. "Oh! Speaking of acting, this is why I stopped by. I have some tickets here for you." Deidre put them on the table and winked. "I thought maybe you could invite that adorable Bianca to see the play with you."

He'd almost forgotten that Deidre and Bianca knew one another. Still, something about her demeanor told him Griff had something to do with this invitation. A test, he wondered, so his old pal could see if the whole "just friends" thing had been true?

"Why didn't you give these to Griff?" he said, tapping the tickets.

"That unsophisticated oaf? He drives me bonkers. One minute he's telling me that he can't abide stage plays. The next, he's announcing that he invited some sweet young thing." She paused, squinted. "How did he put that? 'A sweet young peach, fresh off the vine.'"

"He actually said that?" Logan laughed. "Fresh off the vine?"

"I know what you're going to say. Believe me, I wasted no time pointing out that peaches grow on trees, not vines." She laughed, then added, "He could probably use a hand minding his young peach. Maybe you can double-date, like you did in high school and college."

"I can ask, but it isn't likely Bianca will say yes. She has a son with special needs, don't forget."

"Yes. Autism. Which is why Bianca never imposes on her mom." Deidre sniffed, then clucked her tongue. "Maddy told me the only reason she moved in with Bianca was to help with Drew, but I don't think she gets to do much of that."

"Might not be Maddy's fault," he said. "Bianca has this idea that because she knows Drew best, no one can handle him as well as she can."

"Hmm. You know, you might be on to something there." She smacked his shoulder. "All the more reason to talk her into it. Back her into a corner if you have to!"

Deidre got to her feet and tapped a long red-painted fingernail on the tickets. "If you can't use them, let me know. I won't have a bit of trouble giving them away."

Hoisting her purse over one shoulder, she waited while Logan opened the door.

"Bet you can't guess what my next stop will be…."

"I have a pretty good idea…. Bianca's house." He stooped to kiss her cheek. "If you survive, give me a call." He picked up the tickets and handed them to her. "And if you're successful, give me a call. I'll stop by to get them back, save you the time and trouble of driving all the way back over here."

"Oh, don't be a big silly. I'm happy to come

back. And when I do, I'll spend a little time with your mother."

"Sandra will appreciate that as much as I will."

Deidre's dark penciled-on brows rose high on her forehead. "Do you think *she'd* like to go? I can get her tickets, too." The brows rose higher still and she inhaled a tiny gasp. "And what about your dad? He's been cooped up in this house forever! Think he'd go if I got him a ticket?"

How often had he heard his mom say, "Carl, you're such a stuffed shirt!" No, Logan couldn't picture his dad sitting front and center at any stage play, let alone a little theater musical production.

Speaking of a production, how like Deidre to make such a big one over her little play. If everyone on her guest list attended, who'd look after Drew and Sam and Nancy?

"I can't speak for my dad or Sandra," he said, "but you're more than welcome to ask them." He held up a hand to silence her objection. "Your tickets, *you* ask. You'll have a lot more luck getting a yes out of them than I will. You're right. It'll do 'em both good to get out of the house. Let me know if they say yes. I'll stay with Mom while they're gone."

"I know you're a pretty amazing young fella, but not even you can be in two places at once. How will you stay with your mom if Bianca says yes?"

Even if he planned on inviting her—and he did not—chances were slim to none that she'd say yes. He'd rather not ask than have to deal with the rejection.

"How many show performances will there be?"

"Six." Then she laughed. "And aren't you a smarty-pants. Of course! You could all go to different showings. That will solve the problem of who'll babysit whom!"

The baby monitor lit up and buzzed, his signal that Nancy was going to remind him of something he'd forgotten. Sure enough, her voice crackled through the speaker. "Logan? Honey, I'm in pain. I need you to call Dr. Hamilton. See if he'll approve an extra dose of morphine. And when you come up, would you please bring me some orange juice? I've been craving it all day."

A moment of blessed silence, and then, "Don't just stand there, silly! Hurry up!"

Deidre shook her head. "Oh, you poor thing," she said, squeezing his hand. "Don't get me wrong, I feel awful about what she's going through. But I'd hate to be you…putting up with that, day and night, night and day."

"It isn't as bad as it sounds," he admitted. "And anyway, I've only been on duty for a week. It's Sandra who's here day and night, night and day."

She shook her head again. "That chemotherapy must have fried Nancy's brain. I'll tell you one thing—if I was as close to meeting my Maker as she is, by golly, I'd start treating people a whole lot better, especially the ones who are taking care of me!"

Her mini tirade rocked him to the core. "Look, Deidre. I mean no disrespect, but I can't let you talk about her that way. Especially not in her own house." Logan was glad she'd already come up with an excuse not to visit his mom. "She's dying, and she knows it. And she's exhausted. Terrified. Someone like you, who's always been healthy as a horse, probably doesn't get that Mom doesn't mean to be rude. It's just the pain talking."

Deidre lifted her chin and laughed. *Laughed.*

Had she been diagnosed with Alzheimer's and nobody told him?

"*That's* what I needed to see! A son who loves his mama, no matter what, and knows that sometimes they say things they don't mean— even when they aren't sick." She punched his shoulder. "I'm proud of you, Logan Murray. Couldn't be more proud if you were my son!"

So…she'd tricked him into defending his mom? But *why?*

She smacked him again. "Oh, don't look so surprised. Sometimes it takes a good swift kick to the bee-hind to make a person see where his true loyalties lie. And you can stow the 'Nancy is a saint' malarkey. Anyone who's known your mother as long as I have will tell you she's *always* been…shall we say…difficult. Opinionated. Now don't get your neck hairs bristlin' all over again, kiddo. I'd never say a thing like that to just anybody. I'm just being up-front with you so you'll know I'm here if you ever want to talk. No judgments. No reprimands."

One last poke. "Just so you'll know it's okay to get mad when she takes advantage of your good nature…that doesn't give you carte blanche to respond in kind."

He remembered plenty of times when Deidre, who'd raised his classmate Brooke and her sister, Beth—may she rest in peace—had marched into the school to give her granddaughters what-for, for forgetting their homework or lunches, for leaving the house without making their beds with no thought to who might be listening. And what about Beth and her husband, Kent's, double funeral, when he'd stood two rows behind Brooke and heard Deidre accuse her—right in front of little Connor—of being self-centered for letting her mind wander during the sermon? She had no room to talk, and only respect for his elders kept a lid on his exasperation.

Deidre breezed out the door with a whirl and a flourish as the scarf fluttered behind her like an oversized cape. If she exited the stage with as much fanfare, no wonder she'd been the talk of Broadway in her day.

Logan climbed the stairs two at a time, then paused in front of his mother's door. She'd asked for orange juice, and now he had to break the bad news: thinking its acidic nature would burn the chemo sores in her mouth, he'd let Sam and Sally drink the last of it with breakfast. He couldn't leave her alone while she was awake, which meant no trip to the corner store for another carton. But rather than explain all that, he walked into the room talking. He talked as he administered the morphine. Talked as he adjusted the television. And he was still talking when she fell asleep half an hour later.

He backed out of the room and quietly pulled the door closed behind him…

…and he nearly leaped out of his skin when his cell phone buzzed against his hip.

"Murray," he whispered, hurrying down the stairs.

"Whoever taught *you* telephone etiquette needs to enforce a refresher course."

He'd recognize his agent's gravelly baritone at rush hour in Penn Station. "Hey, Knute. How goes it?"

"It goes. How's your mom?"

"Holding her own. Considering."

"The dreaded day is getting close, eh? Sorry. I know it isn't easy."

Knute's dad had died of lung cancer a few years back, so the guy really did understand.

"Hate to lay this on you with your mom in such awful shape, but we need to talk, like, yesterday. How soon can you get out here?"

"To California? You're kidding, right?"

Knute muttered something unintelligible

under his breath. "All right. So if I came there, could you give me, say, two hours?"

Knute measured everything by nanoseconds, not hours, and he hated to fly. If he was willing to hop a plane to Baltimore…

Logan began to pace. "You're worrying me, pal."

"Schweetheart," he said, doing a horrible Bogart impersonation, "you don't have a thing to worry about." He paused. "Trust me."

Logan heard paper rattling. The click of a ballpoint. One side of a muffled conversation.

"Okay. Alice says she can get me into Baltimore day after tomorrow. This lazy secretary of mine wants to know what hotel you'd recommend."

He could almost picture Knute's wife aiming a dirty look at her partner.

Grinning, he said, "Tell Alice I said hey," and then rattled off a few high-rises near the Inner Harbor. "You need me to pick you up at the airport?"

"Nah. More important that you stay with your mom. I'll grab a limo. Alice will email the itinerary." A pause. More whispering, then, "Will you be available all day?"

"You said two hours."

"Well, yeah, the you-and-me part of this conference will take a couple hours. But we'll need to do some long-distance stuff. Internet. Teleconferencing. All that techno-mumbo stuff. So it might be more like six…if I can't get all the high muckety-mucks in the same place at the same time."

Sandra couldn't have timed her homecoming better. "So I guess we'll play it by ear."

"Yep. Oh. And Alice says we need to make dinner reservations."

Alice, being half-Italian, would love Chiaparelli's. "Best gnocchi on this side of the pond. But what's up with all this 'we' stuff?"

"You'll find out soon enough. See you in a couple days. Oh. And you might want to start shopping for a leather briefcase."

"A leather brief—" He shook his head. "For what?"

"Because mine's on its last legs, and you're gonna want to buy me a nice, pricy thank-you gift when this is over." On the heels of rib-racking laughter, his agent hung up.

Logan repocketed his phone, wondering why, instead of sharing the agent's enthusiasm, a strange sense of dread closed around him. Last time he'd felt this way had been in the waiting room outside Stan Fletcher's office. The announcement that sent that first domino toppling had led to a long line of dark and dangerous choices.

The timer dinged, his signal to administer Nancy's antinausea meds. On the way to her room, he replayed the conversation in his mind, then muttered, "This had better be good news, Knute…."

Because he didn't know if he could bounce back from that kind of trouble again.

CHAPTER NINETEEN

KNUTE TIPPED THE goblet right, then left. "I love watching the cling-and-release value of a good red." He glanced at the Monet-like paintings that decorated the restaurant's brick-walled alcove. "A charming place, Murray old boy. You were right. The gnocchi was excellent."

Logan sipped his iced tea, knowing full well that Knute felt duty-bound to test his sobriety every chance he got. "Can't be too careful," he'd said, time and again, "with a client like you."

In other words, a former boozehound whose drunken exploits had made the news…and cost him his last agent.

Knute had met every attempt to get on with things with an assortment of excuses. Turbulence had been terrible, and the airline had lost his luggage. Though why the man had needed to check bags for a simple overnight trip, Logan couldn't say.

"So how's the Hotel Monaco?"

"Everything the website promised and more." Knute snickered. "Better be, at those prices."

"Speaking of prices…" Logan glanced at his watch. "You know the old saying, time is money, so how 'bout we cut to the chase? I need to get home and let the dog out."

Knute put down his wine goblet. "Okay. So here's the deal." He leaned forward and lowered his voice. "Got a call from one of my Hollyweird insiders about a script and a role that's very hush-hush. It's a sitcom," he said, "that features a former NFL quarterback who hit rock bottom before rising to the top again, doing commercials and voice-overs, playing supporting roles in a couple of major motion pictures…"

Logan opened his phone and pretended to dial. Maybe a well-timed joke, rather than prickly impatience, would convince Knute to just spill it.

The agent frowned but said, "Oh, I get it. Calling to check on your mom?"

"Nope. My lawyer. I'm thinkin' instead of signing to do a series with these schmoes, I might want to sue 'em."

"Sue 'em? For what?"

"Because it sounds like they wrote my life right out from under me."

Knute loosened his tie. "Ha ha. You're a regular Jeff Dunham, aren't you?"

"I hate to point out the obvious, but if I'm Jeff, that makes you... What's the grouchy old dummy's name...?"

"Oh, you're on a roll tonight."

But he was smiling when he said it, so Logan put his phone away. "Have you worked with these people before?"

"Once. I've checked them out. They seem like stand-up guys. Well, as stand-up as you can get in Tinseltown." Knute described the storyline. "In the pilot, a has-been quarterback gets a frantic call from his brother. White-collar crimes put the brother and his wife in prison. Five years. Meaning their kids—"

"Let me guess. If the has-been doesn't take them in, they'll be farmed out to some Dickens-type orphanage." Logan frowned. "I thought this was a sitcom."

"It is."

"I haven't heard anything funny so far."

"Balance, Murray. If it's *all* hilarity, viewers will get bored. That's precisely why the brother guilt-trips the has-been into trading sunny California for some Podunk town in Maryland, to play Mr. Mom to twin teen girls and a ten-year-old who makes Dennis the Menace look like Little Lord Fauntleroy."

Now Logan could see the potential for humor *and* drama. He hated to admit it, but the idea was beginning to appeal to him. Especially when he acknowledged that things like this took time. Years, in most cases. He could probably accept the role, spend as much time as possible with his mom and get the school up and running long before they filmed the pilot.

"But wait a minute. This whole thing sounds too signed-and-sealed. Is this meeting supposed to be my preparation for the online conferences you were talking about?"

"You're too new to the game to be so jaded. But I hear ya. Suffice it to say in this wacky business, a lot can change in a little while. When I called you the other day, the whole thing was a big fat ball of vague. Now we've got a shoot location. Costars. Director. Writers. Heck, they've started building sets for the house where the has-been will live. Trust me. It's a sweet deal. If you so much as consider saying no, I'm personally gonna sign you into the nearest funny farm. And insist that they do a vasectomy so there's no chance an idiot like you will ever reproduce." Knute drained his wine. "We already have too many fools in the world."

Okay, so he was serious. But it was a lot to absorb in just a few minutes. Logan stacked their plates and flatware, and remembering his days as a waiter, slid them to the edge of the table to make them easier to reach.

"So why the hesitation?"

Logan leaned back and crossed both arms over his chest. "The reviewers went easy on me in the past, but I'm not fool enough to think it was based on my talent. I got lucky, working with some of the industry's best." He slid the napkin off his thigh, balled it up and tossed it onto the pile. "Something doesn't smell right here. Why *me,* when half the population of L.A. is made up of *real* actors? Actors who'd sell their sainted grannies for a primo role like this."

"Do you *work* at being a buzzkill, or have you been out of the spotlight so long that it just comes naturally?" He refilled his glass. "Don't look at me like that. I'm not driving."

He blamed his guilty conscience for making it seem Knute wanted to tack on an AA reference.

"They want you, baby. Haven't even considered anyone else for the role. I don't know why. Who *cares* why? Say yes, and you'll be set for life."

"And so will you."

Knute laughed. "Well, yeah, but—"

"I'm already 'set.' So if it's really *me* they want, here's how it'll have to go...."

Logan demanded script approval. On *all* scripts. And costar approval. Credit as a producer, which meant he'd own a piece of the show. "I want them to commit to three seasons minimum. Good for me, the rest of the cast, the crew..." That way, even if the show was a flop, it stood a good chance of being syndicated. And if that happened, the cast and crew would make a few bucks every month off the residuals, and Logan stood to earn tens of millions. "I get to write a couple of episodes. Direct a couple, too. I want a house near the studio. And a car. Scratch that. I remember what L.A. traffic is like. I want a *driver*."

"When did you go all prima donna on me?" Knute shook his head. "Think for a minute, Logan. They *might* make a deal like that for a movie…if they really, *really* believe they'll get a return on their investment. But for TV?" He shoved back from the table. "You ask for all that, you might just be asking yourself right out of the competition."

Logan nearly choked on his iced tea. "What competition? You said they didn't even consider anyone else."

"True." Knute stroked his chin. "True."

Logan didn't expect the decision-makers to give him everything he'd asked for. But he knew it *would* be a sweet deal. He read Knute's silence to mean he knew it, too. Logan didn't need to be a mind reader to know that Knute was doing math in his head, trying to figure out his cut. He wondered how Bianca would feel about him spending the equivalent of half a year on the left coast.

The thought shook him. She'd been the furthest thing from his mind. What *was* it about the woman that made her pop into his head at the oddest moments?

Focus, he told himself. *Think about what you can do with all that money.*

For starters, he could institute before- and after-school programs, to make things easier for working parents, and provide some therapy sessions to help harried moms and dads cope.

"So you're serious. You want me to take all those points to the table."

He met his agent's eyes. "Serious as a cage full of pit bulls."

"A cage full of..." Knute groaned and slapped a palm over his eyes. "And he wants to write and direct episodes."

The waiter delivered the check, and Logan grabbed it.

"I told you I'd pick up the tab," Knute said.

"Way I see it," Logan said, "buying dinner beats having to shop for your man bag."

"Briefcase."

"Potatoes, potahtoes."

The men shared a round of hearty laughter, and then Logan got to his feet. "Bet now you're wishing we'd done all this by phone like I suggested."

"No. Things like this? Always better face-to-face." Knute got up, too. "Besides, I need to check up on you from time to time. Make sure you're still walking the straight and narrow."

Despite the grin and wink, Logan knew Knute was only half kidding. He couldn't blame him, though. Considering what was at stake here—for him *and* for Knute—it made perfect sense to get firsthand assurances that Logan was still clean and sober.

He reached into his pocket and pulled out his newest AA coin. The front of the gold-rimmed navy medallion said TO THINE OWN SELF BE TRUE. He flipped it over, scanned the Serenity Prayer and handed it to Knute.

"'Six years sober,'" he read. "Last time you showed me one of these, it had a five in the triangle." He handed it back. "I'm proud of you. You should be proud, too."

Logan repocketed the coin. It had taken willpower he hadn't known he had to overcome his love affair with whiskey. If the day ever came when he wasn't tempted by booze, *then* he'd allow himself to feel a little impressed with himself.

During the short drive between Chiaparelli's and the Hotel Monaco, Knute promised to have Alice type up Logan's list of requests and have it couriered to the producers. He reminded Logan that things like this sometimes took weeks, months even.

"If it looks like they might cooperate, even a little, make sure they know I won't leave Baltimore with my mom in the shape she's in."

"Goes without saying. But stay close to your phone for the next few days, just in case."

Knute opened the passenger door as Logan said, "I appreciate this, Knute." And it was true.

"I understand your reluctance. Wasn't easy earning that AA coin. And because living in L.A. is what got you into trouble in the first place, I understand your reluctance."

"I'm not reluctant. Exactly. But in all fairness, I can't blame L.A. for my own stupidity." Better to let the guy think fear of backsliding was responsible for his lack of enthusiasm than admit the truth: he didn't like the idea of putting two thousand miles, five-hour flights and a three-hour time difference between him and Bianca.

He wanted to thump himself in the forehead. He'd been thinking between him and the *school*. So why had *Bianca's* name come up? Again!

Maybe he *was* an idiot, as Knute had inferred. Why else would anyone with a fully functioning brain feel this way about a woman he barely knew, one he'd never even kissed?

"I appreciate everything, Knute. The opportunity. You, braving the friendly skies to deliver the news… Means a lot that you believe in me this much."

"Aw, jeez. You're not gonna go all huggy-kissy on me, are ya, and spoil your image as a big tough football player?"

"Close the door," he said, waving a hand in front of his face. "You're letting in a hoard of moths."

"Hoard?"

"Okay, flock."

"Eclipse. Don't ask me why I know. But that's what you've got there, hovering around your dome light. An eclipse of moths."

"Well, there's *my* something new for the day." Logan smirked. "Now get out. And take your eclipse with you."

The agent unfolded himself from the front seat and leaned back into the car to say, "My best to your mom." He straightened, leaned in again. "Remember…stay near the phone."

"Got it."

Knute slammed the door and gave the thumbs-up sign, and after a brief conversation with the doorman, he disappeared into the hotel.

Logan made it home in record time…twenty-one minutes. He stood on his deck, watching as

Poe sniffed the perimeter of the fenced back-yard. The house seemed too quiet after spending a week with Sally and Sam and his mom and dad. At least out here he could listen to the tree toads and crickets. The dog bounded up and sat at the French doors, head cocked and paw raised as if to say, *You gonna stand there all night, staring at nothing?*

He squatted, ruffled the fur on her expressive face. She squinted as a moth flit between them. "Better get in," he said, "before we're eclipsed."

Poe trotted alongside him into the house, sat in front of the cabinet where he stored her treats and barked.

He gave her a thumb-sized bone, and she carried it to the sofa-shaped doggy cushion beside his recliner. He'd never owned a pet before bringing her home all those months ago, and at first, Logan had worried he didn't have what it took to care for a four-legged, nonverbal family member. These days, the only thing he worried about was how he'd cope if anything happened to her. As usual, she stopped chewing and looked up at him as if she sensed that he had been thinking about her.

"Quarter of nine," he said. "What do you think? Too late to call Griff?"

Poe answered with a whispery bark and went back to chomping her treat.

"One way to find out," he said aloud, scrolling to his friend's number.

It rang only once before Griff said, "You haven't forgotten how to tell time, have you?"

Laughing, Logan said, "I could ask the same question. It's not even nine yet!"

"Hey. Judge not, and all that. I had a tough day, and I was up half the night."

"Ah-ha. With the juiciest peach on the vine?"

A beat of silence passed. "Been talking to my landlady, I see."

"Yeah, but that was last week. This must be serious."

"Nothing serious about it. Two dates. End of story." Griff yawned. "So what was so important that you interrupted my beauty sleep?"

Logan rehashed the dinner meeting with Knute, being careful not to mention how many times Bianca had come to mind during the meal. "Just thought I'd get your input before I sign the contract."

"I think you're forgetting…I'm not an entertainment attorney."

"I trust your judgment."

"Okay, for starters, do you really think those Tinseltown tycoons will meet all your demands?"

"Not all of 'em, but they'll meet enough."

"So you're gonna do this, then…. Leave Baltimore, this time for good?"

"I'll never leave for good. This is where my family is." *And Bianca…*

And there she was again, invading his thoughts. Logan shook his head.

"And what does *Bianca* think about a long-distance relationship?"

"How would I know?"

"Well, the way you said her name just now…"

He didn't realize he'd said it out loud. *Dude, you're in trouble…with a capital* B.

"Remember the summer when we worked for that moving company?"

Logan groaned just thinking about it. "How could I forget. Pianos. Safes. Cast-iron woodstoves. We probably could have qualified as Olympic weight lifters when we cashed our last paycheck."

"Still have the lumbar belt the boss made us wear?"

It was on the top shelf of his closet in a box

marked COLLEGE. "You bet I do. Dumb thing cost me forty bucks."

"I'd dust it off if I were you."

It took a second, but Logan knew where this was going.

"...so you won't pull a muscle hefting her emotional baggage."

"It's touching the way you worry about me," he teased, "but you can relax. There's nothing going on. And even if there was, she doesn't have any more baggage than you do."

Silence, and then, "Nothing going on?"

"Nope."

"So you're saying the two of you aren't dating."

"Yep, that's what I'm saying." That, at least, was true.

"And you haven't seen her since the coffee shop?"

"Well, yeah. She's looking into getting a dog like Poe for her kid. So I dropped off some brochures. And she's gonna job share with Sandra, get some of the groundwork out of the way for me, so I can hit the ground running."

"Working for you? In the office at your house?"

"Of course not. At her place." He frowned. "I set her up with some office equipment and—"

"So you were over there. Alone. Plugging stuff in, together?"

He pictured her in the blue pj's she was wearing during his first visit, the dusty sweat suit she'd had on when he'd invited her to the Mother's Day party.

"Hey. What are you doing on Mother's Day?"

"Nothing."

Griff's mom had passed away shortly after he had earned his law degree, and he hadn't been a big fan of the holiday since.

"This will be my mom's last one, so I'm thinking we'll have a cookout. And if the weather is crummy, we'll have a cook-*in*. I know she'd love it if you were there."

"Sounds good. Who else is going?"

"Sandra and the kids, of course, and Susan is flying in from Colorado. Deidre, me. Bianca and her son and mother. And—"

"Stop right there," Griff said. "Why is she gonna be there?"

"She works for me, that's why. And I happen to like her kid. I'm hoping he'll get along with Sam."

"This better not be the start of another Willow fiasco...."

"It isn't." Another truth, because the only thing Bianca and Willow had in common was their gender.

Griff yawned again. "Call me tomorrow. When I'm awake. If I'm in a decent mood, I'll tell you all about the peach."

Logan thought about that last comment long after the call ended. Griff would never admit it, but his first marriage had inflicted Willow-like damage to his ego. And no one—not even Deidre—knew the real reason he'd taken up residence in the garage apartment: the split had finally cost Griff his home, and once the repairs were made and the exterminators were gone, he'd have to sell or file for bankruptcy.

Memory of those hard days—first Griff's, then his own—made him want to hear Bianca's voice and listen to her level-headed advice. He reached for the house phone but hesitated. Warning bells sounded in his head. Didn't take a genius to figure out why he'd stalled in the confirmed bachelor lane: he didn't trust himself to make smart relationship decisions, so he steered clear of them. Meaningless flirtations that went nowhere were insurance against heartache and humiliation.

Bianca, who'd make any sacrifice to build a good life for her boy, was nothing like Willow or the women who had followed in her wake. The terrifying truth? If he took things to the next level and he was wrong about her, he might just find out that he hadn't really hit bottom after the team dropped him and Willow dumped him, all in a few short months.

But what could it hurt, giving her a call? She'd said herself that they were friends, right?

It was only nine. No doubt she'd be awake, performing any one of a hundred household chores. Would she appreciate a break from the work or resent the intrusion?

"One way to find out," he said for the second time that day.

Like Griff, Bianca picked up on the first ring.

The instant he heard her whispered hello, Logan regretted giving in to his impulse.

"Sorry," he said, meaning it. "Didn't wake anyone, did I?"

"Logan?" Her soft voice melted his tension. Would she have the power to do that…if she was just a pal? "Everyone's sound asleep. I'm painting."

"Oh. Sorry," he repeated. "You weren't standing on a chair, I hope."

"Excuse me?"

"To reach some high corner or something. Which room are you painting?"

She laughed, and its music set his heart to beating double time. "Not that kind of painting. Easel and canvas painting."

"Oh. Right. Jason's portrait?" Weird. His tension returned instantly.

"As a matter of fact, yes. I'm trying to figure out how to put affection into his eyes in the hope that when Drew looks at it, he'll believe me when I say his dad loved him. Because he did, in his strange way." She sighed. "But it's been hard, so I tried diverting my attention from it, thinking if I worked on something else, I'd figure out why I can't seem to make that happen."

He knew her husband hadn't reacted well to the news that his son was different from other kids. That he might *always* be different. But to behave in such a way that Drew thought his own father didn't love him? Disgusted, Logan shook his head.

"Another portrait?" he asked. "Still life?"

"No. It's a covered bridge."

Logan winced. The big blowup that had finally brought things to an end between him and Willow had happened during the sixth—or was it the seventh?—viewing of *The Bridges of Madison County*. Her favorite movie. Made perfect sense…in hindsight.

Logan shook off the unpleasant memory. "Looking forward to seeing it," he fibbed.

If he told her about his meeting with Knute, would she agree it was an offer too good to refuse?

"I, ah, I have an idea I'd like to run by you. Wondered if I could stop by."

"Now?"

"No, no. 'Course not. It's too late. Tomorrow, maybe, or—"

"No…tonight is fine."

Something told him the only reason she hadn't added "Let's get it over with" was because she was too nice.

"I'm too wound up to sleep," she said. "This painting is driving me crazy."

The husband thing again. Three years gone, and she was still hung up on him? In one moment, he admired her loyalty. In the next, he envied Jason.

"Okay if I bring my dog?" he asked. "She's been spending a lot of time alone lately."

"Sure. I'll put on a pot of decaf for us and fill a bowl of water for Poe. Maybe your idea will spark one in my head, and I'll figure out how to solve this *eyes* problem."

He hung up, grabbed his keys and Poe's leash and aimed the car toward her house. The familiar logo of the local doughnut shop came into view, and he pulled into the drive-through lane. Just one traffic light between here and her place, and as he waited for the red light to go green, a dozen doughnuts in the passenger seat, Poe draped herself over the console and rested her chin on his thigh. "Think I should tell Bianca about the Hollywood deal?"

Brows twitching, she lifted her head.

"Don't worry. We'll drive to California." He'd heard too many horror stories of dogs being misrouted to airports in Europe or Asia. "No way I'd take a chance like that with my best girl."

A perplexing awareness swirled inside him as he patted the dog's head. He loved Poe…

…but for some crazy reason, he wanted Bianca to be his best girl.

CHAPTER TWENTY

As Poe followed him up the walk and onto Bianca's porch, a pang of guilt seized Logan. When they started filming, he'd either have to leave Poe home alone, or expose her to the lights, noise and activity on the set. And if the producers decided to film in front of a live audience, she'd have to cope with applause and laughter, too. He *did* have a choice, though....

When he raised his arm to knock, the door swung open. And there she stood, smiling, waving him inside, whispering, "Come on in."

He held out the box of doughnuts. "Something to go with the coffee."

But she didn't take it. In fact, she didn't even see it because she'd crouched to take Poe's face in her hands.

"Oh, my goodness. Aren't you gorgeous, yes, you are! You know that? Gorgeous!"

Poe responded with a big doggy smile and, tail wagging, followed Bianca to the kitchen.

The dog stayed at her side as she took cups from the cupboard and as she filled them with coffee and put them on the table. And when she sat down, Poe flopped beside her chair.

Logan walked over to the easel, which stood near the French doors. "I still say that looks just like a photograph."

"And I still say the eyes are all wrong."

He stood back, studied her husband's likeness. High forehead, thick dark hair and eyebrows, hazel eyes, slightly crooked smile. A decent-looking guy, he supposed, but she was right; the eyes were expressionless. Lucky for Drew, he favored his mom.

Logan stepped up to the table and looked at the painting she'd been working on there. When she'd mentioned the bridge earlier, he'd thought of the night when Willow—who'd consented to share his life and give him children—admitted that, like Meryl Streep's character in her favorite movie, she'd been unfaithful. *Why?* he'd asked. And in a blithe, matter-of-fact voice, she'd said, *I don't like you without football.* Bianca's painted bridge, made of stone and steel, looked sturdy enough to survive a lifetime of storms, like the artist herself.

He felt her watching him, sensed her concern and consciously relaxed to erase the frown from his forehead. And that's when it hit him.

"It's the eyebrows," he said, looking back at Jason's portrait.

She joined him at the easel. "What do you mean?"

"He looks cocky. Arrogant." He grinned. "Like a lawyer."

She inhaled a sharp little breath and pressed her fingertips to her lips.

"Oh, hell," he said, slapping a hand to the back of his neck. "I'm sorry. That was insensitive. I had no business saying—"

"There's nothing to apologize for. Because you're right. He does look...smug." Hands clasped under her chin, she said, "I can't believe I didn't see it."

"You would have eventually. Because you're good. Really good." *And maybe still in love with him,* Logan thought.

"No, just a big copycat who paints what she sees," she said, pouring them each a cup of coffee.

"If I painted what I saw, well, let's just say it wouldn't look like *that*." He pointed at the bridge. "I love that one. I can almost hear the water rushing downstream."

Grinning, she covered the palette with plastic wrap, then wiped her brushes clean.

"Can't paint with prying eyes in the room, eh? Well, that's a darned shame. I'd love to watch you work."

She smiled, sat and took a sip of her coffee. "So how's your mom?"

"As well as can be expected. It was a good week. I wouldn't admit it to just anybody, but I'm sorry it's over."

"Says a lot about you." Bianca helped herself to a plain doughnut and, breaking off a chunk, said, "Did Sandra have a good time in the mountains?"

"She signed up for just about every activity. Don't know how she got any rest, but she looked fantastic when she got home."

"I'm not surprised." A wistful smile lit up her face. "A whole week doing only as she pleased, whenever she wanted to, with no one to answer to…"

Frowning slightly, she shook her head. "Listen to me, whining like a spoiled brat. But the truth is, I'm a little jealous. Ridiculous, because everyone knows the only reason I don't get more 'me' time is because I refuse to take it."

Evidence that she was a control freak? Or proof that she'd been let down too many times?

"So what's this idea you wanted to run by me?" she asked.

He couldn't decide whether to tell her about the offer Knute had brought him or Deidre's theater tickets. Poe inched closer, rested her chin on Bianca's thigh.

Traitor, he thought, grinning as an idea formed.

"Well, actually, there are a couple of things. Deidre stopped by the other day with tickets to her play. Seems a shame to waste them. We could go together. If you have time. If you want to, that is."

Shut up, he told himself. Even if she had a mind to say yes, why would she want to spend an evening with a guy with all the how-about-a-date finesse of a knock-kneed schoolboy?

"What play?"

"I forget. A musical, I think."

She laughed. "Well, it doesn't really matter. There's Drew, y'know?"

"Your mom could handle a meltdown...if one happened on her watch, right?"

"I have no idea." She pursed her lips. "I've never really given her the chance to find out."

"Doesn't have to be the play. We could take Drew on an outing."

"What kind of outing?"

Logan thought of the things he'd done with Sam. "Science Center? Aquarium? B&O Railroad Museum?"

"Oh, he loves trains. I think he'd love the museum…if we could find a day and time when it wasn't too crowded."

He got the feeling there were a lot of *ifs* in Bianca Wright's life. If Griff wanted to define that as baggage, so be it.

"The tickets weren't the only reason I wanted to talk to you," he said. "I had a meeting with my agent, and—"

Drew's voice, high-pitched and hysterical, crackled through the baby monitor. "Mommy! Mommy! Mo-o-mmy!"

She was on her feet and halfway up the stairs before Logan could say, "What's wrong?"

Maddy rushed into the hall, tying the belt of a flowery robe around her middle as she did, and squealed when she saw Logan. "Good grief, Bianca. Really? At this hour?" She patted her hair. "You could at least have given me a heads-up."

"I'll apologize later after I get Drew calmed down, okay?"

She burst into the boy's room without waiting for an answer and closed the door behind her. Within seconds, the boy's cries subsided.

"Sorry about that, Logan," Maddy said. "But then, I guess you understand things like that since you have a nephew like Drew."

"Yeah," he said. "It is what it is," he said, staring at the boy's closed door. He turned his attention to Maddy. "Well, we both know this could take a while. There's coffee downstairs. And doughnuts. Why don't you keep me company while Bianca puts Drew back to sleep?"

In the kitchen, Maddy stooped to pat the dog's head. "Well, aren't you just gorgeous?"

Like mother, like daughter.

Maddy sat in Bianca's chair and grabbed a doughnut. Smiling, she wiggled her eyebrows. "So what brings you here at this hour?"

Logan sat across from her. "Can I trust you, Maddy?"

"I suppose." She sipped from Bianca's mug. "It depends, I guess, on whether it's good for my girl."

"Fair enough," he said. "I don't know how

much Bianca has told you about the job offer I made her."

Maddy ran down what she knew about the position that his sister and her daughter would share and the information they'd gather, each from separate home offices he'd set up.

"I really like the way Bianca balances home and work and Drew," he admitted, "but I'm worried that asking her to help was selfish. Do you think she's up to it? I'm worried I added the thing that will act as the proverbial straw that could break her back."

Maddy blinked. Spun her wedding rings round and round on her finger. "She's an intelligent, capable woman who knows her limitations. Which is precisely why there isn't a man in her life." She took a bite of her doughnut and, grinning, said around it, "Now, if the *right* man came along..."

Well, since she'd opened the door...

"You know I'm kinda fond of her, right?"

"What do you mean, *fond?*"

He heaved a heavy sigh. "I admire her. Think she's a terrific mom. A good daughter. With a work ethic that's hard to match." Logan pictured Bianca, ponytails askew, tugging at the hem of her girlish pj's. He cleared his throat. "And she's drop-dead gorgeous."

Maddy patted his hand. "If you're asking my permission to ask her out, you've got it." On her feet now, she aimed a forefinger at him. "But just so you know—if you toss her aside like you did all those girls in the entertainment magazines…" She wadded a napkin in her fist. "Just…just *don't*. Got it?"

"Got it."

She plucked another napkin from the basket on the table and helped herself to a second doughnut. On the way to the hall, she hesitated. "Her favorite color is green, she loves chocolate-covered cherries and her favorite movie is *Secondhand Lions*." She winked. "Just so you know."

And Logan got that, too.

CHAPTER TWENTY-ONE

"Deidre," Logan said, opening his front door. "What brings you out on a day like this?"

She shook off her umbrella and stood it in the corner. "Pish-posh. A little rain isn't going to hurt me. I'm not made of sugar!"

"A little rain? It's storming to beat the band out there!"

She led the way to his family room and sat in his recliner. Poe didn't like that and woofed her disapproval. "Oh, hush," Deidre told her. "Is that any way to treat a guest?"

The dog looked at Logan, who said, "It's okay, girl. She isn't staying long."

"That's no way to win the Subtlety Award," Deidre shot back, laughing.

"So what can I do for you?"

"I want to know what you did to Maddy Wright."

"Maddy? What're you talking about?"

"She was the best volunteer personal assistant I ever had…until you got hold of her. Now all she wants to do is stay home, cooking and cleaning and spending time with her daughter and grandson."

Logan grinned. "No kiddin'?" A selfish thought flit through his head: Did it mean Bianca would have time for a man in her life? "I'm happy for Bianca, because she can use the help…if she'll take it…but I had nothing to do with Maddy's decision."

"That isn't how she tells it." She waved a hand, as if swatting an irksome mosquito. "But what's this I hear about you building a school for kids like Drew? You're all wrapped up in something that big, and you don't say a word to me about it? I'm crushed!"

Deidre got to her feet. "I have something to show you." She linked her arm with his and led him to the door. Once there, she flung it open. "Better grab a jacket, handsome. It's raining cats and dogs out there."

"Why? Where are we going?"

"That's for me to know and you to find out."

Moments later, he found himself strapped into the passenger seat of her shiny black Cadillac and holding on for dear life as she wove in and out of traffic, talking a blue streak the whole way.

Finally, she turned off the main road, and as she drove up the narrow, winding drive, Deidre said, "This land belonged to Percy's family. He was the last in a long line of Richardsons, so when he passed, it reverted to my control. I hate it," she admitted, "but it seems a shame to let it go to waste. You'd be doing me a favor by taking it off my hands."

Deidre drew his attention to the corral and the pastures and riding trails beyond them. "That," she said, pointing, "is the original barn, where Percy's grandparents raised prized quarter horses." In its day, she explained, the farm was self-sufficient because the Richardsons grew their own oats and hay.

Next, the silo came into view. To its left stood a row of small cottages where, Deidre explained, the farm hands had lived with their families. To the right of them he spied a sprawling Georgian mansion.

"Whoa," he said, admiring the stately columns and dozens of multipaned windows. "How many rooms?"

"I have no idea. Like I said, I never liked it

here, so Percy and I lived in my house. But if I had to guess, I'd say twenty, twenty-five."

"Any idea how old it is?"

"Percy's grandfather built it in the twenties. I'm terrible at math, so you figure it out. Let's look inside."

As she gave him the grand tour, Logan envisioned some of the rooms as classrooms, a gymnasium, a library. Science and art outings on the grounds. They built things to last back then, and unless an inspector found extensive termite damage, the place would only need minor repairs and fresh paint.

On the way home, Deidre agreed to let Logan drive.

"Touchy subject," he began, "but have you ever considered selling the place?"

"Only every other day!"

"Has it been appraised?"

"Not recently." She turned to face him. "Why?"

"We should do that, then. Because I'm willing to pay the going rate."

"Still suffering the after-effects of all those concussions, I see."

"Huh?"

Laughing, she said, "See there!" She gave his

forearm a grandmotherly squeeze. "I brought you out here because I want you to take it off my hands. Please. I don't want anything for it. It's costing me a fortune in taxes, what with the boardinghouse and theater. And don't give me that big-eyed, 'you're kidding' look. I'm not a fool. The tax write-off is appealing but not as much as all the kudos I'll get when people hear I've donated the estate to your project." She applauded herself. "Perfect timing, too, to promote my theater. I'll be on the cover of every periodical in the mid-Atlantic!"

Logan only half heard her because mentally he was composing the list of questions he'd need to ask Griff. Things like the transfer of deed and filing the place as a charitable foundation.

"Maddy said you wanted to name the place after the little girl who owned Poe. Commendable, to be sure, but I'm afraid I have to insist you name it after Percy. Whether you use his first or last name is up to you. You can put Holly's name on the library. Or the cafeteria. And you can put my name on the theater."

"Theater?"

"You can't expect those kids to read and

write and do math all day. They'll need a place to make music and put on plays."

Logan told Deidre how Holly had loved her piano. "She was one of those rare and special kids who could hear a song once," he said, "and she could duplicate it, note for note." He nodded. "Maybe we'll turn the ballroom into a music room."

"Makes perfect sense to name it after Holly," Deidre said. "And as long as I'm alive, I'll help with every play the kids put on."

"They'll be lucky to have you as a mentor."

"Flatterer…"

"Just tellin' it like it is."

"Have you told Bianca yet that you're going to be a big TV star?"

He parked in her driveway and, grabbing her big black umbrella, ran around to her side of the car. When she opened the door, he said, "Your tenant is a blabbermouth."

Either Deidre hadn't heard him over the rain, or she'd chosen to ignore the comment.

"So how soon can you start work on the old place?"

Once he saw her safely inside, he'd head home and get Griff on the phone. "Yesterday," he said with a grin. "Day before that, if I can manage it."

Despite the umbrella, they both got soaked. Deidre invited him to stay for coffee, and he might have…if his cell phone hadn't buzzed. "Sandra," he said, reading the caller ID display.

"Oh, my…" Deidre said, staring at him and then his phone screen. "Don't tell me…"

Sandra's text message was succinct: GET TO ER ASAP.

Logan gave Deidre a huge, heartfelt hug. "I don't know what to say," he told her. "'Thank you' sounds insignificant after what you offered today."

"I meant it when I said you'd be doing me a favor. Now get to the hospital." She gave him a gentle shove. "First chance you get, give me a call."

"Will do. Now change into some dry clothes before you catch your death."

"You're too young to talk like an old poop. Now go. Anyone you want me to call?"

If she meant Bianca, he could answer in a syllable. "No." Bianca was one person he needed to tell in person—the good news about the school building and possibly the bad news about his mom. To help him cope as only she could.

Deidre was shivering, and he was torn between staying to make sure she got into warm, dry clothes and racing over to the hospital.

She'd refused to give in to technology, so he doubted Deidre had stored her most-called numbers in her cell phone.

"Where's your phone book?"

"In the kitchen drawer. Right under the phone." She followed him into the kitchen. "Why?"

He'd found Brooke's number and dialed it before Deidre stepped up beside him.

"Hey, Brooke," he told the answering machine, "Logan Murray. I'm at your grandmother's house. She got soaked to the skin this morning, and now she can't stop shaking. I'm going to throw a blanket around her, but I can't stay. Family emergency. I'll call Griff, let him know, too. But I thought you should know."

Logan hung up and, after taking one look at Deidre, said, "Is there an electric blanket on your bed?"

"Not that it's any of your business what's on my bed, but yes."

He scooped her up and carried her to her

room, where he gently deposited her in the bed-side chair. After tossing back the covers, he removed her shoes and the damp sweater and moved her to the bed.

"You stay put until Brooke gets here, you hear?" he said, flapping the blanket into place. "Or Griff. Or Brooke's better half."

"Hunter has been a lovely husband to my granddaughter," Deidre said, "but he is not her better half!"

"If you say so." Logan moved Deidre to the bed, removed her shoes and pulled up the covers. "I'll be back in five," he said, setting the blanket to Medium.

He'd make her a cup of tea and dig through that suitcase she called a purse to find her cell phone. With any luck, Griff or Brooke or Hunter would be here before he brought the tea and phone to Deidre. In the off chance they didn't, at least Deidre would have a way to call for help if she needed it. And hopefully, she wouldn't need it.

While he prepared the tea—one milk, two sugars, just as she'd taught him when he'd lived here—he redialed Brooke and left a second message. He left a message in Hunter's voice mail, too, as an added precaution.

He put the tea on her nightstand. "Promise me you won't get up."

"Why? There isn't a blessed thing wrong with me."

He disagreed as he took in her wan complexion and chattering teeth.

"Just humor me, will ya? I need to get to the hospital, but I can't leave knowing you could take a header down that *Gone with the Wind* staircase of yours."

She huffed. "Oh, all right. I promise to stay in bed. Now go. Or I *will* get up…and kick you out myself!"

Logan was halfway to the road when Hunter's pickup truck met him going the other way.

Both vehicles stopped, side by side on the driveway, drivers' windows open.

Logan brought Deidre's grandson-in-law up to speed, explained why he couldn't stay and hurried down the road. It was a thirty-minute drive from there to Johns Hopkins Oncology. He wasn't much of a praying man, but he prayed now.

Because despite months of preparation and dozens of lectures from her doctors, he didn't know how to say a final goodbye to his mother.

CHAPTER TWENTY-TWO

THE STAFF RELAXED the rules because Nancy's condition was grave and allowed the family to drag chairs in from the hall. And all but one was occupied.

After leafing through every dog-eared magazine in the waiting room, Logan built a tower from alphabet blocks in the kids' corner. Then, cross-legged on the floor, he played every game on the activity cube. Then he made a cafeteria run, and after delivering coffee and soda and bags of chips and cookies, his mom's tray table, nightstand and windowsill resembled grocery store display shelves.

Logan sat on the radiator, pretending to watch *The Price is Right* on the fuzzy TV hanging from the ceiling. Peripheral vision allowed him to see that even Sam had sensed the seriousness of the situation and sat quietly playing with a handheld video game. Susan's iridescent knitting needles flashed purple and pink as yarn whispered from her tote bag. He couldn't make out the title of Sandra's novel and Sally was reading something on her Kindle. But only his dad, snoring softly in the pink recliner beside the hospital bed, looked even remotely comfortable.

"Could someone get me some ice chips?" Nancy croaked.

"I'll get it," Logan offered, and darted into the hall. He knew exactly where to find ice but took his time getting to the little room down the hall.

A freckle-faced nurse, going the other way, said, "Can I help you find something?"

He held up the green plastic cup he'd grabbed on the way out of his mother's room. "No, thanks. Just getting some ice for my mom." With a nod, he indicated his mom's hospital room.

"If you or your family needs anything, let us know." With that, she disappeared around the corner.

He stopped at the water fountain near the elevators and took his time slurping from the watery arc. For an instant, he considered sticking his face into it. But that was a dumb idea because sadness and grief couldn't be washed away that easily.

"Can't be washed away at all," he muttered.

"What can't be washed away?"

Bianca? Impossible. She'd be at the station this time of day. Straightening, Logan turned, expecting to find he'd imagined her voice.

Instead, there she stood, smiling sweetly and carrying a plate of chocolate chip cookies. If he'd ever been more relieved to see a person, Logan didn't know when.

"How'd you find out, you know…?"

"Grown-up phone tag," she said. "Deidre told Griff, who called Brooke, who called me. Griff says to tell you he'll come straight over here from the courthouse."

"Put that down."

Her eyebrows and the plate rose at the same time. "What? This?"

He took it from her, put it on the seat of the nearest chair and gathered her close. "Thought I was hallucinating or something," he whispered into her hair. Then, holding her at arm's length, he said, "I can't believe you're here. What about Drew?"

"Mom offered to scoop him up from school."

She shrugged. Grinned slightly. "I know, I know...hard to believe, but I said yes."

"It won't throw him off, having someone else pick him up?"

"She's going to tell him, before he has a chance to wig out, that she's treating him to ice cream. So I think he'll be okay with it." The grin became a smile. "Sweet of you to worry, though."

Logan cupped her face in his hands, thumbs tracing the contours of her freckled cheeks. "I can't believe you're here," he repeated.

Bianca tilted her head. "Why are you so surprised? If it had been my mom, you would have come, right?"

"In a heartbeat. Because...we're friends."

Liar, he told himself. He'd be there for her, and he was glad she was here for him, and friendship had nothing to do with it. Because, despite Griff's warnings and his own reservations, he'd fallen for her. Hard.

Something came over him as he acknowledged that simple fact, and it compelled him to press a kiss to her forehead, her chin, the tip of her nose. His mother's room overflowed with supportive, loving family members...who watched his every move with a wary eye, wondering which disappointment or defeat would be the one to send him spiraling downward again. In their shoes, he'd do the same. But that didn't make it easier, knowing his battle with the bottle had forever fractured their faith in him. His descent into the hell of alcoholism had been all over the news for a while there. Surely Bianca had read all about it. And yet…

…and yet, here she was.

"Thanks for coming," he said as Sandra stepped into the hall.

"Logan? Mom is asking for you."

He grabbed Bianca's hand, an unspoken invitation to follow, but she resisted.

"This is family time. I don't belong in there." She picked up the cookie plate and put it into his hands. "I only came to deliver these. Something to nibble on while you're…"

While they were waiting. The fact that she couldn't say it was precisely why, in his opinion, she *did* belong here.

With Sandra standing there in the open doorway, he couldn't explain why, but he knew that he loved her. How much more *family* could you get!

Sandra joined them. "We haven't had the

pleasure yet," she said, extending a hand. "It's good to meet you finally, partner."

Then she surprised Logan by taking Bianca's hand and leading her into their mother's room. One arm around Bianca's waist, she said, "Hey, everybody, this is Bianca Wright. Logan's girlfriend."

Every head turned toward her, and one by one, they smiled. Said hello. Told her they were happy to meet her. And Bianca, being Bianca, took it in stride. While they chatted, Nancy waved Logan closer. "Is something wrong with her?" she whispered into his ear.

"No. She's perfect."

"Then why wait until I'm half-dead to bring her around?"

"I haven't known her all that long. And I've been busy. And—"

"Save it," she teased. "I knew there was something.... Just couldn't put my finger on it." Nancy glanced at Bianca, smiling, doling out cookies. "I get it now." She squeezed his hand. "I *get* it now.

"Sandra. Carl."

When her husband and daughter looked over, Nancy said, "Take them all outside. I'd like a few minutes alone with Bianca."

As they filed from the room, everyone looked shocked, maybe even a little afraid. Everyone except Bianca, that is. Though they'd touched on the subject of friendship, Logan and Bianca hadn't discussed anything beyond their working relationship. His stupefied silence had led his mom to believe it was more than that. And now, because of Nancy's condition, Bianca would feel obliged to go along with it. Not an easy feat for a person who had no idea what was about to happen to her.

He planted his feet, a signal to both women that he intended to stay. Not that he felt they needed a referee. Still, because he'd started this ball rolling…

"Go," Bianca said, "we'll be fine."

"She's right, son. Go. Take your time. Drag the lot of them down to the cafeteria. Have some pie. Eat slowly." She winked. "Don't worry. I promise not to die while you're gone."

Logan cringed. "Holy mackerel, Mom. What a thing to say!"

"Sorry. But I don't have time to beat around the bush." She flicked her fingers, effectively dismissing him. "Bring me an ice cream when you come back."

He stepped into the hall and handed Sandra two twenty-dollar bills. He told her to treat everyone to something and bring back frozen custard for their mom. And when the elevator doors closed behind them, Logan stood just outside his mother's door, out of sight but within earshot, just in case.

"Please," Nancy said. "Sit. Right here."

He heard the side rail drop.

"Do you love him?"

He thought he heard a quiet gasp above the beep of the monitors and the hiss of the oxygen machine.

"Sorry to be so blunt, but as I said, time's a-wastin'. Although, I suppose I could have put that a bit more delicately." She laughed softly. "So let me rephrase that. How do you feel about my son?"

"I—I like him."

"Well, of course you do. What's not to like?" Another quiet laugh. "Has he told you how he feels about you yet?"

Logan's heart thundered, and it took every bit of his willpower to stay put.

"No...."

"Trust me. I know my boy. He loves you. Don't look so surprised. Deidre told me all about you. I can't tell you how pleased I am that he finally found a woman who's interested in something other than his connections." She chuckled. "Or his pretty face."

Logan held his breath. If the information came from Deidre, there was no telling what his mom had heard about Bianca. Now he had two excuses to call his elderly friend when he left the hospital: to see how she was feeling and find out how the subject of Bianca had come up in the first place.

"I think it's admirable the way you moved forward after your husband died," his mom said. "Raising kids is tough enough, but one with a learning disorder? Alone?"

"Sandra is doing the same, so you know as well as I do that it can be done."

Way to go, Bianca! Logan thought.

"So," his mom said, "you invited your mom to move in after your father died?"

She must have nodded a response, because Nancy continued with "Logan hasn't had much luck with women, so I'm not surprised that he's moving slowly."

A pause. A *long* pause.

"How much do you know about his past?"

"His publicist put together a very thorough bio," Bianca said, "and I read every word."

"So you know he's an alcoholic."

"I do."

"And that doesn't worry you?"

"I don't know what you mean."

"You're not concerned your little boy will get attached to him, think of him as a dad, and Logan will fall off the wagon?"

"Believe me, I've given that a lot of thought. And yes, it was a big concern…until I admitted all he has overcome in his life. He's strong, so I don't believe he'll backslide."

Her admission came as such a relief that Logan wanted to run in there, take her in his arms and tell her how much she'd come to mean to him.

And then his mom said, "But you know the line… 'Once an alcoholic, always an alcoholic.' And that even he doesn't know what it might take to drive him over the edge."

Silence. Brutal, unbearable, brittle silence. Logan hung his head, bracing himself for Bianca's reply. Instead, he heard his mom say, "You need to know what you're dealing with. For your good, for your son's, for Logan's sake, too. Because another failed relationship could break him."

"Anything is possible, Mrs. Murray."

"And yet you love him."

Another tiny gasp and then, "I never said...
I—I don't..."

"I'm sorry. Didn't mean to put you on the
spot. Logan will come clean about his feelings for you, eventually, and when he does,
you won't have to worry about becoming another name on his long list of conquests. Those
women were...a smoke screen. My big tough
football-playing son hid behind them, biding
his time until someone like you came along.
I'm only sorry I won't be around to see you
two walk down the—"

"Mom!" Logan burst into the room. "Do you
think maybe you should get some rest before
the rest of the gang gets back?"

"Yeah, I guess I am a little tired." Nancy
reached for Bianca's hand. "Thank you, dear,"
she said, giving it a squeeze. "You did this sick
old lady a lot of good."

"It was my pleasure." Bianca glanced at
Logan. "I should go, find out how much ice
cream Mom gave Drew."

He caught her hand as she passed by on
her way out of the room and gave it a gentle squeeze. He wanted to say, *Thanks. You're*

something else. I'm crazy about you. But she was gone before he found his voice.

"You look tired," his mom said when he approached the hospital bed.

"Look who's talking."

"Hush. And do me a favor?"

"Anything." He'd walk to hell and back if she asked it of him. "Ice chips? An extra blanket?"

"Tell that girl you love her."

"That's..." He slid the ugly pink recliner closer and sat down. "That's your favor?"

"So it's true?"

He nodded. "Yeah. I think so."

"You *think* so...."

Logan couldn't imagine a scenario where Bianca would hurt or disappoint him. Couldn't imagine life without her. "Yeah. Yeah, I guess I do."

"Then ask her to marry you."

"I've only known her a couple of months." He shook his head. "And her entire world revolves around that little boy. Besides, you heard her. She read my bio word for word. What makes you think she'd say yes?"

"You eavesdropped on our entire conversation, so you already know the answer."

She grimaced and gripped the blankets so tightly her knuckles turned white.

"I'll get a nurse. Must be time for more morphine."

"No. I don't want any more of that. I want to be awake and alert until…"

They heard the soft *ding* of the elevator.

"That's probably the family. Quick…before they all barge in here, promise me."

"Promise what?"

"Say you'll marry her. So I can go to my Maker knowing someone will keep you in line."

A sob ached in his throat as he said, "Promise."

"Promise what?" Sandra wanted to know.

"She wants more ice chips," he said, grabbing the cup. "Be right back."

In the hallway, he nearly collided with Bianca, who'd just stepped out of the ladies' room. One look into her big, caring eyes was all it took to loosen the last of his self-control. And when she held out her arms, Logan willingly filled them. The gesture was no guarantee that she felt the same as he did. But a guy could hope.

And for the first time in many long years, the tough ex-quarterback broke down and bawled like a little boy.

CHAPTER TWENTY-THREE

DURING THOSE FIRST weeks after his mother's funeral, Logan spent more time at Bianca's house than his own. Then, on Mother's Day, after making lunch that he jokingly referred to as "my famous J.O. Spice crab cakes," he spent the rest of the day with his dad. Commendable, Maddy said when he'd left, that he'd shared even that small portion of his first Mother's Day without Nancy.

Bianca remembered feeling out of sorts that first Father's Day after her dad had died. Firsts of any kind were hard: the first Christmas, the first birthday and, the most painful of all, that first anniversary of a loved one's death. She'd survived all of those, and now Logan had to learn to do the same. And she had to fight her urge to pamper and protect him in the hope of making those firsts more bearable.

He'd spent most of the month of June jetting back and forth between Baltimore and L.A., and on the few occasions when they did manage to connect, he spent as much time *on* the phone as off, discussing the secret business venture. Well, he thought it was a secret. Bianca had overheard enough of the one-sided conversations to know he was considering some sort of an acting role. How long, she wondered, before he let her in on the details? She knew this: until he did, she couldn't risk letting Drew get too attached to him. July brought a series of fierce thunderstorms that canceled Independence Day parades, barbecues and fireworks. But Logan found better ways to celebrate…indoors. And for a reason she couldn't explain, Bianca went along with it. She could only hope she wasn't making the biggest mistake of Drew's life.

Somehow, Logan talked Drew into visiting the aquarium, on a busy summer Saturday, no less. The success of the outing had been the result of hours of research, during which he'd learned that the buzz and flicker of fluorescent lighting—things the average person doesn't even notice—upset and distracted some kids on the spectrum. So he bought Drew a pair of yellow earphones. He also gave him a plastic drinking straw and instructed him to tap it against his thigh when sensory overload threatened a meltdown. Amazingly, it worked.

So in August they took a dinner cruise on the Lady Baltimore and spent one afternoon at the B&O Railroad Museum and another at the Science Center. Drew lost his cool half a dozen times as he learned to cope with the big world outside his realm. And when he did, Logan averted possible injury by picking him up, holding him tight and humming softly until Drew was calm again. If he noticed the sometimes stern stares of people who didn't understand autism, Logan showed no signs of it. Bianca admired him for that. Admired him, too, because unlike her, Logan had no obligation to the boy at all.

By mid-September, when he left on yet another trip to California, Bianca more or less accepted that he wasn't ready to share the details about his hush-hush Hollywood deal. Then, as the month was drawing to a close, the traveling abruptly stopped, and in the weeks that passed, she put it out of her mind.

Logan invited her and Drew to join him for a drive in the country. The minute she saw the massive sign that read PERCY MOORE

ACADEMY, Bianca's heart pounded with excitement.

As he walked them through parlors and pantries, dining halls and dens that were slowly being turned into classrooms in the beautiful Georgian mansion, her relief was so overwhelming that she didn't mind the cold wind or the thick grey clouds. Not only because his enthusiasm was contagious, but also because she realized this was the secret he'd been keeping!

Bianca stood in the middle of the room that would soon become the cafeteria, where blueprints blanketed a makeshift table. "I can't believe Deidre kept this to herself all these months."

"She probably wouldn't have," Logan said, "if she'd been healthy."

Deidre's lengthy bout with pneumonia that began on the day Nancy was rushed to the hospital had scared them all, and when at last their elderly friend rallied, she made the decision to take life easier. Deidre hired Griff to manage the place and hired grandson-in-law Hunter's contracting company to turn some unused office space on the first floor of her theater into a two-bedroom apartment. Everyone was happy…

…except for Logan.

Now that she'd seen the school, Bianca didn't understand why he seemed so distant. Had he been seeing someone in California, someone who'd broken things off…and broken his heart? But since that theory didn't jive with things she'd overheard, like "time on the set," "scripts" and "short-term contract," she made up her mind that tonight, as soon as Drew and Maddy were upstairs for the night, she'd get the truth out of him, once and for all.

Bianca and Logan had been alone less than an hour when he turned on the TV.

Marty had stayed late at the station, as he often did when fierce storms threatened the entire mid-Atlantic region. He was on the screen now, pointing at a huge, ominous-looking orange-and-red swirl and the dime-sized eye that was whirling ever closer to shore. The hurricane was a category 2 storm, packing winds as high as 110 mph. If the storm picked up enough warmth from the Atlantic, it could easily churn out 155-mph gusts.

"But," Marty said, "the beast is a couple hours out to sea."

It could build steam or fizzle, but that didn't stop the station from stationing reporters in every resort from Myrtle Beach to Cape May and interviewing the owners of condos, restaurants and Boardwalk shops who were busy placing sandbags and boarding up their windows.

"If it hits the Chesapeake," Logan said, his serious tone echoing her mood, "my neighborhood will flood. No doubt about it."

She pictured his rambling glass-and-wood contemporary. It sat a mere twenty yards from the Patapsco River, which had a tendency to overflow its banks during heavy rains.

He stood and started for the door. "I'd better get home. Do what those shopkeepers are doing." He patted his thigh. "C'mon, Poe. Let's go." The dog was beside him before he added, "I need to stow the deck furniture and make sure the boat is tied up."

"Why don't you leave her with me?" Bianca suggested. "She'll be safer here, and you won't have to worry she might get into something she shouldn't." *Besides,* she thought, *if she's here, you'll have to come back for her.*

"Good idea. I have some of her stuff in the car," he said. "Leash, extra collar, food and treats. Enough to last until I come back for her anyway. Right, Poe?"

When he went outside, the dog started to follow. Even before the door closed behind him, she changed her mind and sat beside Bianca instead. "Aw, I love you, too," she said, kissing the top of her head.

A moment later, Logan returned. "It's already started," he said, leaning against the door. "Bet those winds are already up to sixty miles an hour."

She joined him in the foyer. "You poor thing—you're drenched! Let me get you a towel."

"No, thanks. Don't want to waste a minute. I can get into dry clothes when I get home." He watched as Poe sniffed the puddle at his feet. "Rats. I'm messing up your rug."

"It isn't a problem." She took a step closer. Would he hug her goodbye?

A second ticked by, but he didn't move. Probably just trying to keep her from getting soaked, she told herself.

"Look. We need to talk. So get the hatches battened down, or whatever it is sailors say, and get back here, safe and sound."

"Talk? About what?"

"It can wait. Just be careful, okay?"

He nodded. "I'll call when I'm on my way back."

And then he was gone.

For hours, the wind rattled the windows and shook the doors, and then the lights went out. Thankfully, Drew slept straight through it. If only Logan's poor dog could do the same. Poe stopped pacing, then whined and flopped at Bianca's feet.

"He'll be okay," she soothed, though she had no idea how he could work without electricity. Hopefully, he wasn't outside in this mess, trying to nail plywood to the first-floor windows. Or worse, on a ladder, securing the latticed roof above his deck.

She dozed in her chair, clutching a pillow to her chest. It was still dark outside when she woke with a stiff neck. No lamplight meant the electricity was still out. Four-fifteen, said her cell phone clock. She scrolled through her calls log, heart pounding when she saw that Logan hadn't left a message.

It was nearly noon when Logan finally called to report that the power at his place was still out. "How are you guys?"

"We're fine. Even Drew."

"Good to hear."

"Our power is back on, so if yours is still out, you're welcome to stay here. I'll make up the sofa bed in the living room for you."

"I might just take you up on that. You're sure Poe isn't any trouble?"

"She's been wonderful. As a matter of fact, she and Drew are cuddled up side by side on the family room floor, watching cartoons together."

"Do you think Maddy would mind keeping an eye on them for an hour or so?"

"I suppose. Why?"

"Thought I'd bring you over here, see how much progress we've made."

"Progress? Where?"

"At the school."

Is *that* where he'd been all this time, while she sat worrying that he'd floated upriver with his house?

"I have a meeting over here with the landscape architect. Afterward, I could swing by, pick you up and walk you through the whole place."

Bianca set her ire aside. He might have forgotten that she wanted to have a heart-to-heart, but she hadn't. "Call you on my way over," he said, and hung up.

She found her mom in the laundry room, ironing. "Mind if I run out for about an hour?" Bianca decided to drive over to the school herself. Not only would it save time, but she'd bring lunch and surprise Logan.

"Where's Drew?"

"In the family room," Bianca said, "watching TV with Poe."

"He gets along great with that pup, doesn't he?"

She smiled. "Yes. Yes, he does."

"Gets along great with Logan, too. Says a lot about the guy. That he can love another man's child, I mean."

Did he love Drew? Or was her boy one more step in getting the school built and filled with students...and putting his name back in the headlines?

She felt a little guilty, thinking he'd use a child—her child—that way. They'd probably etch She Made Mountains Out of Molehills on her tombstone. It was time to get a grip. Time to quit jumping to conclusions and assuming the worst. Time to get to the bottom of things, even if it hurt like crazy.

"I'll have my cell phone, of course, in case he has a meltdown."

"He won't." Maddy went back to creasing a pair of Drew's jeans. "But if he does, I'll handle it."

"I know you will." She smiled. "I'll be at the new school. How about if I pick up a pizza on the way home?"

Maddy nodded. "Is Logan coming back with you?"

Fear panged in her gut. The answer to that would depend entirely on how he reacted to the questions she intended to ask him.

"I'm not sure."

"Everything okay?"

"Sure. Of course. Why do you ask?"

"No reason. Pizza sounds good."

"Poe will need to go out in an hour or so. Whatever you do, don't let Drew go with her or they'll *both* get soaking wet and muddy."

Maddy grinned. "If we go out and make a mess, we'll clean it up." She stood the iron on its end and walked to Bianca's side of the ironing board. "Now go upstairs. Put on a little lipstick. And maybe those pretty hair combs Drew gave you for Mother's Day. They bring out the blue of your eyes."

The roads were littered with fallen branches and tree leaves, and every few blocks she saw one of the power company's trucks, buckets extended high in the air to repair the downed lines. When she turned up the driveway at the school, it surprised her to see so many vehicles out front. Two pickup trucks bearing the same plumbing company's logo, a painter's panel van, a big white box truck that belonged to the landscaper and a plain black SUV.

She parked between Logan's car and the painter's van and grabbed the insulated cooler she'd packed on the way out the door. Chilled water, sandwiches, green grapes and a slice of pie—all of Logan's favorites. She grinned, anticipating his reaction to her unannounced visit. Slinging her hobo bag over one shoulder, she slammed the car door and jogged up the flagstone steps. Logan had replaced the big wooden entry doors with brass and glass. Bold gold letters on the left door said PERCY MOORE, and on the right, ACADEMY. It should have said Deidre O'Toole and Logan Murray in smaller print because without them, the facility wouldn't have existed.

The main office was the first sign on the left. She heard voices and, not wanting to interrupt Logan's meeting, took a seat on the heavy carved wooden bench just outside the open door.

"Who's this woman in the photograph?" said a voice she didn't recognize.

"You wouldn't know her. She's the mother of one of the students."

She recognized *that* voice: Logan. She smiled as the other man cut loose with a wolf whistle.

"Can't fool me, Murray. She's more than that. I can tell by the way you're looking at that picture. Not that I blame you. She's mighty easy on the eyes. Is she a natural blonde? Or haven't you got far enough yet to know for sure?" He laughed, an annoying, juvenile titter.

"Grow up, Vinnie. We're not in high school anymore."

Bianca was tempted to lean left and peek into the office for a look at the crude man with the gravelly voice. Instead, she crossed her legs and tidied the hem of her skirt.

"I wish some of your good luck would rub off on me."

Logan laughed, and oh, how she loved the sound of it! She had to remind herself that the reasons for her visit were twofold: deliver lunch, and find out what he'd been hiding from her.

"Luck? What are you yammerin' about now, Vinnie?"

"You have it all. Good looks, fame, the money to get any gorgeous gal you want—like that one, there, with the cute kid in her lap. So did it work?"

"Did what work?"

"Buddying up to her and her special-needs kid to get the funding for this place."

"I funded the place. Period. No need to buddy up to anyone." He snorted. "Besides, who are you to talk," Logan shot back, "married to the governor's daughter."

"Being married to the governor's daughter doesn't do me any good, and you know it. I'm little more than a puppet. I do what I'm told, when I'm told to do it. Period. I so much as *think* about using my connections to her daddy, and I'm as gone as a Civil War soldier." The man laughed. "But you? You get to keep right on schmoozing with the Tinseltown crowd thanks to this place, and one of the reasons you have this place is your connection to that pretty little blonde. If that ain't luck, I don't know what is."

"Connection?"

"Let me rephrase that. Photo op. Is that accurate enough for ya? She and her kid are insurance that this place will put your name back in the headlines for something other than being drunk and disorderly?"

In the moment of silence that followed, things began to make sense. Why he'd insisted on taking Drew to every one of Baltimore's top tourist spots, for starters, taking lots of pictures at every one. Was that what all the whispered phone meetings were all about? He was making Drew the poster boy for his fancy tuition-free school?

She waited, hoping to hear Logan deny it. When she didn't, Bianca leaped up, dropping the cooler as her shoes click-clacked across the tiles.

"Bianca!" Logan shouted. "Bianca, wait up!"

Tears stung her eyes as she struggled to open the heavy doors. His mother had been wrong. Dead wrong. And *she'd* been a fool.

Had anything he'd said or done been genuine? Was Holly, whose death had inspired the idea for this school in the first place, a lie? Were his feelings for Drew and Maddy—for *her*—fiction as well?

The moment Drew was diagnosed, people had started calling her Tiger Mama because she'd fight anything or anyone who stood in the way of what was best for her little boy.

Not this time.

She'd turned into a woman so desperate for affection and attention that she'd done what was best for her—not what was best for Drew.

"Bianca, wait up. I didn't realize you were here."

"Obviously," she said, finally summoning the strength to open the door.

"Bianca. Stop. Tell me what's wrong!"

He was close, too close, so she picked up the pace. Thankfully, she hadn't locked the car.

"Vinnie is an idiot. And he doesn't know what he's talking about."

So he knew that she'd overheard the conversation.

"You've got it all wrong."

Did she?

The truth hit hard as she slid behind the wheel and slammed the door: Logan hadn't humiliated her; she'd done that to herself.

The need to confront him seemed less important right now than getting her thoughts in order. And to do that, she needed to get away, far away from here.

She threw the car into Reverse, took her foot off the brake…

…and plowed into the passenger door of the plumber's van, bumping her head on the steering wheel.

"Hey, lady," the driver bellowed, "are ya blind or just stupid?"

Oh, stupid, for sure, she thought, *and not only because I didn't look where I was going.* Come to think of it, not thinking about where she was going had caused the mess she was in with Logan, and the position she'd put Drew in with him, too.

Bianca wanted to flee now more than ever. But trapped between two parked vehicles and the irate plumber, she couldn't even get out of the car, let alone escape.

Logan held up a hand, effectively silencing the guy. "Take it easy, pal," he said. "It's just a small dent." He handed the man a business card and promised to take care of everything. It all happened so fast that she felt a little dizzy. And then, before she knew what was happening, Logan opened her driver's-side door.

"Get out of there," Logan said as the van drove away, "so I can make sure you're all right."

Bianca didn't know why, but like an obedient child, that's exactly what she did.

She felt him, watching as she bent to run her fingers across the slight indentation in her bumper. Thankfully, it wasn't as bad as it had sounded. And not so bad that it would require an expensive trip to the paint shop.

Gently, Logan grasped her shoulders and stood her upright. "You're bleeding."

She'd hit her lip when the impact bounced her head from the headrest to the steering wheel. She ran her tongue over it.

"Let me have a look at it," he said, cupping her chin in his big hand.

Oh, he was quite the actor, all right. He'd made his voice tremble, just a little, so he'd sound sincere.

She jerked free of his grasp. "I'm fine," she snapped. *Unless a bruised ego counts.* "I need to go. Mom and Drew will wonder where I am. And I have to contact my insurance company, in case—"

"I told the guy I'd handle it, and I meant it."

She stared him down. "The way you handled me so that you could use Drew as the star of your ad campaign?"

"I didn't. That isn't even close to the truth."

"Is the truth in California?"

His face paled as his mouth formed a small O. "I've been meaning to talk to you about that. I was just trying to dot all the i's and cross all the t's before I—"

Bianca got into her car and quickly locked the door behind her. And this time, she took great care backing out of the spot. The ache of a sob pulsed in her throat, but she refused to give in to self-pity. *You will not cry. You. Will. Not. Cry!*

One glance in the rearview mirror was all it took to wake overwhelming sadness and regret in her because there he stood, slump-shouldered and alone in the parking lot, looking every bit as miserable as she felt. More evidence of his acting skills? Or had she misjudged the situation?

There'd be plenty of time to puzzle it out at home.

Home, the only place she felt truly safe.

Bianca took the ramp to Route 100, which would take her there…

…if she didn't crash into something *else* first.

CHAPTER TWENTY-FOUR

LOGAN THOUGHT IT was Bianca calling. It surprised him to hear Drew's voice instead.

"How's school, kiddo? Mrs. Peterson treating you well?"

"Yes. But I just don't understand why you haven't come to visit in so long. Poe misses you."

"I miss her, too." And he did. "Miss you more, though."

"I think she wonders if you forgot about her."

Since the storm had all but leveled his house, he'd been staying in one of Deidre's guest rooms, a small, cramped little space up on the third floor that had no closet and no private bathroom. Poe would have been miserable cooped up in a place like that.

"You tell that silly pup that I could never do that. I love her too much."

"Then if you love her, why haven't you come to visit in so long?"

And there, Logan thought, was one of the characteristics of autism: fixation on one subject. One of the most difficult...especially when the question was a tough one.

"Remember that big storm we had the other day?"

"When the lights went out and we couldn't watch *Mr. Action?*"

He had to tread carefully here. Too much information, and Drew would worry himself to death. Not enough, and he'd fixate on *that*.

"Yeah. That night. Well, the wind did some damage to my house. Broke a few windows, blew down a couple of trees. I've been busy cleaning up and fixing stuff. Plus working at my regular jobs." And jetting between Baltimore and L.A. to finalize the sitcom. "That's why I haven't been around much."

"You haven't been around *at all.*"

Good point, but there weren't enough words in the English language to explain why a grown man was afraid to face a woman Bianca's size.

"Is your garage broken?"

"A little bit."

"And your kitchen?"

"And the kitchen."

"Your bedroom?"

Fact was, the wind had toppled an ancient weeping willow that had all but destroyed the second floor.

"Yeah. The bedroom, too."

"What about your bed?"

"I guess you'd say that's ruined, too."

"Then where are you sleeping?"

"I'm renting a room."

"What's *renting?*"

"It means I pay Miss Deidre money to sleep in one of the rooms at her house. That's why I can't come and get Poe just yet. It's very small and crowded, and she'd hate it here."

"Do you hate it?"

"Yeah, yeah, I guess I do." What he hated more was the way the conversation seemed to be agitating Drew. "But it's okay. It's only temporary. Before we know it, everything will be back to normal."

Including the rift between him and Bianca? Logan didn't know how that could happen if she refused to let him explain.

"Where's your mom?"

"She's in the kitchen. Painting."

That blasted portrait again. Well, maybe she'd finally succeeded in giving Jason the face of a loving father.

"How's she doing?"

"She's sad. I don't know why. But it makes me sad, too."

He felt like a heel, because he knew why. She'd misunderstood the conversation between him and Vinnie. At first, he'd about worn a callus on his finger calling to explain and to tell her the truth. Then things had heated up out in L.A., and he thought maybe it was better this way. Putting time and space between them would make it easier for her to accept that she'd linked herself to an idiot. He felt bad, knowing she'd waited three years to start a new relationship. Who knew how long it might be before she risked it again. So he'd go to California, do the show, invest every dollar earned in the Moore Academy, so that indefinitely, Drew and kids like him could attend a school built from the ground up with their needs in mind. Bianca would get over this. Even her mom talked about her toughness, her resilience.

"I have to go," Drew said. And just like that, he hung up.

Another characteristic of autism: when you're done with something, you're done. Period. It made him grin a little, wondering what the world would be like if everyone just told the plain truth, all the time, the way kids on the spectrum did.

"Mom?"

"Shh, Drew," she whispered, pointing at her cell phone. "I'm talking."

"I know. I can see the phone. And I can hear you talking."

Bianca turned slightly, hoping to improve her concentration on what his teacher was saying. "That's great news, Mrs. Peterson."

Drew tugged at her sleeve. "Logan's house is broken."

She nodded and aimed her pointer finger at the ceiling. "Give me a minute, Drew, okay?"

"Okay. But Logan's house is broken, and I don't want him sleeping in a crowded room at Miss Deidre's. Poe and me, we want him to stay in my room."

Mrs. Peterson had called to share her excitement at Drew's success taking the same tests as the rest of the kids in his class.

"I can't thank you enough for all you're doing," she told the teacher. "None of this would have been possible without your dedication. He's very lucky that you decided to teach second grade this year."

Now Drew took Bianca's hand. "If Logan slept in the extra bed in my room," he continued, "Poe could be with him *and* me. And they wouldn't miss each other."

"Drew, please. I'm on the phone, remember?"

"Yes. I remember. I can see it. So can he? Can Logan sleep in the extra bed in my room? So him and Poe could be together and not miss each other?"

Mrs. Peterson was outlining this year's plan for Drew. It would include more time with the class, and less one-on-one with his aide.

"All right, Drew!"

He ran from the room, chanting happily as he picked up the house phone. "Mom said yes," he said, dialing Logan's number. "Mom said yes!" he said when Logan answered. "Mom said yes. Mom said *yes!*"

"To be honest," he said when Maddy led him upstairs, "I was shocked when Drew called with the news."

"Well, Bianca didn't say anything to me about it, either. She's been swamped at work lately, and putting in a lot of volunteer hours at Drew's school. I keep telling myself that's why she's seemed, I don't know, a little *off* these past couple of weeks. I hope she's not coming down with one of those bugs that are going around."

So Bianca hadn't told her mom what had happened at the school, he realized. Maybe it meant she'd thought things through, realized she'd jumped to conclusions, but didn't know how to reconnect after so much time had gone by. In Drew's room, Maddy opened the closet door. "I cleared space in here for you to hang a few shirts, and emptied the nightstand drawers in case you want to put your socks and underwear in there. You're only steps from the bathroom across the hall. It'll almost be like a private bath because Drew uses the master bath to shower and brush his teeth. So that Bianca can supervise, you know?" She chuckled quietly. "If you need something in there and don't find it, let me know, okay?"

"Thanks, Maddy. You're the best. I promise, this is temporary. Already have a Realtor looking for places."

"Stop. Please. We'll enjoy having you. When you've unpacked, come on downstairs. I'll fix you some lunch."

That sounded great; he hadn't eaten a bite since breakfast, yesterday. "I'll do that."

When he'd returned from that last trip to L.A. and learned that the county had condemned his house—along with three of his neighbors' houses—Logan had to pull a few favors for permission to go inside long enough to grab a few personal items. A family portrait buried under a collapsed wall. One of Poe's favorite toys. The fishing rod and reel his paternal grandpa had given him.

Fortunately, he'd always stored important papers in stylish file boxes on the shelves beside his office fireplace. After transferring them to plastic bins, he stowed them in his car trunk, along with his framed Knights jersey and Super Bowl ring. Ironically, he'd been looking into adding coverage to his homeowner's policy, and it had been on his desk when the storm hit. Now, it lay in a soggy heap at the foot of the stairs. He added it to the stack of antique books that had decorated the mantel and added it to the trunk. All of that would be safe in the car, thanks to darkened windows and an ear-piercing alarm system. For now, at least.

Logan hung two suits, two white shirts and two ties in the space Maddy had cleared in Drew's closet. After sliding a pair of sneakers and his dress shoes onto the shelf above, he placed his duffel bag on the bed that would be his and hung his shaving kit on the hook behind the bathroom door, then joined Maddy in the kitchen.

Poe hadn't left his side since he'd arrived "I still can't believe Bianca suggested this arrangement," he said, ruffling the dog's fur.

"Sometimes," Maddy said, "just going about your business as if the argument never took place is the best way to resolve things." She laughed. "One of a handful of things I learned from thirty years of marriage."

After wolfing down a sandwich, he squatted near the front door and gave Poe a hearty hug. "I have a couple loose ends to tie up," he said over the dog's head. "You have my cell number, right?"

Maddy nodded. "It's on the whiteboard beside the kitchen phone."

"What time did you say dinner will be ready?"

"Six. Though these days, Bianca's schedule has me reheating things for her at seven eight o'clock, even. If we didn't have to stick so closely to Drew's schedule..." She shrugged "Anyway, he'll be thrilled to see you when he gets home. You have no idea how much he missed you!"

It had only been a couple of weeks since the big misunderstanding. If it felt like three times that to him, he could only imagine how much longer it seemed to Drew.

"I'll try to be home around five, see if maybe I can help him with homework, or throw a football around the backyard, or whatever. But don't say anything to him, just in case my meetings run overtime. If that happens, I'll let you know. Thanks again for lunch. For everything."

Had the separation seemed like months to Bianca, too?

"See you at five, then," Maddy said.

Guess that's when you'll find out….

BY THE TIME Bianca got home from the autism fundraiser, Maddy and Drew were in bed. Normally, she wouldn't have attended. But a flurry of things had prevented them from participating in the Autism Walk back in April, and she couldn't in good conscience miss this, too.

She thought about tiptoeing into Drew's room to kiss him goodnight but decided against it. It wasn't likely he'd wake up, but exhausted as she was, Bianca didn't want to risk a tantrum. She'd wait until morning instead and surprise him with his favorite wakeup call: butterfly kisses while she sang the "Good Morning" song.

Six hours later, Bianca's alarm buzzed, and for a moment—only a moment—she thought Jason was beside her. She blamed the exasperating painting. After looking into his larger-than-life likeness all these months, the only surprise was that she hadn't seen him in every dark-haired man's face.

All but Logan's, that is.

Kismet had led her to the school that day. If she hadn't overheard the conversation, who knows how much longer she might have cooperated with his farce? Not that all her memories of her time with Logan had been negative. He'd made her admit that, despite three years' worth of claims to the contrary, she did want a man in her life. If that was in the cards, she was open to it now. More important were the changes he'd brought about in Drew: being called "friend" by a man who was a movie and sports hero all rolled into one had given Drew a new confidence in himself.

One of her favorite things about Saturday

mornings was lolling around in her robe and slippers, reading the paper and sipping coffee from her favorite mug while Drew watched his favorite cartoons.

Yawning and stretching, she tiptoed down the hall to have a peek at his sweet sleeping face before heading downstairs…

…and plowed into Logan.

A myriad of questions—from how he'd got in, to why he was standing in her upstairs hall wearing nothing but a white T-shirt and blue plaid boxers—flashed in her mind. How dare he look so sweet and sexy with his sleep-rumpled hair and sheet wrinkles on his right cheek? And why did he look so happy to see her?

She grabbed his forearm and led him to the bottom of the stairs, well out of earshot of Drew's room. And one by one, she fired off the questions:

"How did you get in here?"

"Maddy."

"When?"

"Yesterday afternoon."

"But…*why?*"

"Because Drew called me. Said it was your idea."

"Said what was my idea?"

"Staying here, so Poe wouldn't miss me. Just until I find a new place."

"What's wrong with your house?"

"The hurricane took out trees that demolished the entire second floor. And the river overflowed its banks, pretty much destroying everything else."

He was looking at her as if she should already know these things. Which made no sense at all. Bianca didn't know whether to be angry with him, Maddy, Drew or all three of them.

"Wait." She rubbed her temples. "Your house was condemned?"

Nodding, Logan crossed both arms over his chest. "Got home from L.A. and found a big sign tacked to the door. And a letter in my P.O. box. Then I called Griff and, based on what he dug up, there's not a blessed legal thing I can do about it."

"Griff." She mimicked his posture. "The guy who's living at Deidre's because his house is infested with wood eaters."

"Wood bores."

He grinned but only a little and only for a second. Because based on her expression and body language, Bianca saw no humor in his correction.

"But, yeah, that's the same Griff. Strictly between you and me, though, the real reason he's at Deidre's is because he lost his shirt in the divorce, not bugs." Logan shrugged. "Can you believe it? A lawyer marrying a former model without drafting a prenup first?"

Bianca ignored the prenuptial crack, mostly because she still didn't understand how Logan had ended up sleeping in Drew's room.

She mimicked his stance. "So let me get this straight. Drew and my mother said it was my idea for you to move in here."

"Yeah, but only until—"

"And for you to sleep in Drew's room."

"Uh-huh."

"Until…?"

"Until I find a more permanent place. Like I told Maddy, I've already got an agent hunting for apartments. Eventually, I'd like to rebuild on the same site. I still own the land, so, once I hire a crew to clear it…"

He followed her into the kitchen.

"I can't think straight. It's too early. And I haven't had any coffee yet."

"Just so you know, I tried to call you after

Drew phoned to extend the invitation. But you didn't answer. And didn't return my texts or voice messages. So I figured you still had your mad on."

She filled the carafe with water. Well, he had her there, now, didn't he?

"And also, just so you know, I didn't hire Vinnie."

Stuffing a filter into the coffeemaker's basket, Bianca echoed, "Vinnie."

"The guy doing all the crazy talk at the school. He was there delivering a bid for insulation. If you hadn't run off like a scared rabbit, you would have heard me tell him to leave because I don't work with cheats. Or liars and gossips, either. You would have heard for yourself that I didn't get close to you so that I could use Drew in some cockeyed ad campaign, or some fool attempt to get my name back in lights. And that crack you made that day, about California? I'll probably turn down one heck of a deal in Tinseltown because..."

She met his steady gaze, blink for blink, waiting for him to complete the sentence. Did he look sincere because she wanted him to, or because every word he'd spoken had been the truth?

"I considered the possibility that I might have overreacted a bit."

He groaned, and she read his expression to mean *A bit?*

"Even if everything *Vinnie* said was bogus," she said, clicking the on switch, "how do you explain the way you've been behaving for *weeks?*"

Logan shrugged. "How have I been behaving?"

"Like you're sorry for getting involved with me. Like you can't stand to be around me."

He lowered his head for a moment, and when he raised it again, Logan said, "Bianca. Honey. Look at me. I'm standing here, whisper-arguing in your kitchen so I won't wake Drew. In my underclothes. Trying to thank you for the invitation that spared me spending who knows how long in Deidre's closet-sized spare room, or some bedbug-infested motel. Hoping like hell that you'll believe me when I say I've never cared about a woman the way I care about you."

He paused, and in the peculiar silence, she wondered why he'd turned to her instead of his family. She was about to phrase the question when he said, "Whoa. Wait a minute here. I know Drew, and he doesn't lie. You must have said something to give him the idea it was okay for me to stay."

Bianca started to deny it, but memory of a phone conversation with Mrs. Peterson stopped her: Drew, repeatedly asking if Logan could move in; her, exasperated with his repeated interruptions, saying yes.

Life could sure be weird, Bianca thought. Just when she screwed up the courage to stand up for herself, *really* stand up for herself, out comes the truth to make her feel small and petty and self-centered. Plus, he'd all but said he loved her.

So why hadn't he?

Logan took a deep breath, let it out slowly. "I should have tried harder to get in touch with you. I'm sorry that I didn't."

"I'm sorry about your house. And for behaving like an insensitive shrew. Of course you can stay. But you don't have to share Drew's tiny room. I'll fix the living room up for you. No one ever uses it. We spend all our time in the kitchen and family room. I could put curtains on the French doors that lead to the foyer, so you'd have some privacy. There's even a closet in there. It's not very big, but, as you pointed out, this is temporary."

Logan studied her face, as if he expected her to lash out again. "I'll pay rent. Contribute to the groceries and the chores. I can mow the lawn and collect the trash. And believe it or not, I'm a fair-to-middlin' cook."

Bianca still wasn't totally convinced of his sincerity, but at least she had her guard up now. Whatever questions remained could be asked—and answered—in the days to come.

"I hate to be rude," she said, "but I think we should get dressed before Mom and Drew wake up."

It seemed he'd forgotten, for the moment, what he'd worn to bed. He looked down at bare toes and, blushing, met her eyes. "I was on the way to the shower when we met in the hall."

He looked confused and hurt as he left the room. Bianca felt the same way.

She poured herself a mug of coffee, and leaning on the counter, stared out the kitchen window. The October wind whipped through the yard, disturbing the blanket of gold-and-burnt-orange leaves. So many things were changing all around her, things she seemed powerless to avoid or control.

Drew walked into the kitchen rubbing sleepy eyes. "Where's Logan?" he asked, hugging her.

"Taking a shower." She tousled his hair. "Want some cereal?"

"No. Logan said he'd make pancakes for breakfast. And you know what? He doesn't even snore!"

"Well, that's good news."

Maddy joined them. "So how'd our house-guest sleep?"

"He looked fine to me," Bianca said. "We need to have a talk." She pointed at Drew. "Later."

For a mere instant, Maddy looked guilty. She wrapped her arms around Drew and Bianca. "My, aren't we just the perfect happy little family?"

Nothing is ever as perfect as it seems, she told herself.

CHAPTER TWENTY-FIVE

"IT'S BECAUSE I'm weird, isn't it?"

Bianca pulled Drew into a loving hug. "Of course not! Where would you get such an idea?"

"From Dad. I remember how you two used to fight all the time because of me."

She kissed the top of his head. "No, Drew. Logan and I aren't fighting."

"Well, if you aren't fighting, then it *has* to be 'cause I'm weird." He looked her square in the eye. "I'm not stupid. I know what I heard. I couldn't say the word back then, but I knew what it meant. Dad. Called. Me. *Weird.*"

He took a few steps away from her and sat on the arm of his favorite easy chair. Cupping his elbows, Drew rocked back and forth. He used to do it all the time…a signal that he was nervous, or frustrated, or afraid. But he hadn't rocked in—

"Logan *told* me," Drew said.

Bianca knelt in front of him and sandwiched his hands between her own. "What, Drew? What did he tell you?"

"That he loves me. Like a son." Eyes narrowed, he tacked on, "And he's not like Dad. *He* doesn't lie."

If only she could be more certain of that....

"Aw, Drew, honey," she said, gathering him close again, "I promise that your dad loved you, just like everyone who meets you. Your father just wasn't very good at showing his emotions. And he wasn't very good at expressing himself, either."

He leaned back and studied her face. "If it isn't my fault that Logan moved out, and you guys didn't fight, then *why did* he leave? I thought he liked it here!"

She needed to exercise caution because Drew really *wasn't* stupid. He'd recognize a fib, even before she finished telling it.

"He's a busy guy. You know that. I'm sure he did love it here. But Logan was used to living in a big beautiful house. It had to be tough, moving into our tiny living room after having all that space."

"Yeah. And sharing *everything*." Drew nodded. Suddenly, he grinned. "He called himself a control freak once."

"Oh?"

"When I asked what it meant, he said, 'It's a person who's afraid if he lets anybody else do stuff, they'll mess up.'"

After a moment of silence, Drew added, "He loves you, you know."

The breath caught in her throat, and she swallowed. Hard. "He...he told you that?"

"Only a couple hundred million times. 'I love your mom's sense of humor.' 'I love her laugh.' 'I love her chocolate chip cookies.'" He rolled his eyes. "And he said if he had a magic wand, he'd wave it over your head to put a spell on you."

"A spell? What kind of spell?"

"I don't know." Drew wriggled free of her hug and said, "I'm hungry."

"So am I." She took his hand and, side by side, they walked into the kitchen, where she poked her head into the fridge. "Peanut butter and jelly or grilled cheese?"

"Ham on rye."

Logan's favorite sandwich...

"With mayo, and lettuce, and a tomato, and salt and pepper. But easy on the salt, please."

Hands folded on the table, he sat up straight, looking very proud of himself for getting all the ingredients right, for remembering to say please, for having figured out how to sit still long enough to get it all out.

"You're in luck, young man. Just so happens I have all the makings of—"

"A Logan Special."

"A what?"

"It's on the menu at the Double D Diner, 'cause when Logan found out Mr. Douglas was almost out of money and might have to close the restaurant, he made a commercial for them for free." Drew bobbed his head. "Guess I'm pretty lucky having a guy that nice sayin' he loves me like a son."

Was it luck, she wondered, laying sandwich fixings on the counter, or wishful thinking on the part of a boy so desperately yearning for a dad?

The phone rang, startling her so badly that she nearly sliced her thumb instead of the tomato. Logan Murray, said the caller ID display. Bianca would have let it go to voice mail if Drew hadn't said, "Can I get it?"

Say no, and defuse his enthusiasm. Say yes, and end up talking to Logan, like it or not. And now that she suspected his mom may have been right after all, she did not like it. At least not until she'd had time to sort things out in her head…and her heart.

"Sure. You know what to do."

"Wright residence, Andrew speaking." His face lit up when he realized it was Logan.

"I'm great.…Uh-huh.…Watchin' Mom make me a Logan Special." He flapped his free hand. "Yeah, okay, hold on.…" He stopped flapping long enough to put his fingers over the mouthpiece. "He wants to talk to you."

"How 'bout you wash your hands?" she said, taking the phone. "With any luck, by the time you're finished, your sandwich will be ready."

Nodding, he walked toward the powder room, chanting, "Warm water, soap, rub-rub-rub, sing the birthday song, rinse-rinse-rinse."

When he was out of earshot, she said, "Hi, Logan. How are you?"

"Better, now."

"Did you call to talk to Drew?"

"No. You."

Bianca put Drew's sandwich on a plate, then put the plate on the table.

"Oh?"

"This is gonna sound corny, but you know what? I don't care."

She plucked a napkin from the basket, and it fluttered to the floor when he said, "What are you doing for the rest of your life?"

CHAPTER TWENTY-SIX

"THE HOUSE looks really nice," Logan said. "Did you do it all by yourself?"

"Actually," she said, "this year, Drew and Mom helped a lot."

"That's a relief. I can just picture you teetering on a ladder, all by yourself, stringing lights on the gutters." He pretended to shiver.

He glanced around the family room. "Looks great in here, too. You know, I've never put up a tree."

"You've lived on your own for, what, fifteen years and never had a Christmas tree?"

"Didn't seem to be much point. Who'd see it?"

"Well, you would…."

"Nah. Mostly the house was a place to sleep and store stuff. Bet I can count on one hand the number of times I used the stove. Or the dishwasher."

"Takeout and paper plates, eh?"

"Yeah. Mostly."

"But the newspapers and magazines made it sound like you had a woman for every night of the week."

"Doesn't mean I brought them *home*."

She hadn't expected him to say that, and it must have shown on her face.

"I'm kidding." He tucked a curl behind her ear. "Don't you know me better than that by now?"

Bianca shrugged. She would have bet her life that Jason would be a terrific father, and she'd been wrong. Would have bet a man like Logan wouldn't give her more than a passing glance, and she'd been wrong about that, too. He'd popped the question, twice, and both times, she'd avoided a straight answer. Tonight, after the school's grand opening, she'd try to explain how she hoped he'd pass the test of time.

But just as nothing in life was as perfect as it seemed, things were never as bleak, either. It was time to step out in faith…

…and pray she wasn't making the biggest mistake of her life.

LOGAN HAD POPPED the question twice, and both times, she'd avoided an answer. Tonight, he was hoping for a little three's-the-charm luck.

"You look so handsome," Maddy said. "I've seen guys in tuxes before, but, Logan Murray, you look like a male cover model!"

"Stop. You'll make me blush. And that wouldn't be good for my image."

He was dying to tell Bianca how amazing she looked. But doing that would spoil his plan, and he didn't want to do that.

"You ready?"

"Just need to grab my coat and purse. Oh, great. I left my cell phone in my room!"

She ran upstairs, and once she'd rounded the corner, he leaned in close to Maddy. "Does she suspect anything?"

"If she does, she hasn't said a word to me." She squeezed his hands. "I'm so excited, I could pop! I wish I could be there to see it."

"Don't worry. You'll see it. The whole thing is being videotaped. From half a dozen camera angles."

"Oh, good heavens. How thrilling. But I'd better go into the kitchen. I'm afraid she'll take one look at me and know something's up."

He kissed her cheek. "I'll see if the video guy can email you a sneak preview. If he can, I'll text you."

She hurried from the room as Bianca came

down the stairs. "Drew, honey, where are you? Logan and I are leaving now."

He thundered down the steps. "Weren't you just upstairs?"

"Yes. To get my cell phone."

"Why didn't you say goodbye while you were up there?"

Bianca laughed. "I guess I didn't think of it." She hugged him. "Besides, don't you want to say hello to Logan?"

Drew met his eyes and, smirking, said, "Hi, Logan. Bye, Logan." And with that, he raced back up to his room.

"Mom...we're leaving...."

Maddy's voice floated to them from the kitchen. "Have fun! I'll probably be asleep when you get home, so goodnight while I'm at it!"

Frowning, Bianca said, "They're plotting something. I don't know what, but they've been acting strangely all day."

"I promised not to tell, but I happen to know they're about to start a party of their own. A sundae party."

Bianca rolled her eyes. "Oh, great. They'll both be bouncing off the walls when we get back."

He shrugged. "Maddy can handle it."

And she smiled. "Yes. You're right. She can, can't she?"

Bianca handed him her coat, and he slipped it over her shoulders. It was killing him not to tell her how fantastic she looked. And smelled. He resisted the urge to bury his face in her shining curls. Instead, he patted her shoulders, then turned her around and opened the door.

"Your carriage awaits, m'lady."

"Logan, a limousine? Oh, my goodness!"

"It's a very special night. So nothing but the best for my lady."

During the drive between her house and the Percy Moore Academy, he told her that their $500-a-plate event at the school had sold out. Every invited politician, athlete and actor had either sent a contribution, or planned to deliver one in person.

He'd shelled out fifty grand to have the place decked out for the holidays. And as they approached the drive, Bianca sighed.

"Oh, it's so beautiful!"

Not anywhere near as beautiful as you.

"I hope someone is taking pictures."

"Don't worry. I hired a photographer and

a videographer. Like I said—this is a special night."

"I can't wait to see Deidre's plaque. She's going to be thrilled and so surprised. I hope you don't make her cry when you make the presentation. You'll never hear the end of it if you make her ruin her mascara."

He shook his head. "Women."

Inside, in the room that would soon be the gymnasium, Logan's decorators had gone all-out.

On the stage, a black podium stood between long, blue-draped tables, and above each, huge temporary chandeliers glittered with bright white lights. The walls were covered with twinkle lights, too, and they'd been shrouded in gauzy white toile. Tiny Christmas trees, each adorned with colored lights and ornaments, served as centerpieces on each round white-clothed table.

"It's breathtaking," she said, turning in a slow circle.

No. You *are breathtaking.*

"I love how they played up the autism awareness colors. Is the whole place decked out this way?"

"Every. Single. Room."

When she looked up at him, Logan didn't know which glittered more brightly...ten thousand twinkle lights or her blue eyes. He grasped her waist and brought her to him. "Better find your seat," he whispered into her ear, "before I mess up your lipstick."

She blinked, then smiled and stepped out of his arms. "Are there name tags on the head table?"

"Of course."

He watched her walk away, then lift the full, blue-velvet skirt of her gown to climb the stairs. When Bianca slipped off the matching cloak, she wriggled her shoulders. The soundman must have already done his test because he heard her tell the woman seated beside her, "It's chilly in here!"

"Don't worry," the lady said. "It'll warm up once everyone gets here. Body heat, you know!"

The women laughed as Logan wondered how Bianca would react when it dawned on her that the woman was the governor's wife. The women shook hands, then Bianca said something that made her tablemates laugh. Smiling, Logan shook his head.

"That's some woman you've got there."

Logan turned and greeted Griff with a hearty handshake.

"This is Callie Fredericks," said his friend. "Callie, meet Logan Murray."

She was nothing like the women Griff usually dated, and first chance he got, he'd congratulate his old pal, because instead of a vapid young thing with too much makeup and not enough dress, Callie exuded elegance...and appeared to be in her early- to mid-thirties.... Griff's age.

"It's a pleasure," Logan said, bowing slightly.

The tables were filling up fast, and as the din of conversation and laughter floated around the room, Logan signaled the string quartet. While they played a Beethoven sonata, a slide show featuring before and after pictures of the school flashed on two big screens that hung in the corners. He tapped the microphone until the guests quieted, then said, "Thanks for joining us, ladies and gentlemen. Our waitstaff is ready to serve your meals, so if you'll take your seats..."

When he sat beside her, Bianca leaned in close. "You look so dapper and dignified that *I'm* tempted to mess up my lipstick."

"I dare you," he growled.

For a minute there, it looked like she might

just do it. Unfortunately, he'd never find out because a white-gloved waiter slid a steaming plate in front of her. All through the meal, Logan did his best to pay equal attention to others seated near him. He had a feeling the night was going to drag like a boring math lecture.

He was wrong. All too soon, dessert was being served. It was time.

He tilted left and whispered into Bianca's ear, "Give me a kiss for good luck?"

At best, he expected a quick peck on the cheek. Instead, she took his face in her hands and said, "I'm so proud of you." Then she gave him a gentle shove. "Now, break a leg."

Grinning, Logan ran a finger under his collar and stepped up to the podium. He adjusted the mic, then tapped the black-sponged bulb. "So. How were the burgers and fries?"

Laughter and applause mingled as the music stopped and the huge video screens went dark.

"The man I'm about to introduce," he began, "has baseball in his blood. Born into a family that loved the game, he played in high school and college and then for the very first U.S. Olympic baseball team. He did a stint for the Brewers before he got his baseball cap on straight and signed with the Os. And there he stayed for the rest of his career, earning the Most Valuable Player title, playing in the Home Run Derby and securing a spot in the Orioles Hall of Fame, just to name a few accolades. These days, though, he's the president of Pathfinders for Autism, founded to support families with kids with autism. Ladies and gentlemen, I give you the man who made The 40 Greatest Orioles of All Time list, number thirty-four, B. J. Surhoff."

People stood to applaud as the tall, slender gentleman took Logan's place at the lectern.

"Welcome," Surhoff said, "to the has-been sports ball."

More laughter and applause as he and Logan shook hands.

"Thanks," Surhoff said, holding up one hand. "Thanks very much." And when all was quiet, he began to speak. "When a bunch of us got together back in 2000, our mission was simple—improve the lives of kids with autism and the people who care for them…and do it for free. Pathfinders helps families—nearly one thousand of them every year—navigate the confusing array of services, treatments and programs.

"We hook people up with the professionals they need, who then work directly with them.

"We're all about training and education, awareness and outreach, and partnering with organizations like the Percy Moore Academy, which will ensure kids receive a complete tuition-free education."

He reached into the podium and pulled out a foot-tall polished chunk of crystal carved into the shape of a puzzle piece.

"Piece by piece, thanks to people like you, we're finding answers to the puzzle that is autism. Piece by piece, we're helping educate children who were once forgotten. Piece by piece, we're providing assistance to the people who love them."

He held the crystal higher. "Tonight, we're here to honor the woman who saw a missing puzzle piece and made up her mind to find it. Whose generosity made this beautiful old building and surrounding grounds available so that Logan Murray, here, could turn his dream into a reality.

"That woman, ladies and gentlemen, is Deidre O'Toole."

People got to their feet again as Deidre rose slowly from her seat on the dais. A bright spotlight followed her. With her every step, light reflected from thousands of sequins covering her floor-length pale blue gown. She took her time crossing the stage, alternately bowing and waving and blowing kisses, and when at last she reached the podium, Deidre grabbed the thin black gooseneck and lowered it until the microphone was even with her lips. She looked right. Left. Straight ahead. There wasn't a sound in the room, save the quiet footsteps of waiters and waitresses, moving among the tables, delivering dessert.

Surhoff repeated, "Ladies and gentlemen, Deidre O'Toole," and amid the standing ovation, he handed her the award and returned to his seat.

Arms high, Deidre commanded silence, and when she achieved it, she scanned the crowd. "Where's the kid with the prompt book? Cue cards? *Some*thing?"

When the laughter faded, she hugged the award to her chest. Tears sparkled in her eyes when she said, "Thank you. From the bottom of my heart, thank you."

She returned to her seat and began to cry softly.

Her tablemates offered tissues, gentle pats on the back and quiet words of encouragement as Logan returned to the microphone.

"I think we're all in agreement when we say, thank *you, Deidre.*"

Following a second standing ovation, Logan said, "In just a moment, our team will take anyone who's interested on a tour of the school. I'm told it's sleeting outside, so for safety's sake, we've canceled the hayride tours of the grounds. But before I let you go, I have one more thing to say."

Logan put his back to Bianca and took a small velvet pouch out of his jacket pocket. When he shook it, a sparkling diamond ring dropped into his hand. The women seated front and center immediately recognized it for what it was, and their oohs and ahhs filtered around the room. He palmed the ring and faced front again.

"Some of you remember me as number seven, the Baltimore Knights quarterback. And some of you know me as the voice of Hikler's Pickles. I played second fiddle to a couple of Hollywood heartthrobs and made a few commercials for America's favorite roadster. What no one knows is that, a few months ago, I was offered the role of a lifetime, playing the lead in a sitcom. Big house, big bucks, big car...the whole nine yards."

He heard the quiet whispers and knew what people were thinking: "What's he blathering about up there?" He heard Bianca's quiet gasp, too, and could see from the corner of his eye that she'd covered her mouth with her fingertips…her go-to move when she was uncomfortable. Or afraid. Or worried. Knowing *he* was the source of her concern touched him. Deeply. And so he continued.

"Saying yes to the TV deal means moving to Hollywood. Saying no means…"

He held out his empty hand and summoned Bianca. It seemed to take an eternity for her to stand beside him.

"Saying no," he continued, "means never leaving this amazing woman, the best thing that ever happened to me."

His hands were shaking as he held the ring between thumb and forefinger. Facing her, he said, "It's up to you, beautiful. Am I staying or am I going?"

Bianca's eyes filled with tears. Lower lip and voice trembling, she said, "Go.…"

Several women in the audience said, "Oh, no!" And a man in the back hollered, "Aw, c'mon, girl. Say yes!"

For a moment, it seemed that time really

could stand still as she looked into his eyes and smiled. She blinked, and one gleaming tear slid down her cheek, and she covered the microphone with one hand. "So much I want to say," she whispered. "So many questions I need to ask."

Logan's heart pounded. He thought he'd prepared himself for a possible rejection. Now that the moment was here and he had to grapple with the actuality, he wished he'd prepared a joke, a speech, something that would allow him to save face until he could walk off this stage, out of the facility, and hide himself away.

Bianca let go of the microphone, took a step closer and curled the fingers of her right hand into a fist.

"Go," she repeated, shaking the fist, "and you'll suffer your *fourth* grade C concussion." Extending her left hand, she waited, and as he slid the ring onto her finger, he couldn't look at her. With the ring in place, there was nothing to do but wait for the cheers and applause to fade away, so they could smile and thank the donors for their support and their congratulations.

Now he looked at her, and when he did, Bianca stepped closer still, and he could see the love shining in her eyes. "I can't wait to tell Drew," she said, "that he finally has a dad."

Then she stood on tiptoe to receive his kiss.

* * * * *

LARGER-PRINT BOOKS!

**GET 2 FREE
LARGER-PRINT NOVELS
PLUS 2 FREE
MYSTERY GIFTS**

Love Inspired

Larger-print novels are now available...